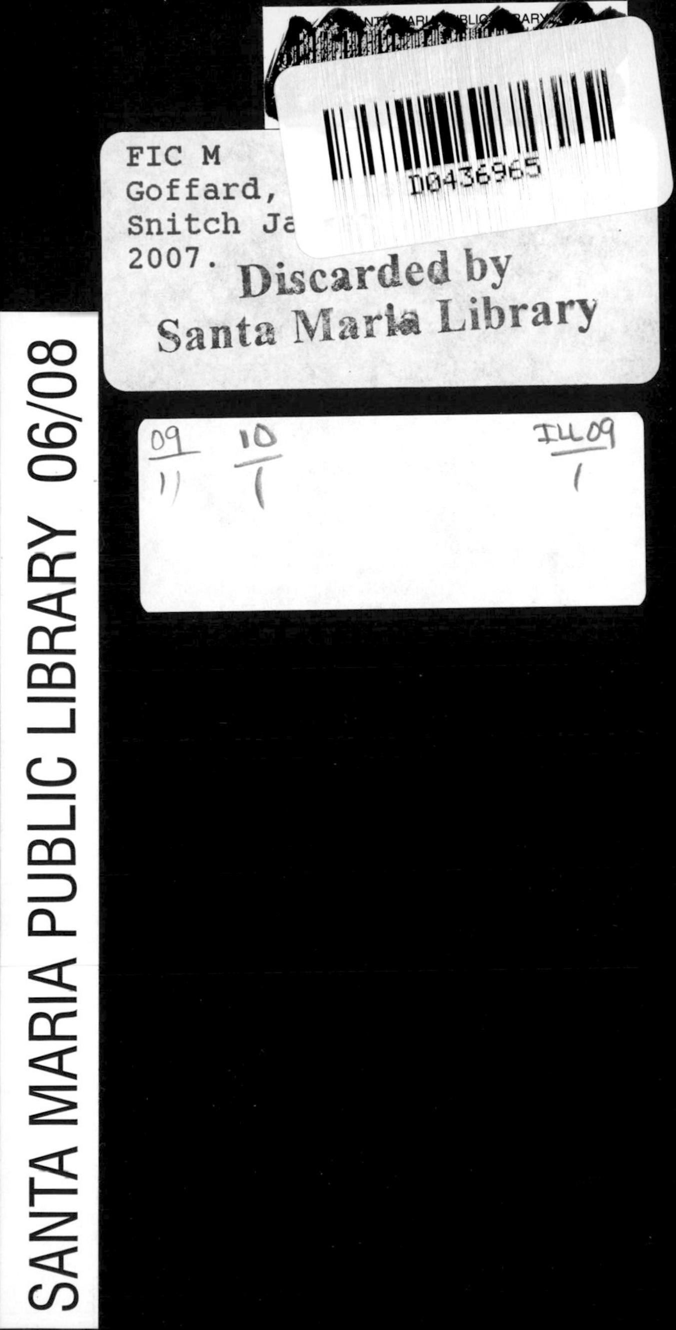

SNITCH JACKET

SNITCH JACKET

Christopher Goffard

Overlook/Rookery
New York, New York

SNITCH JACKET

This edition first published in The United States of America in 2007 by
The Rookery Press, Tracy Carns Ltd.
in association with The Overlook Press
141 Wooster Street
New York, NY 10012
www.therookerypress.com

This is a work of fiction. Names, characters, places, and incidents are either the product of the author's imagination or are used fictitiously, and any resemblance to actual persons, living or dead, business establishments, events, or locales is entirely coincidental.

Cataloging-in-Publication Data is on file at the Library of Congress

Printed in the United States of America
FIRST EDITION

ISBN 1-58567-954-2
ISBN-13 978-1-58567-954-6

9 8 7 6 5 4 3 2 1

To Jennifer, Julia, Sophia
& my parents

ACKNOWLEDGMENTS

The author wishes to thank the following people for their friendship, feedback, and/or random gifts of inspiration, which proved invaluable in writing this book: Jesse Wilson, Danny Wein, Andy Conn, Chuck Natanson, Will Fischbach, Bill Varian, Mark and Anne Albracht, Graham and Nicole Brink, Robert Eldred, Darren Madigan, Gary and Inge Bortolus, Jamal and Sami Thalji, Charley Demosthenous, Sean Keefe; special thanks to Seth Jaret, my manager; my agents Phil Patterson and Luke Speed; James Gurbutt, my editor; my parents; and my wife Jennifer, above all.

snitch jacket \'snich 'ja-ket\ noun: slang term denoting the state of being an informer; believed to have a jailhouse origin stemming from the distinctive colors worn by informers in protective custody; considered pejorative; see also: *snitch, informer, confidential informant, C.I., sing, stool pigeon, squealer, squeaker, squawker, narc, songbird, rat*

'Snitches are a dying breed.' – Outlaw Biker saying

PART I

THE OUTLAW

CHAPTER 1

The big man lived in the janitor's closet behind the bar, and through the night you could hear him building birdhouses. He sawed and hammered in his tiny room, using scraps of pine and cedar and aluminum foraged from flea markets and junk piles. His knuckles grew together in knobby masses, they'd been broken so many times, but over the wood his hands ran rhythmically, sanding and smoothing. Finished, the birdhouses looked as fragile and crushable, cradled in those lumpy sledgehammer mitts, as the eggs of the phantom fowl they were supposedly meant for. They hung from the ceiling and piled up on his padlocked ice-chest and foot-locker, alongside his cigar box of war souvenirs and photos of Army buddies. By daybreak he'd be flat on his mattress gazing dead-eyed at the empty aviaries, each one dustily returning his stare with the single neat blind eye he'd bored in its middle. By mid-morning he'd be asleep, sawdust filming his beard and the gray coat of his ancient dog, Jesse James, dozing beside him on a Mexican blanket.

No one knew for sure, but we supposed the big man had picked up his hobby in some prison woodshop, the same way his body had collected ink from Soledad to Starke. He wore patriotic eagles and vampire bitches, Old Testament prophets and pitchfork devils. His tattoos were like stickers commemorating ports of call on an enormous, beaten suitcase. They crowded each other, overlapped, got jumbled up. The names he'd worn over the years sometimes got jumbled up too. By the time he came to live in the bar he was calling himself Gus Miller.

Mad Dog Miller's legend preceded him. 'Mad Dog lobotomized a whole squad of Vietcong with a chopstick,' people whispered. And: 'Mad Dog survived six weeks in the Khe-Sanh mountains on his own urine.' The first look you got of him – the gimlet eyes blazing through crooked glasses, the crimson face with the riot of exploded veins, the gigantic tar-streaked Norse-god beard – well, you could even believe it. Bedlam in the bones, his face proclaimed.

One of his birdhouses, a nice little Tudor cottage job, is sitting now on the sill of the 11-by-7½-foot cell where I'm writing this as a guest of the State of California. It makes me miss the big man, though of course I wouldn't be in this brick-and-razorwire snakepit if he hadn't lumbered into the Greasy Tuesday with his dog and his million stories and his movie-house sentimentality.

The night I first saw him, he was throwing his war medals against the wall and wearing a necklace of human ears. I knew right away I wanted to be his friend.

CHAPTER 2

My public defender's name is Walter Goins. You'd think it rhymes with loins, from the spelling, but it's pronounced go-*ins*. Gut, combover, firesale suit, Looney Tunes tie: he does not inspire confidence.

We're sitting in an interview room with a stainless-steel table between us and I'm trying to make him understand the horrible wrongness of my situation. I share a filthy brick cell, and a lidless toilet, with three other guys awaiting trial: a gabby junky with sores on his arms; a schoolteacher facing vehicular manslaughter who weeps in his sleep; and a swastika-covered teenager who stabbed his girlfriend's mom with a chlorine-filled syringe. They're all resigned to it, one way or another. You can see it in their eyes, the knowledge that their lives pointed here, right here, all along; it's a kind of comfort to arrive.

'I'm not like these others,' I tell Goins. 'I don't belong here.'

'You've been in lockup before, right?' Goins says.

'Few months in county jail here and there,' I say. 'I can hack it for a while. But state prison? Christ, Goins, they send me there, you could measure my life with an egg-timer.'

First they push you into a broom closet. Then they bust out your teeth and take turns while you kneel. Then they cut out your tongue and say, 'You won't talk to pigs no more, even in hell.' Then they slip the shank, and by then, you're glad to say: So long.

Goins is all that's standing between me and that broom closet.

But his tie is making me insanely insecure, a reminder of how utterly fucked I am. Clear sign he's a public defender – no one would *hire* an attorney in a Looney Tunes tie – and he wears it like a defiant sneer.

'What are you, a pediatrician?' I say in a half-joking tone meant to conceal my nervousness. 'Of course, my broke ass, I get you *gratis*, so who am I to complain how you dress?'

'It's a grim life,' Goins says flatly, fingering the tie. 'Why not?'

'A little sartorial whimsy, sure, I appreciate that. Life is pretty grim. Except mine is in your hands here, Goins. You understand? *Mine is in your hands.*'

'I take my responsibility to my clients very seriously, but I try not to take myself too seriously. There's a distinction, you know.'

He watches me with chill, suspicious eyes as if I were some kind of repellent rodent. The look tells me I'm just another imbecile client, tells me Goins sees what almost everyone else sees: a short, unscrubbed man with bad posture, bad teeth, and jittery, chemically damaged eyes that are set a little too close together – the kind of guy he unconsciously edges away from in the elevator, one no Girl Scout ever approached with a box of cookies. An antisocial personality who, save for the manacles bolting his hands to the table, might lunge across and stick a Bic pen in his lawyer's eye.

'I'm not at all what you think,' I say in a kind of angry panic. 'I always had ambitions.'

I explain that I could've been a lot of things, had I put my mind to it. Maybe a history professor. I love history. I know a lot about it.

'In a game of Trivial Pursuit,' I say, 'I'm pretty sure I could go toe-to-toe with you, even though you're almost a lawyer and I'm just an ex-dishwasher at a Mexican restaurant facing Murder One. Did you know the Aztecs imbibed their beer anally during religious festivals? Aztec Empire, 1325 to 1521. Good to know history.'

A cop is another thing I could've been, I explain, really the main thing I wanted to be. One of those detectives who swishes into a crime scene – he's got a bad-ass overcoat, so he swishes – and sees what everyone else misses. 'What we need on these bullets,' he says, 'is some Neutron Activation Analysis. And don't forget to run the ICPs.' I tell Goins that's short for Inductively Coupled Plasma Optimal Emission Spectroscopy Analysis.

'I bet you never had a client who knew that, have you, Goins?'

'I guess not.'

'It's good to know science.'

'Why are you telling me this?'

'I'm not one of these low-lifes,' I say. 'You think I couldn't be a lawyer, if I'd put my mind to it? Not just a PD, either: a real one. Double-breasted suits, new tie every day of the year, Mont Blanc pens – that's the name of a high-end pen – with a few little diamonds in it, maybe, that flashed when I pulled it out to sign something. Cufflinks with double Bs: Benny Bunt. My watch? Emporio Armani job, cutting edge: no numbers, no hands. Maybe a Timex in my pocket to actually tell the time with. Salvatore Ferragamo, Louis Vuitton: Italians crawling in every orifice. That's what I'd look like, if I were a lawyer.'

He doesn't find any of this funny. Cuttingly I add: 'Always figured I'd be a prosecutor, on the side of the good guys.'

He smiles icily. 'Well,' he says, 'it's the *good guys* who want to stick a needle in your arm filled with sodium chloride. The scientific term is "joy juice".'

He seems to sense that I've been testing his stones, trying to measure the fight in him.

'Look,' I say, 'I didn't mean to insult you. The truth is, I'm embarrassed by how much I want you to like me. You're my Destroyer Lawyer. You're my Demon Barrister. And I have absolute faith,' I lie, 'that you're going to find a way to get me out.'

Goins's eyes don't change; his face doesn't twitch; he genuinely doesn't care whether I believe in him or not. I fear I have already alienated him beyond repair, squandered what little goodwill he might have brought to the table.

'You seem to have some education,' Goins says.

'Three semesters at Costa Mesa Community College. I was going for a degree in Criminal Justice.'

'What happened?'

There's a lot I could tell Goins. Like how by the time I enrolled, in my mid-twenties, I'd been surviving on my own for 10 years, drifting in and out of juvie halls and county lockups, mostly on charges related to an on-again, off-again attachment to crystal meth. I could tell him how it's tough to concentrate on your midterms when you've been up for 50 hours straight, fingering nuts and bolts, dismantling your roommate's toaster, and clawing through Dumpsters for aluminum cans (not for the pennies they bring, although this helps buy more powder, but to satisfy the mysterious tactile jones every meth monster knows).

No, college wasn't for me. I could tell Goins about all I learned from a guy I met at the Van Nuys public library, a retired professor named Ray Castle, whose couch I crashed on until I realized he had ancient Greek notions of what a mentor–pupil relationship should be. I could tell him about the six different law-enforcement agencies that rejected my applications for employment, as cop, as dispatcher, even as clerk. I could catalogue for him the jobs I've worked and lost – short-order cook, furniture-hauler, lawn boy, telemarketer, Blockbuster Video clerk, assistant at a one-hour photomat, ice-cream scooper at Baskin Robbins, Radio Shack stock boy – and point out how a rap sheet and no degree makes it tough to get much better.

Or I could admit that I've always found a kind of security in dead-end jobs, because as long as I could tell myself I was just slumming, just logging time in a temporary gig that didn't come close to defining me, well, maybe I wasn't out of the ballgame yet. Like an actor who'd rather wait tables than teach junior-high drama: the first job means he's waiting to arrive, the second that he's given up all hope of arriving. Instead I say, 'I wasn't a college type of guy. Plus, two jobs in the world let you do all the reading you want. One's bum. The other's jailbird. I've been both. Once read a dictionary page-by-page during a six-month jail stint, made it all the way to the Rs. Got the idea from Malcolm X.'

He flips open a yellow pad. He says, 'Well, let me stack it up for you. We have a man in the Mojave Desert with a bullet in him, and your prints on the gun. We have another guy burned beyond recognition, and you the last person seen in his company. And we have a third guy being thawed out now like a Neanderthal in an ice-slab, found in a vehicle you were driving. In short, Benny, the stage is ass-deep in corpses. And *you're* ass-deep in trouble. First-degree murder, felony murder, conspiracy to commit murder—'

Suddenly it's hard to breathe, and I say, 'Goins – Goins – that's not me.'

He looks at me, blinking, as if astounded by the zeal of my denial.

'Okay,' he says. 'Alright. I'd like to believe you. All I can do is ask you to tell me the truth. I don't really expect you to – no one does – but it's you who gets the screwing if you lie. We've got exactly four days till your prelim. That's where the state puts on a preview of its case, and the judge decides whether there's probable cause to bind it over to Superior Court for trial.'

'I know what a prelim is.'

'It's our chance to blow the case out of water, early. Although I'm not gonna lie about the odds.'

'What do you need from me?'

'Everything you can tell me – anything even remotely relevant to the case. Anything else that'll help me understand the world from inside your skull. If I'm going to make a judge and jury empathize, I need to feel it. I mean, I can fake it, but I like to feel it. I want to be able to write a book about you. Pretend I'm a bird on your shoulder, seeing and hearing everything. Alright? So start. Start where it starts.'

'The Greasy Tuesday.'

He clicks his pen and starts writing. 'It started on a Tuesday?'

'I couldn't say, Goins. I'm telling you the place's name.'

CHAPTER 3

The Greasy Tuesday is a one-room, sawdust-floor dive on Harbor Boulevard in Costa Mesa, on a block the Orange County Chamber of Commerce will never allow to blight a postcard. Scrub shops, check-cashing joints, a Chinese rub-down palace, a porn emporium, a Church's Chicken, a 99-cent fish-taco stand: you get the picture.

On the corner squats a wholesale wig outlet, and in my Bad Benny days – I mean my adventures-in-amphetamine days – I found myself standing in horror before the display window, with its cloned ranks of bodiless heads. I'd listen to them muttering, trying to form words with their painted mouths. With a meth-fiend's paranoia, I believed they were denouncing me, talking some kind of shit. Other times I wept at their helplessness and believed they just wanted a listener, wanted desperately to explain how they wound up in such an asinine limbo. And I'd think, 'You poor bastards, you're not alone.'

People say John Wayne used to drink at the Greasy Tuesday. For years he owned a mansion down the hill in Newport Beach, so it was possible, just possible, but I never believed it. Framed behind the cash register hangs a black-and-white photo of the Duke – the leathery older Duke – leaning over a bottle at the scarred, horseshoe-shaped counter of this very bar. Some regulars think the Duke's head sits at a funny angle on the body, like someone cut it out of a book and glued it on. But they don't say this around Little Junior, the owner. A rabid Duke-loving American, Junior is, though a terrible failure at eradicating his New Zealand upbringing from his voice.

There might or might not have been all kinds of colorful pistoleros and desperadoes who also figured in the bar's history. A card shark named Anaheim Ames, who gambled away (and won back) his glass eye a couple of times a year, and whose best friend stabbed him to death over a misheard word . . . a quadriplegic hit-man, Nick 'Piranha' Pranwitcz, who lured you close with his one working finger, as if to whisper a secret, only to seize your jugular in the unbreakable vise of his jaws . . . a dwarfish cat-burglar, Hugo Mink, who locked eyes with his heart's truest yen – a tall, busty, ample-assed woman – the moment his head emerged from the AC vent over her bed, the same tragic Mink who later asphyxiated going down a chimney to steal her an engagement ring . . . a gambler with powers of precognition, Tony the Money, whose hands shook violently when he saw the future and who shot himself after calling a Kentucky Derby superfecta because no one would front him a dime to put on it, his curse being that he couldn't stay away from the track even when his strange gift wasn't working . . . and Mad Dog Miller, who persuaded his VC torturers to let him eat his maggoty rice with a chopstick, then used the humble utensil to dispatch the lot of them . . . each name doing service as a kind of empty gigantic foot-locker where people who felt like talking had been putting their stories for years . . .

In the mornings, before the sun burns away the fog that rolls in from the ocean down the hill, the maintenance hands and labor-pool men arrive in their pickups and utility vans. They load up on three-buck breakfasts of whiskey-spiked black coffee and eggs with Tabasco sauce, before rattling off to whatever kidney-shaped pool or strip of expensive lawn or patch of Mediterranean roof they're working that day in Newport. All afternoon the bar drowses in the cool, smoky dimness; a few old rummies push around pieces on a checkerboard; unshaven men work up doomed schemes on napkins and coasters. At sunset the laborers come straggling back with the day's stinks and resentments, trading punches and complaints about the rich. And at night the vampires slink out of their 55-dollar-a-night motels and one-room efficiencies, folding hands the color of the Dead Sea Scrolls across the counter, with their purple lips and eyes that don't line up and armpits that sweat gin through the night. Side by side, their slouching bodies look like some kind of slumscape, a row of rat-gnawed tenements. The sight tended to cheer me up.

I never knew how the bar got its name. It probably had to do with the cost-efficiency of tacking a couple of letters to the front of a prior, prettier one, judging from the Frankenstein neon hanging now above the grimed, mustard-colored façade: GR*Easy Tuesday*.

One night after my shift at the restaurant (Mexican, sink) I found myself dreading the prospect of home, of another evening confined with my wife and the gibber of the TV. In no time my bicycle had taken me across town and parked me in front of the bar, and then I was moving down the long, smoky hallway at the entrance toward the blur of bodies and dim crimson illumination in the main room, suddenly depressed that I had no place else to go, that I felt at home only here. It couldn't reflect well on me. Already the familiar smell assailed me – the bar's fetid compost of alcoholic sweat, sawdust, Kmart cologne, Brylcreem, cigarette ash, piss, intestinal bile, domestic beer – and already I was becoming part of the smell, augmenting it with all the bad sweat and misery coming out of me. I drifted down the hall like a man carried by a powerful invisible current, propelled toward the sweetly alluring sin-lights of the bar, not even conscious of working my legs toward them.

I had slipped down this tunnel so many times, lived in this smell so many years, the passage was automatic; I believed my ghost would be doing it long after my body departed, just like

Tony the Money and the other trapped shades. It occurred to me, not for the first time, that I was going to die here, I was going to die just another bad smell, among the mole men, no better than any of them. I knew every inch of this bar's scabrous skin, and it knew every inch of mine. We owned each other and understood each other. We were like one of those bitter old couples you see, she and I, hating each other even as we wrapped our bored bones around each other one more time – a hideous nightly dry-hump, lacking passion or even pleasure. Nevertheless I was hers and she was mine and there was some comfort in that.

The tunnel opened into the main room, and I stepped through the vertical sheets of smoke toward the counter, moving past the 10 or 12 cheap stools arrayed around the horseshoe. The stools that weren't sticky with beer were spilling stuffing from gouges in their surfaces or patched with masking tape. I found my favorite stool at the far end of the bar and hunkered down to wait for my drink. Familiar faces around the bar: trajectories doomward as my own.

Telly Grimes was back tonight, after six months in lockup. He wore his favorite uniform of snakeskin boots, Levis, Western longsleeve shirt with pearly snap-buttons, and Texas bronco-buckle. It was good to see him. He was sitting beside his best friend, Sal Chamusco.

'I tell them, "Officers, fer crissakes, it ain't my shit,"' Telly said. 'What kinda dumb-ass keeps fifty hot volleyballs in his back seat? I say, "When you gonna leave a man alone in this country?" I say, "*You* put 'em there, you fascist fucks. I know how far you'll go . . ."'

Telly was recounting his latest arrest, drinking Coors, chain-smoking 405s and saying fucking-pigs this, fucking-pigs that. He was an ex-radioman with a voice all bass and gravel, textured with 35 years of fumy carcinogens. Gaunt and bent, with gapped fanglike choppers and gray, moistureless skin, he was easier to imagine hanging upside-down in a cave than sleeping in any human habitation.

A one-man clearance center for all kinds of random black-market trade, Telly spent a lot of time slouching against the fence at soccer games and loitering near labor pools, hawking cheap-jack green cards and drivers' licenses. Mexicans called him 'El Chupacabra,' after the legendary beast that swept down from the hills to spirit away cows and drink from their jugulars. Telly believed it was an endearing term of some kind, maybe Spanish for 'dude' or 'pal.' Once, with the aim of peddling a 'miracle' to the faithful, he went through a half-dozen lighters failing to burn the recognizable likeness of the Virgin of Guadalupe on a flour tortilla.

Telly was on his second pair of lungs and needed a third. Three years ago, an ice-slick sent a Mormon teenager through a windshield and saved Telly from emphysema. He was certain he didn't deserve the new lungs; it seemed an awful injustice the kid should be snuffed out so that Telly, who knew he was one of God's sorrier sons, could kick around larcenously for another decade or so. He vowed to beat his vices and do his best to obey the law. He bought walking shoes. He went to AA. He tried to develop a Personal Relationship With Jesus Christ. He quit smoking and lectured on its evils, twitchily spitting bag after bag of sunflower seeds into the sawdust. His friends found him insufferable.

Raging with tears, and with a Michelob bottle trembling threateningly in his grip, Sal Chamusco finally told Telly that he missed his best friend, that he'd rather see him dead than replaced by this seed-spitting psalm-sucker who'd taken him over like a pod creature.

They embraced then, hot tears filling the cystic pits on Telly's cheeks. Sal lit a cigarette and thrust it at the thin, purple gash of his friend's mouth; the men looked at each other silently for a long time until, slowly parting, the lips received. Apart from jail stints, Telly had not been without a cigarette since.

Right now they were sitting beside each other and fixedly avoiding each other's eyes. Sal was a squat, nervous man who wore a baggy Members Only jacket and a mustache that refused to meet in the middle.

'Why'd the pork stop you in the first place?' Sal asked. He carried a Bic lighter snug in his sweaty palm, like a sick man with his hand on the call nurse's button. When he was depressed, especially around the holidays, he torched Dumpsters to make himself feel better. I was never a lover of fire myself, but in certain black moods I could admire the purity of the fuck-you it represented.

'Tag,' Telly said wearily. 'Tag's expired. Who can jump through those DMV hoops anyway? Miserable fucking luck! And I tell them, "I didn't loot the fucking Sports Authority! I got these offa some wetbacks! You can't connect me to that shit!"'

'You accuse the cops of planting those balls,' Sal said.

'Bet your ass I did,' Telly said.

'Then you say some Mexicans sold 'em to you.'

'Right.'

'Maybe you deserve to get jacked-up, story like that.'

Their posture resembled two men having a conversation in a car, watching something distasteful through the windshield, rather than each other.

'Six months of my life's nothing to laugh about,' Telly said. 'This is a joke to you? You know what they feed you in the Orange County jail?'

'Goats'd puke their guts,' I said. 'I've been three times.'

'Thank you, Benny,' Telly said. 'Benny's been three times.'

'Hear you ate a lot of salad in there,' Sal told Telly. 'Hear they got an all-you-can-eat salad bar.'

Drunks sputtered and wheezed in amusement. Telly looked wounded. He cut his eyes to his Coors.

Little Junior walked over and said in his cheery Kiwi lilt, 'They torture you with greens, huh? What's so bad about—'

'He means ass-eating,' I said. 'Don't ask me who thought it up. Reminded some inmate of a nice bed of Romaine, and there you are.'

Junior hurried away to find some glasses to towel off.

Telly to Sal: 'I siddown tonight, six months in the dungeon, what do I get? Everyone else is, "Hey, Telly," and "Good to have you back, Telly," and you're like, "Hey." That's it. "Hey." Not a hug, not a handshake, just the fuckin' stink-eye all night.'

'You been stink-eyin' me!'

'Well, maybe I hate you, you greasy guinea fuck!'

'Maybe I hate you too, you fuckin' salad eater!'

In this fashion they made up. Soon they were sitting with their arms around each other's shoulders – long, bony Telly and fire-plug Sal, cursing each other and shaking with laughter.

Suddenly I was as invisible as the drifting smoke. Seeing them in that brotherly, almost amorous huddle – these two gnarled hoodlums, these low-rent lepers who didn't know half the things that I did – I felt a familiar kid-alone-in-the-cafeteria ache. It seemed unfair they should enjoy such a bond.

It's like trying to be friendly with an ugly, kicked-around dog you believe would appreciate your attention. You say, 'Come here, boy,' but all the mutt does is show you its ass. You watch his balls bounce away, and suddenly you're a lower thing than he is.

'We're a proud people,' Sal said. 'We made up the Sistine Chapel and vendettas.'

'Wops got the God racket, I'll give you that,' Telly said. 'But you stole it from the Heebs.'

Soon Sal was quietly apprising Telly of recent commerce. Eddie the Chink was trying to move some hot Björk tickets, a shipment of luffas, a set of *Star Trek: The Wrath of Khan* collectible plates, six reclining plastic nativity lambs, and three cases of ben-wah walls; Balboa Bill was on the hunt for some animated Japanese splatterporn; a dude in Newport wanted to unload some Swedish furniture, Brazilian exercise videos, and South American fighting fish . . .

I sat listening, looking as harmless and inconspicuous as an empty bar stool. My only real talent: listening, filing away what I hear using memory tricks I picked up in magazines (since a man didn't want to be seen taking notes amid loose talk of larceny). There's a gigantic old Southern plantation house in my head with 10,000 rooms where I deposited what I picked up, street names of underworld players, accomplices, cribs, cross streets, car types, girlfriends, pimps. Benny Bunt's Fabulous Memory Palace, I call it, and there are things kicking around in those rooms – recipes for failed drinks and bad limericks and obscure words from 15 years of vocabulary calendars, and data on long-dead batting champions and the Turn Ons and Turn Offs of Eighties Playmates – that I sometimes wish would clear out and make room for better tenants. Maybe it's low on the scale of important gifts a man should possess in the world, this memory stuff, but it made me ferocious at Trivial Pursuit, particularly because I'd flawlessly memorized all the cards ahead of time. And it helped pay the bills.

I'm a snitch.

Not one of these low-lifes at all. You must've mistaken me, sir! No: a spy, a man on a mission, an agent of higher authorities merely posing as a lower life form. A soldier behind enemy lines.

I could remember the smell of those fine, white, regulation-size volleyballs when Telly brought them in last year, three in each arm, factory-fresh in their packages. He passed them around, but found no takers, the bar's regulars not being known for their athleticism. (By mysterious channels he'd also acquired eight pairs of Chuck Norris crotch-flex jeans that we snapped up immediately. Snug inside them, you were supposed to be able to throw head-level axe-kicks 'without hindrance from the superflexible fabric,' as Telly put it. 'A confidence builder in any dangerous situation.' So clad, we spent the next half-hour out back kicking up packing crates with savage martial grunts and howls. Sal Chamusco hurt himself the worst, ambitiously trying to get his leg above his waist; the rest of us settled for knee-level and below.)

That day I excused myself from the bar, found a payphone down the block, and called Detective Al Munoz. El Guapo. I gave him the license plate of Telly's 1978 DeVille – retrieved from one of the rooms in my brain labeled 'Potential Useful Stuff' – and told him about the hot volleyballs he could find in it. The wonderful Norris jeans I didn't mention. 'Keep the tips coming, Cowboy,' Munoz told me. 'I'll pass it on to Property Crimes and make sure you get a few bills. And lemme know when you hit some gold.' He meant something better than a stash of hot sporting goods, something a homicide man like himself could use. Munoz was always calling me Cowboy. We had a special understanding.

Graffiti carved into the bar's counter top:

I smell bacon, I smell grease
I smell the Costa Mesa police

'Those jackboot pigfuckers, I'd like to, I dunno what,' Telly was saying bitterly, scanning the bar for the comfort of shared bitterness. 'But I'd like to do something to 'em.'

'We'd all like to do something to 'em,' I said. With a flourish I peeled back the sleeve of my shirt to show the six-inch scar across my forearm, where I cut myself colliding with a fence (schnapps, Schwinn). 'Last time they picked me up, I got this souvenir. Some men are blessed by luck, but I don't see any such man at this bar.'

From the end of the bar, Old Larry Swet muttered in outrage at the cops' treatment of his pals Benny and Telly, making a noise that sounded like, 'Uhhhfuggin fuggin caz! Gugdammit peegahs! Nug blaggah!' He was in his seventies, wasted to the shanks and barely capable of human speech anymore, but his watery eyes followed people's mouths when they spoke. Outrage shuddered through his brittle old body, and, shaking his head slowly, he looked between me and Telly sympathetically. It was good to have his love.

'Larry knows,' Telly said.

'A man who's logged some mileage on the unluck highway,' Sal said.

'Look, Telly,' I said. 'Those Nazis stole six months of your life you won't get back, and they gave me this gash, but there's no sense dwelling on it too much. God knows we've got the right. *God knows*. But you're back in the land of the drinking now, and I'd like to put one in your paws to celebrate.'

Telly was touched. 'Shit, that's pretty decent of you, Benny.'

'Least I could do. And one for Sal and Larry too.'

Junior brought the drinks. Telly and Sal and Larry raised their glasses to me and cursed the Man. I raised mine in solidarity, shouting, 'Fuck the fucking Man!' We drank, and it was a beautiful moment, the sense of brotherhood in the room almost enough to bring tears to a man's eyes.

It was a fine thing, to be here in the cool, smoky dark with the other ugly men, none of us even ugly in the shadows, our bad yellow teeth unseen and our cracked veins nearly invisible. The love we shared was a true love, the strange family love of moles for fellow denizens of the tunnels.

With such emotions in my chest I told myself that I snitched on them for their own good. Freedom was bad for them. They didn't know what to do with it. Lockup kept them from drinking and smoking themselves to death. I was doing them a kindness. Without some time away in lockup, besides, tender reunions like these would be impossible.

'How's your woman?' Telly asked me. 'She letting you in these days?'

'Sure,' I said. 'Twice a year I go to the mines. Bring your pick and shovel and get down to work.'

A man shouldn't malign his woman this way. I'm against it on principle, and have no respect for men who do it. But Telly laughed, and Sal laughed, and Old Larry made a half-gurgling, half-choking noise that was probably laughter, and they were all raising their drinks again to witty Benny, smiling in boozy brotherhood at me over the scum of their glasses.

Every day I said to myself, 'I will not talk shit about my woman today.' But it's easy to betray your principles for a little love. Still, you could've asked these guys: I was still about the biggest-hearted human being you ever met. 'Benny Bunt might not be so easy on the eyes,' they'd say, 'but he is one big-hearted motherfucker.' They all remembered me staking them drinks when they were hard up. Among the chronically hard-up, that coin went a long way.

CHAPTER 4

I couldn't say when Gus Miller walked in, because I didn't see him. In fact he just seemed to materialize in the smoke around midnight, like some kind of demon-bear in the misty woods. I looked up from my fourth or fifth or sixth beer, and there he was across the bar, this enormous stranger with shaggy gray hair pulled together in a ponytail that hung down his back through the opening of a Yankees cap, and his bare arms so thick with tattoos that for a moment I thought he was wearing sleeves. Sal and Telly and Old Larry cackled at some story he was telling.

'Who's that big Willie Nelson motherfucker over there?' I asked Junior. 'Look at all that scribbling on him. He looks like a toilet stall.'

'I dunno.'

'I suppose he's being funny. He's the new funny guy around here.'

'Take it easy, Benny. A bar has room for more than one. Have another.'

He brought me another drink and I carried it over to where the gray-haired stranger was holding court. At his feet lay the world's sorriest-looking mutt. A rangy, smoky-gray dog that looked to me like a German shepherd, although the stranger was saying it had strains of wild Canadian steppe-wolf in it.

'Why'd you call him Jesse James?' Telly asked Gus Miller.

'Got an outlaw soul, like mine,' said Gus. It sounded like he'd said this with pleasure more than a few times before.

The big guy carried some old prison muscle, some once-serious fuck-you muscle that now sagged with fatty layering. He had shoulders that would fill a doorway and a garrulous deep-throated cigarette voice, and the long-suffering face of a sinful Santa Claus who might have spent his best years in a maximum-security prison. A hand-rolled cigarette slanted from the gash in his nicotine-yellow beard, the smoke dribbling upward into the climbing curtains of gray fume made by the men up and down the bar. There was so much smoke around him that for a moment I thought of a corpulent, disheveled djinn that had just slipped from its lantern to perch on this undersized stool.

When the smoke purled away from his face, leaving momentary fissures through which I could glimpse his broad, flat features, I noticed the pair of square glasses that hung slightly crooked, from a missing nose-guard on the left side. He wore a Taco Bell give-away T-shirt with a picture of a chihuahua on it, the sleeves scissored off high so that you could see the unbroken mural of tattoos running from the top of each shoulder down to the backs of his hands. The usual ex-con shit: snakes, screaming skulls, naked sluts, patriotic eagles, bleeding Christ, Satan, Confederate stars and bars, Indian stuff, mythic heroes, Chinese characters. The right tricep said: 'PLAY IT LOUD,' 'HARDSCRABBLE MAN,' and 'HARDLUCK BASTARD,' while a forearm that said: 'JOHN 3:16' (a prop, I guessed, to impress some parole board), '13½' (meaning: 12 jurors, one judge, and one-half of a chance), and 'ONE PERCENTER' (denoting proud membership in society's worst 1 percent). The left arm said: 'POW/MIA,' 'VFW,' and '173rd' and had a bunch of other military emblems. Some of the ink seemed new and bright. As with a lot of guys who go in for tats, his skin was a schizoid mess, like a cave decorated with the iconography of one tribe and then scrawled over with the totems of its enemies. The arms themselves were cable-thick, but lacking any noticeable muscle-tone, and the Bud longneck he nursed looked tiny in the lumpy mitt of his hand. His fingernails were a half-inch long and scummed with dirt.

Enormous twin jets of smoke spilled from his nostrils as he stroked his dog and said: 'There's pieces of state troopers in his colon.'

Scars crossed the dog's coarse-haired body, a map of lots of bad road traveled. The tip of the dog's left ear was missing, as if chewed off, and drool hung in a constant strand from his mawful of rotten teeth. He refused to eat much besides tacos and burritos, the stranger explained, and he frequently shat himself. Clouded with cataracts, the dog's eyes nevertheless seemed weirdly alert. Sal, always uncomfortable around dogs (a chow once lunged for his testicles), seemed especially wary around Jesse James; I could hear the click-click-click of his Bic.

'This old boy has special senses,' Gus said, his pale gray eyes following us through his crooked glasses. 'Even more'n other dogs, who all got them. Anyone who knows shit about dogs knows this. Jesse James can smell cops from a couple miles away. Some kinda mutant thing. Don't ask me how, but he picks up pig-whiff on the wind. He starts that real deep growling down in his guts, a minute later a black and white cruises by. Anyone means me harm, he knows before I do. This time in Phoenix? I'm breaking break with a hobo. Nice enough hobo, no clue he might be queer. My guard's down. And old Jesse starts that growling . . .'

Through Gus's closed mouth, the growl came, remarkably doglike, murderously threatening. 'His hand's gone into his pocket, and I ain't even noticed. "What the hell is it, old boy? What the hell?" And then Jesse's just a blur going for the dude's hand, and you know what's coming outta that pocket while Jesse's teeth are sinking in? A fish-boning knife. A hobo after Gus Miller's tender cornhole itself. Evil's in a man's sweat, it lives there, Jesse smells it oozing outta you. Old boy's peepers ain't so terrific anymore, but he's got other senses. Like those blind old masters on *Kung Fu Theater* who can snag arrows out of the air based on the vibrations, whooshwhooshwhoosh!'

'I've heard dogs smell, like, ten thousand times what we do,' Telly said.

'More like fifty,' Gus said. 'And that's a normal dog. Mine's twice, three times that. You're an open book to Jesse James.'

The dog was angling his snout into Larry Swet's buttocks. Old Larry stared with his blasted face, twisting his body to monitor the dog's progress into his prostate, too frightened to touch the dog with his frozen, outstretched palm.

'Well now, old boy,' Gus said. 'I don't think it's that kinda bar.'

'Why's he doing that?' Sal said, his lighter going click-click-click.

'Says he smells a cop,' Gus said. 'Got any LAPD in there, friend?'

Gus tugged his dog away, then gave terror-pallid Larry a rough, good-natured thwack on the back. A smile cracked through the stranger's beard, showing chipped yellow teeth. Old Larry looked uncertain for a moment, then his shriveled cheeks filled with color and his toothless old gums hung wide open. He couldn't stop smiling, glowing with sweet relief, making a sound like 'Ugmadaawg mugga.'

'To a dog, see, a bunghole's like a signature,' expounded Gus, a professor now, the bar freaks hushing like delegates at a UN forum, 'or a fingerprint or a snowflake. No two exactly alike. A dog's more intelligent than a human being. It's ancient tribal dog-wisdom. Your glands tell a dog what you're made of. A man, on the other hand, shit: he's stupid and easily betrayed. He'll believe another man's words, or his eyes, and before he knows it there's a shiv in his fucking ribs.'

As he stood to lift the dog onto his lap, stretching himself to his full height, I perceived Gus's enormous – and enormously uneven – dimensions. In his leather military shit-kickers he stood a few inches over six feet tall, with a sagging barrel chest and a gut like a heavyweight's medicine ball. He gave the impression of being able to consume entire chicken coops, if not chicken farms, and of the capacity to shit really unreasonable quantities – avalanches, Pompeii-drowning cataracts of shit. Propping up all this weight were a pair of small, overtaxed legs. A big, square Dumpster of an upper half attached to a set of wobbly Q-tips down below. His Yankees cap, which he wore with a sharp peak, was a cheap bootleg knockoff of Major League Baseball-licensed merchandise. He'd sweated through the cap's gray cloth so that it was permanently black in a rim around the crown. Crumbs of what might have been pretzel or peanut infested several strata of his big yellow beard, which started high on his cheekbones and hung shaggily over his throat.

'It's Jesse's Apache and Blackfoot ancestors,' Gus said, elaborating on the dog's powers. 'He's bred from a race of proud warrior-dogs that ate the white man and the white man's soft yogurt-eating dogs for breakfast.'

'I thought you said he's from Canada,' Sal said.

'On his mamma's side, brother,' Gus said. 'Daddy's side's pure Apache and Blackfoot from way back. Ain't you listening?'

'The big guy's right,' I said. 'Some dogs are telepathic over short distances. There're studies on it.' Inventing one on the spot, I added: 'Conway-Kane, University of Minnesota, 1992.'

'Matter of fact,' Gus said with a slow nod, 'they wanted Jesse James for that one. I said, "Over my fat dead carcass am I gonna let you poke him and electrode him, you government maggots."'

Muscles twitched in Old Larry's leathery cheek and his shrunken fist slammed the bar top. 'Mufukkin gummint!' he cried.

'CIA gets their hands on him, what do you think they'd do? Exploit him as a weapon of war, same as they did me,' Gus said. 'An assassin of indigenous populations. I've worked for the government – shit I can't really talk about – and I know how their thinking runs. I've been there! Covert missions! Lookit this!' He pointed to a tattoo on his meat-slab forearm, nestled between a Satanic biker slut and a pair of dice. In bold square letters, it read, 'BLACK OPS.'

'What does this tell you?' he said. 'It tells you I've *been there*.'

Gus had taken my fictional Minnesota study and given himself a personal encounter with it. I waited for a wink from him, a smirk, something that said we were pulling a little harmless jabberwocky on the rest of them. When none came, I began to wonder whether he believed there was such a study. Was he insane?

'Hey,' Telly said, 'they're throwing hands over there.'

Two large, drunk men with stupid hair – a mullet, a rat-tail – were taking wild, grunting swipes at each other over the pool table. Then they picked up pool sticks and began to have a sword-fight. 'Come on, bitch!' one cried. 'Bring it, bitch!' cried the other. 'Step up, bitch!' shouted the first. Soon it became a ham-fisted wrestling match, the two of them tumbling sideways onto the pool table and holding each other in a furious, panting, spittle-streaked clench. Bets were placed on the outcome.

It wasn't until a pool ball came flying over the counter and into the mirror that Little Junior decided to stop it. The jockey-sized barkeep was too cheap to hire a bouncer and forever picking up drubbings as a result. The combatants stood there with their stupid hair mussed, snarling, winded, and red-faced, while he ordered them out.

Each man had 70 or 80 pounds of muscle on Little Junior. They were offended that he had interrupted their fun.

'Couple friends can't mix it up a little bit?' panted Rathead, wiping a string of his friend's saliva from his forehead. 'Who laid down that law?'

'My bar's blue-collar, not white trash,' Junior said. 'Jerry Springer's waiting for you on the sidewalk with a contract.'

'Your voice is funny,' Mullet told Junior. 'What *are* you?'

'I'm American,' Junior said defensively.

'He ain't,' Mullet said. 'I can hear it in his throat. I can't pretend I didn't. And I won't.'

'This is Orange County, California,' Rathead said.

'If it was riverdance night,' Mullet said, 'the sign should say, "Riverdance Night."'

'He's Australian, like the Crocodile Hunter!' Sal shouted. 'But he's American.'

'This,' Junior said firmly, 'is John Wayne, Jesus Christ-country. The Duke used to drink here.'

'The Duke was a draft-dodger,' Mullet said. 'Plus a queen. Why do you think he walked that way?'

Junior looked furious, uncertain. 'Riding horses,' he said.

'He hated horses,' Mullet said. 'He had to remind himself to say "ain't."'

'You're a goddamn liar,' Junior said.

'It was the gay rights crowd,' Mullet said, 'that got that airport in Irvine named after him. I can show you the article.'

'I'll show you the fuckin' curb!' Junior screamed.

There are little guys who seem a lot bigger than they are, when they climb up on their bluster. And there are little guys who seem exactly the same size, no matter how much they scream, and only embolden enemies when they do it. Junior was the second kind of little guy.

An unfortunate thing happened to him then, the same unfortunate thing that always seemed to happen when he tried to exert physical force on those larger than himself, which is everybody larger than a jockey. He got his ass kicked. You hoped there'd be patrons to step in to stop this from happening, considering how Junior was a much-loved neighborhood treasure who cashed social security checks to keep people in drinking money and sold Durals for a quarter a smoke. Shame for a man to put his life into a bar only to get his ass kicked in it all the time.

Everyone knew Junior's story. How he inherited the bar from his dad, Dick Dorsey Sr., who was famous for his fistwork. How the old man was an Army boxer and Vietnam vet who looked runty and harmless behind thick Buddy Holly glasses, but could aim his uppercut like a scoped rifle. How he deployed that rifle fist on any man who even vaguely disrespected his bar, but might feed the same man free drinks till the ambulance came, toss him a loan, or let him crash in the janitor's closet. That was old Dorsey, right next to the Duke, in a photo behind the counter, grinning in his Army beret and dress greens and thick glasses. When oldsters told stories of his dad, as they often did – of his violence and generosity and deceptive runtiness – Junior's face got this far-away look. His posture straightened with pride a little, and he had to turn away to hide the mist in his eyes.

But no matter how much he tried to emulate his lost dead pop, the barkeep succeeded only in emulating those World Wrestling patsies in plain tights with names like John Johnson or Don Smith who served as whipping posts for the spectacularly caped-and-monikered steroidal greats.

Tonight all of us just watched as poor Junior once more martyred his little body on the rack of filial longing. Rathead hoisted him by the crotch over his head (Junior's sneering, startled face suspended there at a humiliating angle) and body-slammed him on the pool table, producing an ugly thumping sound and a collective 'Oooof!' throughout the room. Junior lay there writhing like a pinned bug, grimacing with impotent hatred at the Budweiser lamp swinging above him.

You hated to see a thing like that, really. And nobody doing a thing, just a lot of people shaking their heads and saying, 'Poor Junior.'

Except Gus Miller. There was a terrific rush of wind as he sprang off his stool, those undersized legs trucking him along with surprising swiftness. If Mullet even caught a glimpse of the big shape rushing toward him, he had no time to react before a pair of fat tattooed arms were tightening like pythons around his neck from behind. His mouth sagged; his eyes flickered up in his skull; he sagged to the sawdust.

Rathead gaped, retreating against a wall. He smashed a

Michelob Lite against a chair and waved three inches of jagged-edged bottle. 'Git away! Git away, fatguts!'

'I did two tours in Nam and served the devil himself,' Gus growled. 'My kill-count's thirty-two men, fifteen women and eight children. Maybe tonight I improve my stats.'

'Don't think I won't cut open those guts!'

Gus's tone was matter-of-fact, humorous, and terrible. 'I will take that bottle from your hand. I will gouge your eyes out with it. I will fuck your sightless skull with my fifty-four-year-old joint. I will fire jizz into your cranium. I will feed your liver to my dog. Then I will cut off your head and hang it from my rearview mirror as a souvenir.'

Rathead's lip began trembling pathetically. 'Live and let live, okay, brother? Let it be, alright?'

'You havin' a John Lennon moment?' Gus said. 'I'm more a Stones man myself. "Let it bleed" is better than "Let it be," don't you think? Let it bleed! Let it bleed! Let it bleed!'

Rathead dropped the bottle and bolted, leaving his friend unconscious on the floor.

'Battlefield desertion,' Gus said. 'People just don't understand a goddamn thing about friendship anymore.'

Grunting and cursing, Junior climbed off the pool table and kicked the sprawled-out Mullet two or three times in the guts. A few regulars dragged the man by the ankles onto the sidewalk.

Junior limped behind the bar and pounded back three drinks. He told Gus Miller he could drink free all night, and Gus, leaning his elbows on the bar, smiled and said, 'Much obliged. I'll take Bud.'

'What about us?' Sal asked.

'I didn't see anyone else do shit,' Junior said.

'After what they said about the Duke,' Telly told them, 'I was pretty close to fucking them up.'

'Every man is alone in this world, even in his own bar,' Junior said.

'I'm hearing some God's honest truth now,' Gus said.

'You showed some heart and hustle out there,' Sal said. 'We love you, Junior. We wouldn't let anything bad happen.'

'Fuck you,' Junior replied. 'And I'm from New Zealand, asshole. Don't ever call me an Australian again.'

Junior came over and stood in front of me wearing a foul, troubled expression. 'You know history, right?' he asked hesitantly. 'That true about the Duke liking other cowboys?'

'That was an ugly lie,' I said. 'But it was true about horses. He hated 'em. And it was true about "ain't." He didn't like to say it. I'm sorry.'

'What about draft-dodging?'

'That's true too,' I said.

'Liberal media horseshit,' Telly said. 'Duke was a great American. He never ran from nothing. Remember that part in *The Searchers* where he shoots out the dead Indian's eyes so he'll wander blind between the winds forever? I mean, just to be a cold motherfucker?'

'Maybe my favorite flick,' Gus said. 'Where he says, "What the Red Man don't understand is, there are some critters that just keep comin' – and I'm one of 'em." Gives me wood, religiously.'

Junior opened a Bud longneck and stood it in front of Gus. 'I'm grateful for the hand, and I mean no disrespect,' Junior told him, 'but you're kind of a scary piece of work.'

'Terrorizing shitbirds gets my nuts off,' Gus said. 'Trouble with a rumpus at fifty-four, you pay for it later. A body don't bounce back. Not when you got arthritis, gout, a gimpy spine, and a bad ticker, and I ain't even gonna tell you about my liver, much less the horror-movie runnin' in my brain . . .' Stroking his dog, he added: 'Hate to see my favorite drinking establishment dissed that way.'

'I've never seen you in here before,' Junior said.

'Been thirty-odd years,' Gus said. 'Back when Dorsey ran it. Giant of a man, Dorsey. When the pintsized bastard was standing on his guts, that is.'

'You knew him?'

'Brothers in Special Ops,' Gus said. 'I sucked a pit viper's venom from his thigh in Da Nang. Men go through a thing like that together, well . . .' He held aloft two meaty, entwined fingers. 'That's the kind of friendship most never know.'

Junior's face filled with questions and a kind of nervous pride. 'That's my pops you're talking about,' he said quietly.

From Gus: a surprised smile. 'Hell, you're Junior? The one whose mama took him overseas? Your pops talked about you all the time.'

The shot glass Junior had been toweling off hung limply at his side. 'What was he like?' he asked. 'I never – never met him, you know. But he's big in my heart and he's why I'm here.'

'A crazy, two-fisted, play-by-his-own-rules sonofabitch,' Gus said. ''Course, the Latin brothers called him "*mojon*," which means "little turd," but they always said it with respect. We did things in that jungle—' He grimaced into the corners of the room, as if recalling something unmentionable. 'Well, maybe some scabs are better left unpicked.'

'Did he kill a lot of gooks?'

'He did his share.'

'That's my pops,' Junior said with emotion.

Gus opened his wallet and put half of an old, torn dollar bill in front of Junior.

'He gave me this, last I saw him,' Gus said. 'Anytime I was down on my luck, he said this buck'd buy me some friendship.'

From a drawer under the register Junior took a small wooden curio box where he kept items of sentimental value left by his dad. He removed half of a dollar bill. Its torn diagonal edge matched perfectly with the half produced by Gus. There was writing on the bill. Assembled, it read: '*Dick to Gus: eternal IOU for my ass*.'

'Well,' Junior said, 'if my daddy gave you this, you bet it's redeemable here.'

'Who are you, big guy?' Telly said. 'We been here all night and don't know your name. I'm Telly. Mexicans call me Chupacabra.'

'Gus,' he said. 'People used to call me Mad Dog, but I like plain Gus these days.'

'Mad Dog Miller?' Sal asked. '*The* Mad Dog Miller?'

'Only one of me,' he said. 'The world never thought to kick around two men that way. World doesn't have a foot big enough.'

We all sat in silence for a moment, digesting that. Junior just stood there with his hands at his sides. Sal worked up the guts to say, 'People said you could tell Mad Dog Miller by his horrific scars.'

Gus turned his big head toward Sal, glaring. 'You take me for some kind of sideshow freak?'

Sal's hand wormed its way into his pocket and came out with the Bic: click-click-click-click—

'Fuck it,' Gus said, slowly standing and peeling his T-shirt up off his enormous belly, up over his sagging man-tits. Someone said: 'Damn.' Another said: 'Holy Christ.'

The whole abdomen crawled with gashes and puncture-wounds and stitch-marks, like the surface of a butcher block. He pulled down his shirt and returned to his beer, saying, 'Horrific enough for your taste?'

'How'd you get 'em?' Telly said.

'Central Highlands, '69,' Gus said. 'Gut-first plunge into a pungi-staked Cong trap. Nearly bled to death, impaled in that godforsaken pit like some kind of hog. Grace of God, monsoons had partially collapsed the trap so I could claw my way out. Found the carcass of a monkey, choked down the rotten flesh to stave off starvation. The maggots? I made a friend of 'em, used 'em to suck out the poison. Finally – this is after three days in the jungle – some American soldiers find me. Come to find out, nobody's been looking for me. My commanders wanted me to disappear. Only two, three people in the military command structure knew the nature of my mission.'

'What sorta mission?' Telly asked.

'Your basic wetworks-type covert shit,' Gus said. 'Assassinations of foreign dignitaries sympathetic to the enemy, with extreme prejudice. You might've heard that phrase in the movies? Actual code. Bona fide. Not supposed to make it back alive. And then I was too dangerous to keep around, so that was the end of my paid vacation in Southeast Asia. Diagnosed Post-Traumatic Stress Disorder, friends: a skullful of fucking demons, screaming monkeys and Napalmed children. Not to mention a ten-percent-shrunken hippocampus. I'm talking about the brain now, brothers. That kinda stress'll shrink it right up. Three months in a VA hospital fighting off infections and then a discharge to the States, where they threw chicken-blood on me and called me a baby-killer and wouldn't give a vet a job . . .'

'Just like my pops,' Junior said. 'It's why he had to open this place.'

'I show up at a flower shop looking for a job,' Gus said. 'Lady's like, "Vets are drunks and dopeheads." She doesn't even want me *shopping* there. I couldn't even spend my own legal-tender *cash* there, that was the thing, the outrage of it. A drunk! Hell, discrimination like that *drove* me to drink! I haven't forgotten that lady. Send her mental hexes whenever I can remember. But that's what it was like, for a man impaled in a filthy Cong pit like a hog on a stick, for a soldier who'd never questioned orders. That was my Welcome Home, Gus . . .'

With such talk he held court for the next couple of hours. His war stories were filled with specific dates, places, battles, regiments, and platoons. They were larded with the kind of sensory detail that threw us into the middle of them. He put us in a Cobra gunship and, pounding the counter with his big hands, made us feel the rattle that went through a man's bones as the machine screamed down at treetop. He put us in hot jungle air impregnated with the stench of a thousand soldiers' burning shit, the day's waste incinerated at night, he explained, with jet fuel in huge tin drums. He spoke of civilian villages torched, atrocities perpetrated. 'They tell us: no witnesses, no survivors,' Gus said. 'Killing becomes a blast of coke in your veins. You need the rush. You don't care anymore. You're a human Terminator. Trained for one thing. Killing. Stealth. Sabotage.'

'That's three things,' said Telly, but Gus didn't seem to hear.

'Uncle Sam'll turn you into a monster,' Gus said. 'But then what? You come home with a dead soul. You can't relate. All you can do is kill. And your fucking noodle's ten percent shrunk, so you lost your impulse-control and can't remember your mamma's face . . . Jesus, if I had my full brain again . . .'

He shook his head at the sawdust floor, as if watching the remains of his gray matter oozing into it. 'I lied to that man,' he muttered disconsolately, 'when I threatened to skull-fuck him. My fifty-four-year-old joint don't even work.'

'Tell about the chopstick incident,' Telly said.

'The what?' Gus asked.

'Braining all those VC,' Telly said.

'And drinking piss in the jungle,' Sal said.

Gus glared darkly at the ground, smoking. 'Chopstick? Piss?'

'We want to hear about it,' Telly insisted.

'Well . . .' said a grim-browed Gus. 'What've you heard?'

'*You* know,' Sal said. 'How you escaped with a chopstick and drank pee.'

'Escaped . . . pee . . .' Gus considered quietly for a long moment, then shook his head and scowled. 'Look: in my condition there's lots I don't recollect perfect. But I'll say this: a man forced to imbibe the water of his own dingus is a desperate bastard. Would I be lying if I said I'd never been such a man? I would . . . I would.'

Deep into the evening – he might have been on his seventh or eighth free longneck – Gus stumbled outside and returned from the parking lot wearing a waist-length, raveled camouflage jacket affixed with patches of the 173rd Airborne. He put a cigar box on the bar top and began taking out war medals: three Purple

Hearts, a Bronze Star Medal, and a Distinguished Service Cross. He pressed them against his cheeks and emotionally recited the names of lost friends. 'PFC Carny "Corndog" Wilson, fragged in Da Nang . . . Second Lt. Teddy "The Pipe" Piper, julienned by a mortar shell in the Mekong Delta . . . Sgt. Micky "Twisty Mick" Mashburn, cut open like a cantaloupe at Khe-Sanh . . . all those brave boys . . .' He unfolded old news clippings detailing the wartime bravery of one Gus Emmett Miller of the 173rd Airborne, tenderly cradling the brittle clips in his rough, sledgehammer paws.

There was an air of dissipated greatness about him, like a crumbling statue in a museum. He made me think in particular of *The Dying Gaul*, which I saw in an art-history book: a warrior bleeding out on the battlefield. Except with Gus, it was a drawn-out, decades-long dying, which he seemed to have a perverse need to display. Bleeding out in a storefront window; a quad who pimped out his stumps.

By about 3 a.m. most of the drinkers had stumbled home, leaving only hard-core regulars like Telly and Sal and myself. Gus seemed eager to keep what was left of his audience. 'I'm no hero!' he bellowed terribly. 'Call me a soldier who did his duty, but don't call me a fuckin' hero! Corndog and Pipe and Twisty Mick and "mojon" Dorsey, those are heroes . . .' He was weeping now, rolling his eyes maniacally. He hurled a pair of medals savagely against the wall. 'I bought these with the blood of innocent civilians! Do I hate the yellow man? No – I never did . . . I never, never did . . .'

From the cigar box he removed a small stash of snapshots and passed them around. There he was, bearded and disheveled, in a long fatigue jacket and khakis, marching solemnly in a parade carrying a sign that read: 'VIETNAM: A BLANK CHECK FOR 58,000 AMERICAN LIVES.'

'Memorial Day in San Diego a couple years ago,' he explained.

There he was in another photo, posing in front of the Vietnam

Veterans Memorial Wall in DC with a group of guys who looked a lot like him: grim, haunted, unshaved, angry, somewhat crazy, all looking like veterans, if not of Nam, then of Alcoholics Anonymous or Narcotics Anonymous.

Gus was proud of one photo in particular, which depicted him in close-up pressing his cheek against The Wall, his fingertips touching the doomed names on that shiny, reflective slab. His long hair poured in a tangle out of a camouflage boonie hat, and his mouth gaped in a soundless wail.

'This one ran in the papers,' he explained, massively drunk now. 'Me and the boys from the vet center held some carwashes and scraped enough together to fly to The Wall. You never go alone to The Wall. The counselors will tell you that, and they're right.'

The last photo showed him planted on a milk-crate on a freeway off-ramp, holding a donation cup and a cardboard sign that read 'NAM VET! HOMELESS ANYTHING HELPS GOD BLESS!' His expression was at once self-pitying, accusatory, and weirdly vainglorious.

'That was a good spot right off the 405,' Gus said. 'Pulled in eighty bucks a day before the pigs ran me off.'

As I handed back the photo, he grabbed my bicep, with more force than was strictly polite, and exclaimed, 'Wait, wait! Lookit this . . .' He rummaged through the box and took out a necklace of what might have been a dozen dried and shriveled mushrooms. But they were not mushrooms. He draped the necklace around his throat and held one of the objects toward me. I touched it. Tough. Rubbery.

'Ever feel a gook ear?' Gus sputtered, leaving a mist of alcohol in my face. I jerked my hand away. 'Souvenirs. Some of my kills. Why you lookin' at me like that? Everybody did it.'

Gus pantomimed slicing motions in the air, and as he did so his upper body began to wobble on the stool. Sal and I caught him under the arms and helped him to his feet. He straightened, tucked his cigar box under his arm, and looked around blearily for Jesse James. 'To the chariot, old man,' Gus said. 'C'mon, Jesse. C'mon to papa. Brave old boy, looking out for big Gus. C'mon.'

The dog followed us out the back door, Sal and I steadying Gus between us while that necklace of ears swung back and forth on his chest. 'Shoulda let him fall,' Telly muttered behind us.

The parking lot was nearly deserted, thick with late-night ocean fog. A rattletrap old van sat against a chain-link fence under fluorescent lamplight. The van was a faded blue Dodge with a ladder running up the back door and an Arizona plate that said LV1NUTR. As we headed toward it, Gus was alternately weeping, cackling, and demanding we find him some coke so he could keep partying. 'Easy, officers,' Gus mumbled. 'Don't do my pussy like that with your nightsticks, officers . . . Want some blow . . . Wanna take a dive in the snow . . .'

He fumbled his key into the back door and lifted Jesse James into the van. From what I could see of the interior, it resembled a bum's upended shopping cart: clothes, plastic bags, food cartons, pill bottles, beer cans, blankets, car parts, birdhouses, a thousand random items, all smelling richly of dog. There was a mattress laid out on the floor in a clearing. Gus collapsed on it, rattling the van's contents. 'Hey,' he said with sudden concern. 'Where's my medals? Someone grab 'em for me.'

I had them in my pocket. I brushed off the sawdust and handed them over. With a grunt he took them and slammed the van door. Heading back into the bar, Sal and I could hear his voice carrying across the parking lot, cursing and singing.

'Big guy alright?' Junior said inside.

'He's crashing in his van,' Sal said. 'Looks like he lives out of it.'

'Goddamn tragedy,' Junior said, shaking his head. 'A goddamn human tragedy.'

'I don't like him,' said Telly, stinko and slurring, when Junior moved away. 'Gook ears. How morbid is that? Wonder what else is in his bag of tricks? How do you top that?'

'You think they're the real McCoy?' Sal asked.

'Tell you what,' Telly said. 'They don't mean shit. I know a guy in Pomona can get 'em for you for a few bills.'

'Rubber ones maybe, but not real,' I said.

'Real ones,' Telly said. 'He's got a girlfriend in the morgue. Dry 'em out, they look just like authentic "I-killed-'em-in-Nam" gook ears. There's a market for everything out there, Benny. And Vietnam shit is always hot.'

'I believe him,' I said. 'He's got the thousand-yard stare. And those medals.'

'All you need to do is get grazed in the ass, you got a Purple Heart,' Telly said. 'Bring home some scrotal fungus from a whorehouse in Saigon, you got two. And you get a Bronze Star just for showing up.'

'Not a Distinguished Service Cross,' I say. 'We had almost three million boys over there and only a thousand came home with the DSC.'

'He hadn't even heard of the chopstick massacre,' Sal said.

'Seriously,' Telly said. 'Who forgets surviving on his piss in the jungle?'

'Cut some slack to a dude with shellshock,' I said. 'I'm telling you, he's got the feel.'

'And I'm saying he talks too damn much. But whatever. Hell with him. He'll be gone tomorrow anyhow.'

As I pedaled home through the fog, drifting past quiet rows of stucco flats with the morning's *Orange County Register* and the *Newport-Mesa Daily Pilot* already waiting dewy on the doorsteps, past all the homes where people were living lives that were not mine, sleeping beside wives who were not mine, I couldn't help it, I cried for the vet in the van, I cried for the 58,000 we lost, I cried for the soldier who died in operatic slo-mo in *Platoon*, and most of all, I guess, I cried for Benjamin Bunt – the pissed-away years that never touched heroism or tragedy in a foxhole or anywhere else – I cried for my squandered little snitch's life.

Gus Miller moved into the Greasy Tuesday the next day.

CHAPTER 5

How did I first slip into the snitch jacket? It happened on a mild Friday afternoon two years earlier. I was sitting in the bleachers at Pomona Park, squinting through a ganja haze and hoping for fistfights as I watched the Mexicans play bloody, breakneck-paced soccer on the pitted dirt field. In my jeans: a few ounces of pot, 10 or 12 skankweed dime bags generously cut with oregano. Sitting near me: a grubby-looking *cholo* with tangly, unwashed hair, greasy whiskers, and a Che Guevara T-shirt tightly engorged with pectorals. Now and then he cupped his hand at his mouth, cursing the players in Spanish. Considering the roughness of the rest of him, the hand he raised looked weirdly delicate and clean, with nails that appeared buffed, a detail that in my befogged state failed to register as the warning it should have been.

'You into Che?' I said. '*Te gusta* Che?'

'*Que?*' he asked.

'Che was a bad-ass,' I said. 'He rode a bike around South America. *Bicicleta*. He did some revolutionary stuff too. *Revolutionario*.'

'*Si, si. Revolutionario.*'

'*Amigo*,' I said. '*Quieres mota?*'

'Marijuana?'

'*Si, si,* marijuana *fantastica*.'

We went behind the bleachers and, as I handed over the weed, he slapped the handcuffs on me. Suddenly his English was perfect. 'Selling weed this shitty,' he said, inspecting my poor product, 'there ought to be an extra charge.'

It turned out he'd been observing me for a few days. He had been staking out the park, watching for perverts. There was always someone disappearing into the park's red-brick bathroom shack, lawyers and stockbrokers and other suits who snuck off on their lunch hour from the nearby business plazas and Newport mansions to blow the local drop-outs. (A few weeks earlier I'd seen a weeping, pleading businessman being led out of the shack in cuffs: shiny black shoes, a wedding ring, a Benz in the lot, and an apostrophe-shaped port-wine stain over his right eye. But it was his infinitely sad expression I remembered. Leading him to an unmarked cop car had been a muscular surfer punk who was, I would learn, Munoz in one of his other guises. For such stings he carried around a department-issued rubber dick.)

Now, as I sat in the back of a squad car, Munoz was telling me in a semi-apologetic tone that he knew the economy was bad, that otherwise law-abiding people were picking up some extra cash. He had none of the usual I'm-a-cop-and-you're-a-leper vibe, so even as he took me back to the station and booked me, I couldn't help liking him. I asked if I could hold his badge, and he didn't hesitate: he let me. It read: DETECTIVE ALBERTO A. MUNOZ. 'Splendid, isn't it?' he said as I felt the weight of it.

'Lighter than I thought,' I said.

'Look,' he said, slipping it back on his belt. 'Maybe I can throw you a line. Tell me who supplies your shit.'

'A line how?'

'We can try to cut your exposure. With your record, possession with intent to sell scores you out to state time. Gimme a hand, maybe you get straight probation.'

'I don't like the idea of being a snitch.'

'I understand. I admire that. I got the feeling you were the kind of guy who had a code. Everyone needs one. The thing is, a snitch is a particular thing. By definition, he does it for the scratch. See? He's after easy money. Whereas you're interested in something else, which is saving your ass.'

'I could tell you stuff that would help you.'

'I know this.'

He gave me a stick of Big Red, and I chewed it till it was dead.

'I wouldn't, strictly speaking, be what you'd call a snitch, then?' I said. 'I mean, if I helped out?'

'It's totally respectable to save your ass. Everyone knows this. Even Sammy the Bull did it.'

'*If* I helped you out . . . if . . . it wouldn't even be for that reason.'

'No?'

'It'd be to get scumbags off the street. Drug-dealers and things. So kids aren't fucked up like I got fucked up. My life . . . I could've done something.'

Munoz nodded. 'I could tell you stories,' he said. 'Kids twelve, thirteen years old – they hook them that young. Girls twelve, thirteen selling themselves for some rock. I'm thinking, "This could be my little niece."' He added with emotion, 'That ain't right. And you know what? I think you know it ain't right.'

'I don't want my name down on any court papers.'

'Nothing like that, buddy. We give you a Confidential Informant number, we put that on our warrants. You won't need to testify, nothing.'

'Starsky and Hutch? They never woulda solved anything without Huggy Bear.'

'You're right. He was one of them. An equal partner.'

'And he was a snitch.'

'No! A confidential informant. Whole different ballpark. Which isn't to say there won't be some change in it down the line. You need to eat.'

He passed me a lined yellow notepad and a pen. I strolled down the halls of that big memory mansion in my head, opening doors, rifling rooms. I filled three pages with names, aliases, addresses, phone numbers, pager numbers, drivers' licenses. I loved the marveling look in his eyes, as he saw it spill out. I realized I had been storing up this information with the half-conscious hope that someone like Munoz would arrive to relieve me of it, make important use of it, redeem the years of sickness and squalor I had trudged through. I gave up the UC Irvine frat boys with the hydroponic rig in their basement who once threatened me with an ass-kicking when I said hello to one of their girls. I gave up the Snell Brothers, redneck meth monsters who kept trailer labs in Anaheim and Santa Ana and who liked to insult me. I gave up a Newport Beach coke dealer who owned a nightclub and refused to let me in the door. Grudges were as good a place as any to start.

'Talent like that, it's about time you started working for the good guys,' Munoz said. 'Nobody shits on your shoes anymore. You don't take *any* disrespect. You and me? We'll fuck this town up a little bit.'

So he recruited me, Munoz did, or – as they say in the streets – 'turned me out.' Which, funnily enough, is the same phrase a pimp uses when he ropes a fresh girl into his stable, teaching her the crucial distinction between a whore and a lady. A whore spreads just for the cash, he tells her. A lady does it because she loves her pimp.

He measured me for the snitch jacket and slipped me snugly inside so it came to feel like a noble second skin.

On police reports, I was Confidential Informant # 8342. On search warrants, when Munoz referred to me as 'a reliable CI,' I never failed to feel a twinge of pride. What I brought him, I learned mostly just by listening, by making myself disappear in the smoke of a dozen dives from Costa Mesa to Huntington Beach where men plotted half-witted break-ins and bragged of stashes of stripped auto parts and discussed the quality of the crops yielded by their basement rigs.

Munoz called himself El Guapo and drove a chocolate Porsche Carrera. When not in disguise he was fond of sleek, loose-fitting sport coats, ribbed muscle-shirts, no socks. He had olive-brown skin and a bleached row of large, feral, cosmetically capped teeth. He vibed sex and weight racks and suicidally dangerous sports. On the walls of his office, along with a series of enlarged newspaper clippings charting his big arrests, he kept photographs of himself dangling from one impossible precipice or another ('Suicide Rock '95' or 'El Cap '97'). While his hands were small, as I said, kind of delicate and bird-boned like a piano player's, his arms were roped with veins and corded with muscle. He had the Latin thing in overdrive: I think you know what I'm talking about. He looked like he hailed from some sub-equatorial zone where, early in the great forward march of coital history, they invented the wheel, the arch, and the alphabet.

One of the clippings in his office called him a 'hero cop.' He became a hero in the traditional cop way: by getting shot. It happened in an alley behind the Ross Dress for Less on Costa Mesa Boulevard. I remember the night. I was there strictly by accident. A piss-drizzly, foggy night in late January soon after I joined his stable of confidential informants. My bike taking me puddle by puddle toward home from a bottle club on the city's north end, and my brain as fog-steeped as the streets. From somewhere in the fog: the *Pop!* of a gunshot, followed by Munoz's angry voice: 'Ah ag ahg! *Cabron*, that's a bitch!' Then someone came rushing out of the fog and collided with me and I found myself on the ground, blinking up into the furious face of a man with an enormous jawbone and a police badge three-quarters concealed on his belt. Before vanishing in the fog he managed to scream, 'No pedaling on the sidewalk, citizen!' Behind the store I found Munoz sitting on the wet ground with his back against a trash bin, smoking.

'Dude?' Munoz said, noticing me.

'Dude,' I said.

'What'd you see, Cowboy?'

'I dunno.'

'You sure?'

'I guess.'

After a long pause, in which he seemed to be making up his mind whether I was telling the truth, he said, 'Well, I'm glad you're here. You're my man. My boy! El Guapo took one in the gut.'

'What does it feel like?'

'Lot worse if my vest hadn't stopped it. Or if I were one of those cruller-sucking slobs like McGorsky or O'Daniels, instead of a cop who does five hundred sit-ups a day. *Still* felt like a Louisville Slugger. So – ahg – tell me what you saw.'

'I don't know.'

'It'd be a great assistance to law enforcement if you could . . . for identification purposes . . .'

From a shirt pocket he produced a mug shot and extended it toward me. It showed a ferocious-looking black guy with dreadlocks dangling over a pitted forehead, crazed eyes, and a scar high on one cheek.

'Ivory "Daddy Glock" Williams,' Munoz said in a confidential buddy-to-buddy tone. 'My man, this is a very bad, very dangerous scumbag. Stone crackhead psycho killer. As you might have been in a position to witness, I was pursuing him through this alley when he turned and fired his Glock at me from a distance of about three yards. As you – ahg – might have clearly seen for yourself, he was standing about where that lamp pole is there. I think you'll agree there's ample illumination for you to have seen, without obstruction, the events you might have seen . . . and probably did see . . .'

I stood under the lamp pole with my right index finger pointed at him and said, 'Blam! Like that?'

'Exactly, except he's a lefty. You probably were at a good vantage to witness his *left* hand firing that Glock.'

'Who was that cop running out of here?'

'Cop? You must have made a mistake.'

Sirens were already screaming toward us in the fog; he had radioed them. After they hustled Munoz into an ambulance, I gave my account to detectives, corroborating his story point by point and helping to furnish the basis for Daddy Glock Williams's arrest warrant. Hours later cops raided his crib and, claiming he refused an order to lower his gun, shot him in the neck, the forehead, and the heart.

The newspapers, which made no mention me, devoted five or six paragraphs to Daddy Glock Williams's criminal record. It was reassuring news. He was indeed a very bad scumbag who was linked to three shootings for which witnesses had all been killed or disappeared.

While Munoz convalesced at Hoag Hospital, the mayor and a state senator posed by his bedside. There he was in the *Pilot* and the *Register*, showing off that bullet-dented Kevlar shield and looking right at the camera from his bed, very steely and undaunted. Standing with him in one of the photos was Capt. Harvey Wein. The stories described Wein as the first cop through the shooter's door, the one who had been forced to waste the sinister Mr. Glock Williams. He possessed the granddaddy of hard-on jaw lines, this Wein – the kind of oceanliner-prow, Dick Tracy mandible you could visualize those man-apes in *2001: A Space Odyssey* picking up to brain each other with. I recognized him immediately as the man who collided with me fleeing from Munoz's shooting.

I was not so stupid that I didn't understand how I'd been used, that Munoz and Wein had staged Munoz's shooting as a pretext to waste Williams, that my accidental presence – and my lie – had abetted a man's death. I did not ask Munoz to come clean with me about the incident; it seemed like a violation of an unspoken pact we had. It was like your dad, on your 15th birthday, wordlessly marching you to a whore's door and handing you a rubber; he would not ask about it when you got home, and you would not need to tell. I believed Munoz was giving me a lesson in the Hard Facts of How the World Worked, and that his willingness to do so was a sign of his trust and respect for me. I'd seen enough cop shows to know you had to skirt the rules to get anything done. Apart from the exhilaration of playing a role in a real-life cop drama, it elevated my sense of self-worth to help law enforcement win a round. I believed loyalty went a long way with a Latin like Munoz. He knew he could count on me, knew whose side I was on.

Having made my peace with my lie, a funny thing happened. After a while I began remembering the back-alley incident as I was supposed to have seen it, not as I really did see it. I began to believe I *had* seen the dreadlocked drug dealer raise his left hand with that gun; I could even remember seeing his eyes. It became an actual memory, and the jut-jawed officer who actually pulled the trigger – *that* fog phantom became a dream.

CHAPTER 6

Dogs ran through your dreams on Pomona Avenue.

Even before dawn, all across the block of low-rent tenements and dirty, laundryline-streaming cinderblock flats, the dogs started going at it: the terriers, the rotts, the pits, the porch chihuahuas and the stray gutter mutts, the reedy altos, tremulous tenors, and mournful crooners sending up their cries, conducting obscure long-running debates, haranguing, reinforcing their hierarchies, the cruel alphas threatening their cringing inferiors with rape and quick death, the whole block moaning for food or sex or sniffable pisspuddles or hydrants to baptize with a raised leg, or whimpering in thrall to cravings that their dog-throats couldn't even name. You learned to sleep though the noise, but it permeated your sleep and sent you dog-themed dreams.

On the morning after I met Gus Miller – Nam vet, Black Ops assassin, and soon to be my best friend – I woke late with my heart hammering in my chest. I lay flat on my back listening to the dogs and staring at the ceiling with its little family of brown water stains. It must have rained the night before, because the splotches seemed to have conquered a few more inches of the stucco. My ceiling has cancer, I thought. My walls sweated nicotine. My woman slept beside me, wheezing. I was 41 years old.

The afterimage of trains – a flash of gorgeously lacquered locomotives in sky blue and candy-apple red – imposed itself for an instant between my eyes and the ceiling. I closed my eyes to retrieve the dream. I was moving through a noisy train-station. All around me crowds streamed into magnificent Crayola-hued trains. I couldn't find my platform: the departure boards melted and slid when I looked at them directly. A blonde woman behind a partition was trying to help me, but the clamor swallowed her voice. I chased a train as it roared away. I screamed, 'Is this the one? Is this mine?' Neat nuclear-family dogs yapped happily from the receding windows; the blonde held one of them.

Now, I never put a lot of stock in dreams, though I don't begrudge the shrinks and shamans and TV writers their gravy-train; you find your livelihood where you can, and a snitch is no one to judge another man's hustle. Still, I felt this particular dream might mean something, if only I knew the identity of the blonde. I felt it was the dream's most important detail, that all the ambiguous emotion in it – panic and longing and dread and hope – was somehow tied to her.

The sun spilled through the cheap, buckled blinds into the apartment's cramped spaces, pitiless light suffusing the Martian towers of unwashed laundry, the milk-crate mountains, the neglected Ab-Flexer and trampoline, the driftwood piles of clothes and magazines and old bills. All around me, the world was sending me its voices. Gwooff-urffurff-arff-uff, cried the dogs. Whump-whump-whump-whump, thumped a boom box. Ploop-plop-ploop, muttered the water drops, falling from the lesions in the ceiling into the Tupperware and Hormell chili cans strategically arrayed around our living room. I heard the shriek of chicano children chasing each other in the street; the tick of car motors in their cages and purr of tire-tread on blacktop; the heavy bad breathing of Donna in her sleep. I lay there, owned by entropy, lashed to my mattress by so many invisible cables.

There was a lot to do, before I was prepared to enter the world. There were certain chemicals to ingest. I already had the first Marlboro going as I padded in my socks to the kitchenette, where

I heated water for Folger's instant. I peeled open a can of Spam, drained the jellied slime and Spam juice, and sliced three thin pieces from the rubbery pink brick. I let them fry in Country Crock, flipping them every 30 seconds and pressing them flat for the death-sizzle. Donna stirred, wheezing, and, in a motion so habitual she didn't even need to wake up to do it, turned her head to hack into a napkin. Her mouth hung open when she slept. Seeing her in this state brought to my heart a spasm of the old tenderness.

To avoid the sound of her lungs – they were in very bad shape – I put on my headphones and listened to some Credence while I ate breakfast. I had tried to get her in shape by hauling home various pieces of exercise equipment that went unused. Last year I bought the little trampoline off Telly brand-new for 15 bucks and brought it home with unreasonably high hopes. Her expression said, *What kind of idiot have you been?* She asked what she was supposed to do with it.

'Jump up and down on it,' I said.

'Why would I want to?' she said.

'To get in shape. It'll get your pulse moving.'

I stepped on, knees slightly bent and legs planted shoulder-width, and started bouncing. It squeaked and creaked and skittered under me. I spun, I touched the ceiling, I did jumping jacks, I pretended to kick like a Rockette, ripping the crotch of my Wranglers.

'Calisthenics,' I said. 'Like the Japanese do before they start on the assembly line, which is why they're kicking our asses.'

'What you're saying is that I'm a repulsive fat-ass and you don't want to be seen on the street with me, and yet you're too cowardly to come out and say so,' she said. 'Are you trying to stage some kind of dumb-ass intervention? Is that it?'

'No, no, no, honey. Of course not.'

She was crying. 'I resent that you feel that way about me! With all I've got wrong with me!'

'I don't!'

'Look at you! You ain't no Adonis! You ain't no Greg Louganis! Maybe I should be ashamed of you, Benny!'

Sleeping, as she was now, my dear Donna was easier to love. I smoked two more cigarettes and began to feel alright, but I needed a half-bowl of cannabis before I would feel alright enough to go outdoors. I broke out the good Oregonian shit, a deep green species that made me contemplative and poet-souled. The first thought it sent me today was a strange one, just a phrase, really. *Benny Bunt's whimpering inarticulate dog soul.* Strangely I found tears in my eyes. I was incredibly moved by this. Like the dream, I didn't know what it meant, yet I was certain it had significance. I wrote it down. Then I wrote, 'What is my train?'

Escaping through the door before Donna woke up, I found my Schwinn 10-speed toppled on its side at the bottom of the back stairwell, where I kept it chained to the steel slats of the railing. Someone had kicked it over again and it lay in a detritus of dead cigarettes and Trojan wrappers. Ass installed in the worn twin craters of the seat-cushion, I pedaled out of the complex and through the alley and onto Pomona, the dog chatter growing fainter and finally disappearing behind me. I cut onto 19th, taking the sidewalk the whole way and watching the cars fly contemptuously by.

Every motorist felt superior to me. Not just the psychotic soccer moms in their Expeditions and the wage slaves in their Tercels, but even the teenagers in 1970s Camaros with mismatched doors and the illegals in their junk-ass Gremlins and Pintos. Yes, even people whose cars turned into blazing death-cages when kicked on the bumper knew for a certainty they were better than me. And they were glad I was there, glad to see me. Hi, Benny! Hi, biketrash! I was good for their self-esteem. In Southern California a man who does not own a car is considered a freak, barely human, and probably dangerous.

Since the repo men yanked my shitheap Datsun a few years ago, I'd racked up about a grand worth of tickets for pedaling on the sidewalk, mostly in Newport, where the cops wear great, even tans and grow sadistic around ugly guys on old bikes, tunnel men, mole men. The law required you to ride right there on the blacktop with the Land Cruisers and Avalanches, right there under the grinning grilles of the semis. This I refused to do. In the world of the car, the authorities do not give a rat's ass for the life of a bike man. Still, when I saw screeching near-misses between cars and people stupid enough to pedal their $3,000, space-alloy machines in the 'bike lane' – I call it the suicide lane – I rooted instinctively for the car.

So I was on my way to work, gliding down the hill out of Costa Mesa toward Pacific Coast Highway, and beyond it I could see the long silent blue of the Pacific, looking so big and friendly from this distance that it was possible to forget the sea was really a great salty puddle waiting to be nudged by an earthquake or asteroid into an annihilating hiccup. It gave me pleasure to think of the sea someday uncoiling its body vertically for a death-run at California. People say they love California, but it occurred to me that maybe everybody would like to see California destroyed, because it's the state Hollywood visits most with its Technicolor Armageddons by fire and water and bomb. I don't know why people should feel this way, except that everyone knows California sunshine is the world's loneliest light. Sailing down the hill, I found myself dreaming of possible apocalypses and of the battles royal I followed in the pages of *The Incredible Hulk*, *The Mighty Thor*, *The Amazing Spider-Man* and *The Fantastic Four*, where muscle-bound demigods yanked up city sidewalks for use as bullwhips and hurled buildings like javelins, the panels raining rubble, though no one ever seemed to die or raise the question of litigation.

Now, as the hill sloped, blue-collar Costa Mesa became silk-scarved Newport Beach, where, among the BMWs and trust-fund princelings and Hoag Hospital cock doctors with monogrammed cuffs, a mole man was instantly more conspicuous. I slid onto PCH and slipped into a familiar fantasy, wondering how far my Schwinn would take me in a day – a week. I imagined that I was not going to work at all, but instead was taking this beautiful coast-straddling highway north as far as it went, past all the dingy, piss-polluted beaches and the few still-pristine ones, the littered gray sands and creamy tangerine ones that comprise the Southern and Central California coastline, past Long Beach and Hermosa, past Santa Monica, Malibu and Point Mugu, past Santa Barbara, Monterey and even San Francisco; going up and up, and on my right the sun rising against my smiling, unshaven cheek.

Instead, being a cowardly Benny, I did what I always did. I found a gas station mini-mart where I parked my bike and stood in line for my daily dozen lottery tickets.

In front of me stood an orange-haired lady in a chinchilla-fur coat. From the top of her expensive-looking handbag emerged the head of a tiny, spotted brown terrier with blue bows tied around its ears. The dog seemed hip to its social status. There might have been a touch of condescension in its expression. But it seemed to be looking at me with empathy, the empathy of one trapped animal for another. I scratched it between the eyes, and it blinked at me. Had I not been stoned, I probably would not have said, to no one in particular: 'That's a beautiful animal.'

The lady turned toward me halfway, appraising me at a glance – the short, unscrubbed man with eyes set too close together – and gave me a polite smile, really just a quick twitching of the corners of her mouth. 'Thank you, dear,' she said.

The lady looked like a washed-up starlet, unreconciled to time's rape of her once-stunning beauty. She was about five feet tall, of indeterminate middle age, Botoxed, face-lifted, drum-taut skin, equipped by surgeons with a nose so tiny it amounted to two vertical skull-slits overhung by negligible rubbery nubs for nostrils. Her eyelids hung sensually low, post-coitally droopy.

Eyebrows were painted high on her brow, like something out of *Shogun*, and her orange hair was stacked on her head in a foot-high pile, kept in place by some miracle of skyscraper engineering. On her finger was a tremendous diamond.

She had an air of great unhappiness about her, of high-strung, imperious authority, a woman accustomed to ordering around armies of illegal maids and nannies, houseboys and pool men, accountants and lawyers. Her breasts were an affront to time and gravity; they belonged to a 19-year-old. Every inch of her sweated money, which carried an unmistakable sexual charge, even as she lugged around her ruined looks like a shameful Quasimodo hump. Money is always young.

I reached out to pet the dog again, saying, 'You're a good boy, aren't you? Who's a good, good boy—'

'Please!' cried the lady, flinching.

'I'm – sorry?'

'This isn't a petting zoo,' she said, 'for everyone with dirty hands.'

She smiled at me again in her curt, unhappy way, and turned back to face the checkout counter. I felt the eyes of the other people in line on me. They regarded me as incredibly stupid. I was only looking for a little love, some lotto tickets and some love, and I had humiliated myself. Again I was conscious of my squalidness, my hovel at the bottom of the socioeconomic kingdom, my unfitness to eat the snots from the canine's nose.

'Look,' I said. 'I'm sorry, lady. I didn't mean to offend you, or anything.'

'Forget it, please.'

'I was just admiring your dog is all.'

'Stop menacing the nice lady, man,' said the guy in line behind me. 'It's not cool.'

The guy had blond eyebrows and wavy golden hair. Sandals, surfer-shades, guava-mango juice in hand. Some kind of yuppie beach freak, body waxed hairless, all muscle and bronze.

'Who are you?' I asked.

'I'm a Good Samaritan,' he said, taking in my face, my posture, my California Angeles jersey, my windbreaker, my inappropriately tight jeans. 'I'm doing my civic duty.'

'You'd crucify a man for friendliness?'

'Keep your friendliness to yourself, dude, no one gets edgy,' he said.

'You're a jerkoff.'

'Oh, I'm a jerkoff now,' he said. 'That kind of language in front of this respectable lady. Pal, I'm here to say it's totally erroneous. Totally.'

Staring at him cold-eyed, I put my hand inside the pocket of my windbreaker, to allow him to consider the possibility that I may have a knife. Men who look like me carry knives. 'Maybe you're a totally erroneous fucking human being,' I said. 'Maybe you're not aware that a slashed femoral artery bleeds out a man's life in fifteen minutes?'

I was about to ask him, as a follow-up, how he would like a disfiguring scar on his pretty face, when he obligingly stepped back a couple of feet, reconsidering the wisdom of heroism. He tried to follow my hands with his eyes. The lady in the chinchilla coat bought a bottle of Perrier and glided briskly out the door with her blueblood mutt. With one eye on the line and a hand still in my pocket, I bought my lotto tickets and strolled out, cool, cool.

Standing beside my bike, I scratched the tickets off with a quarter against the side of a payphone. All losers; not even a $2 or $4 winner. A minute later the Good Samaritan exited with his fruit juice and slipped his hairless body quickly into a gleaming silver Expedition. As he zipped away to his private tennis courts and indoor lap pool and beautiful girlfriend or whatever pleasure-filled life awaited him up PCH, I imagined how the SUV would look, compressed into a neat junkyard cube with his bones twisted in among the metal.

'Are you packing?'

I turned and the chinchilla lady was looking up at me, she and the cradled terrier watching with their nervous money-faces. Her small, knobby fingers made rapid circles in the dog's fur.

'I'm sorry?' I said.

'You're a dangerous character,' she said, those racy eyes squinting as if at an esoteric specimen in a museum. 'Rough trade. A nasty little number right out of Casting Central.'

I blinked at her. 'I said I was sorry, lady. You don't need to insult me.'

'You would have cut off his balls, wouldn't you? Even though he's twice your size. *Rrrripppp!* Brutality is second nature to you. You exude it.'

'I don't mean you any harm, ma'am. I've had enough problems with the cops without you calling them on me.'

'Of course you have,' she said excitedly, pushing closer so that I became aware of the stench of alcohol on her breath. 'A man like yourself is forever at odds with the authorities. Of course you have!'

It dawned on me that it cost her an effort of will to approach me, that she was fighting to keep her nerve. And there was something besides twitchy curiosity in her manner. There was some other, definite motive, some subject she was trying to work toward.

'Tell me,' she said. 'What is it you're packing? A switchblade? A blackjack? Brass knuckles? Or maybe a gun?'

'I don't pack,' I said.

She looked incredulous for a moment, then said: 'I imagine it's dangerous, particularly if you're on – what is it, parole? Probation? I can never keep them straight. That man – you bluffed him. You read him in a second, and you knew he wouldn't risk a tussle. And he knew you would.'

We just stood there, watching each other for a while. There was more than idle friendliness in her voice. She wanted to say something more, but it seemed to me a bad idea to wait around for her to get to it. She made me nervous, with her big rock and chinchilla coat and expensive wonders-of-science parts that were created in silicon labs or snatched from the corpses of young accident victims. She could scream 'Mugger!' and a dozen people would come running to pummel me. Stoned as I was, I had little confidence that the conversation I thought I was having with her corresponded to the conversation she thought she was having with me.

'Well,' I said, picking up my bike. 'I've gotta get to work.'

'Of course – "work."' Her tight little smile hung quotation marks around the word. 'The kind those cocksuckers at the IRS never hear about, right?'

'I work in a restaurant.'

'Who was the writer – the one who talked about the White Negro? Norman Mailer?'

'Sorry?'

'The darker impulses, blood and instinct, and all that. Mailer was himself a Jew from a nice part of Brooklyn.'

'I don't know what you—'

'My world, it's – different,' she said. 'If there's a thorn in your toe – an intractable problem – you call your lawyer. And your lawyer makes threats. He promises to tort them till their rectums hemorrhage. Of course, this only works with people rational enough to know what they have to lose. You see the limitations. You see what a headache it becomes. But in *your* world – your antisocial, Molotov-cocktail world – the solution is simple and quick, a slashed artery.' Pressing her lips toward my ear, she whispered with great intensity: 'Yet how often do our worlds collide? How often do they inter*sect*?'

In her low-lidded eyes I glimpsed a hint of what I suddenly perceived as her true motive: a smoldering sexual eagerness. Yes, this is what she'd been driving at. This was the salve she sought for her rich-lady blues. I began to suspect there might be something in this for me. If I heard her correctly, she believed me to be a black man. I was not about to disabuse her of this notion, which could work to my advantage. I smiled. I now had a read on this lady. She imagined herself as one of those romance paperback covergirls, limp in the grasp of some cruel, dusky-chested Fabio. I could picture her watching the windows from her oversized satin bed at night, some shriveled millionaire sad sack snoring beside her while she fantasized about masked intruders.

Maybe she would pay me absurd amounts of money to carry out such a scenario.

'I've read all about ladies like you,' I said.

'Yes?' she said, ambiguously hopeful.

'Trapped in some big old Newport mansion with a priceless Ming Dynasty dildo and a withered old husband with a colostomy bag, right? You want someone from the wrong side of the tracks? Little danger, little excitement?'

First, her mouth opened in a little O. Then, as her features contracted into a tight, furious circle, like a sheet of paper crushed in a fist, her hand flashed out to sting my cheek. I realized my mistake.

She emitted a tortured-bird squawk. 'You verminous, vomitous—'

'I'm sorry, lady,' I said, palms out pleadingly.

'You malignancy! You anthrax spore!'

'I didn't mean – I misunderstood – I thought—'

'Do you have any notion of—? I'm a woman who – why—' She sputtered, 'I have a daughter at Juilliard! I'm on the museum board! You believe I'd allow – someone like *you*—'

People were starting to turn their heads from their gas pumps. The lady's hand flailed in my face like one of those New Orleans voodoo chicken-claws. Wild-eyed and tossing its head, the terrier was barking, or trying to bark: the sound that emerged from its throat was more like a wheezy smoker's cough, an oldster gasping with emphysema.

Shakily I straddled my Schwinn and jumped the curve,

maneuvering through the maze of cars at the pump-station. Flashing by, I got a glimpse of three or four faces in tinted sunglasses watching me from the safety of their SUVs and over the glinting hoods of their Beemers. Someone shouted, 'The Mexican mugged that old lady!' And another voice: 'Somebody do something!' All of them making private risk–benefit calculations, debating whether apprehending an absconding wetback was worth a broken jaw, a gouged eye, death. But all these potential urban heroes, like the Good Samaritan before them, remained immobile, their instant of action lost.

'*Cobardes! Putos cobardes!*' I cried, hitting the sidewalk and peeling away. I booked 15 or 20 blocks, legs pumping, before I was confident no one was following me. Probably overkill, but there was still the paranoid whispering of that good cannabis in my brain.

I leaned my bike against an alley wall to catch my breath, aware that the confrontation had unhinged me on a number of levels. We were having different conversations, she and I. So much of the trouble between people is just that. They're on different drugs, and they think they're on the same drug.

It was not just that I misread a situation so badly – not unusual for me – although I wondered what clues I missed in discerning the lady's real intentions. And I was disturbed at all those people watching and none of them coming to the aid of that shrieking lady. Don't they have mothers? Wasn't I menacing her? At a mini-mart in Costa Mesa – parts of that city, at least – I'd be swarmed in an instant and dangled from the ankles. But of course the moneyed had so much more to lose. They had their cars and hot tubs and all those years of terrific athletic fucking with multiple partners to lose. They possessed no rational reason to risk violent death from a nasty little number like Benny Bunt. I couldn't blame them; nevertheless I despised them.

Maybe one or two of those frozen bystanders were suffering now, having learned they were cowards. The moment for action came – an innocent lady in jeopardy – and they failed, they blew it, they just stood and watched. How could they have known, on waking this morning, they would find themselves passive poltroons in some Kitty Genovese microdrama? I read a 40-page comic book adaptation of *Lord Jim* once. I'm thinking of the moment Captain Jim ditches his imperiled ship, the single moment that wrecks his life with the self-knowledge it brings. It all hinges on those unexpected split-seconds (it's going down NOW!). You act before you think and learn what you're made of, and then you're chained to that knowledge forever. Who knows that one of those moments isn't waiting for all of us before we're through?

Then I realized the strangest thing about the incident: the terrier in the crook of the lady's arm. How it made no dog-sounds at all, not a single woof or yap or yawp, even as its maw snapped open and shut and the eyes rolled furiously in its head. No, there was just that eerie asthmatic rasping. Like the poor dog was trapped in one of those nightmares where you need to talk, you need to scream, and you can't. As if the orange-haired lady had put it on mute.

Puzzling over these thoughts, I pedaled toward work, late for my shift. In my headphones Motley Crue were singing about blowing some bastard's head off. Normally the lyrics would hearten me. But already it had been a rough and bewildering day, and there were times when even Nikki Sixx and Vince Neal in their prime could not speak to me.

It would be six weeks before I saw the old lady's face again, in a photograph several hundred miles away, and came to understand what she'd wanted from me.

CHAPTER 7

It was still daylight when I finished my restaurant shift and pedaled over to the Greasy Tuesday, breaking one of my how-to-outsmart-alcoholism rules – I had a thousand of them – which was: Don't start drinking while the sun's out. (In the end, it only made you despise the sun.)

I arrived to find Gus Miller moving into the little cubbyhole behind the bar. It was really just a janitor's closet that had been cluttered with old stools and jukebox parts and cobwebby bric-a-brac for years. Gus hauled all this junk to the trash bin and ran a broom along the floor and went through a full can of Raid, methodically slaughtering roaches. Then he carried his bedding from his van to the room, his narrow bachelor-sized mattress balanced on one of his broad shoulders as effortlessly as a little pillow. He threw down some Mexican blankets for Jesse James and put out his water bowl and a squealing chew-toy. (The dog needed no food bowl, eating only take-out Mexican.) He put in a foot-locker and a small Sony AM/FM cassette player. On the particleboard shelves overhead he stacked a bunch of paperbacks and old hardcovers: James Michener's *Hawaii*, *Alaska* and *Centennial*; Michael Herr's *Dispatches*; Homer W. Smith's *Man and His Gods*; Mac Bolan and Tom Clancy adventures; a bunch of true-crime books about the mob, serial killers, and high-profile murders. He pinned up all the Vietnam veteran photos, and carefully set his war medals out on top of the cigar box.

His heaviest piece of furniture was a padlocked, waist-high, battery-powered freezer, which Junior and I helped him carry from the van to a corner of his room. 'How else does a homeless man keep his venison cold?' Gus grumbled, when Junior asked what it was for. Junior sputtered an apology; he meant no insult to the homeless. Gus explained that a few months ago he and some buddies bagged four bucks in the Northwest with a bow and arrow and he'd been living off the meat ever since. There had been many nights in the desert, a hundred miles from any human light, when a good slab of campfire-seared deer is all that kept his heart from despair.

'My new pimp pap,' Gus said, pulling the chain on the naked light bulb hanging from the ceiling to illuminate the cubbyhole.

'How'd you swing this?' I said.

'Reptile cunning,' Gus replied. 'I said I'd be Junior's bouncer, keep the riffraff out.'

'But everyone's riffraff here.'

'I can't argue with rent-free digs. Actually, it was his idea.'

Gus rubbed his hands together thoughtfully, with an expression stone-sober, tranquilized, and bloodless. 'Bring a little order in the establishment,' Gus said, mumbling so softly it was tough to hear him.

'A man starts toppling at the bar and before anyone can yell "timber," he's safe in bed,' I said. 'Nice arrangement.'

'I just hope I don't wake up thinking I'm back in lockup. Some shit might get broken. Some people too. My head's a bad neighborhood you don't wanna drive through at night, brother.'

'How long were you in lockup?'

'Few here, few there.'

'What for?'

'Killing some motherfuckers, this and that,' he said casually.

He pulled off the light and we walked back to the bar counter, where Junior was cleaning the well. Jesse James was curled on the sawdust under the legs of the pool table. The dog lifted his head from his forepaws and seemed to regard me with some intensity, his good ear and his bad ear both pointing straight up on his head, and his black nostrils quivering, undoubtedly picking up the distinctive emanations of my rectum. This made me very nervous, irrationally nervous; in the back of my throat I tasted a compound of dread and guilt that, from here on, would never fail to manifest itself in the presence of Jesse James.

A man will spend years crossing the street to avoid a particular building on no grounds other than it brings a bad feeling to his gut. I always assumed these are the sites of slayings or suicides that happened or will happen. The ragged old dog gave me something like that feeling. Maybe Gus's boasts about the dog's mutant olfactory-telepathic powers touched some guilty nerve in me; maybe I suspected that even now Jesse James was alerting his master to my professional-Judas nature, warning him that, despite my surface amiability, I was the one dude in the bar he shouldn't trust. I genuinely did not want to betray Gus Miller; I wanted to be his friend. But the dog, perhaps sensing my poor record with friendship, seemed to have developed a quick animosity toward me. His eyes were cold and vicious; he belonged on the leash of an SS man.

Whatever suspicions he may have harbored, however, Jesse James lowered his head and began licking himself under the scrotum.

Late-afternoon sunlight diffused through the bar from the front and back doors, which were propped open with rubber wedges so that the crossbreeze could carry away some of last night's residual corruption. It was the first time I'd seen the bar's interior exposed to raw daylight, and I experienced the strange, protective urge to bolt the doors against the intrusion, like Nosferatu's keeper. A bar in natural light is an unspeakably forlorn and depressing place, and you should never have to see it. Everything looks wrong. Every blemish shows. It becomes a hole in the ordered universe, an un-place or anti-place.

Something else was strange. The nicked wooden horseshoe of the bar top was clean. The vinyl stools were shiny. The ubiquitous pissreek and remnants of bile and spilled beer and all the other mingled stenches, never more than perfunctorily scrubbed away by Junior, had been replaced by a pungent ammonia odor. There was even a little green fragrance-tree hanging from the mirror.

'This place is all wrong,' I said, sniffing the air with a frown. 'It's unsettling. I come here for the squalor. Is rose blossom pot-pourri next?'

'I landed tidy-up detail,' Gus said. 'Throw around some Comet and some Lysol and march Mr. Clean into action and we're in business.'

'Gus is our new all-around handyman,' Junior said proudly.

'You know I appreciate it,' Gus replied.

'For a war hero and a friend of my pops, it's the least I can do.'

'I wish more people in this country felt that way.'

Junior shook his head. 'It's men like you that it's all built on,' he said. 'After what you went through, to come home and have those hippies spitting on you, and Hanoi Jane and all the others . . . it just burns me . . .'

'Sometimes you have to be from somewhere else to know what America's about,' Gus told the Kiwi.

Junior nodded, creasing his lips emotionally and hooking a thumb at his chest. 'It's what's in there,' he said.

'It's American as shit of you to give me this chance.'

'A man who's flown million-dollar gunships, I know I can entrust with this kind of responsibility,' Junior said. 'This place – this place—' He waved his hand, taking in the gouged, shiny stools, the splotched walls and the array of decapitated pool sticks. 'All my old man had to pass on, you know. They say he couldn't stand to see it disrespected, and neither can I.'

'I won't let you down, Junior. And I know your pops would be proud you're helping his old pal.'

Junior's eyes shone, slightly wet. He clasped Gus's hand and looked soulfully into the wide, red, grizzled, dissipated face. I could tell Junior had been practicing this – the look, the handshake, and what he said next: 'Welcome home, soldier.'

All night Gus Miller crammed Percocets and other pills in his craw and washed them down with Bud. By midnight he was asleep snorelessly on his forearms at the bar, bearlike, and the drinking went on around him. I was drunk and feeling piss-mean, brooding over the day's indignities. Across the horseshoe I saw Telly and Sal and Old Larry. Ah, my friends. But tonight I didn't love them at all. In my spleen I experienced a moment of clarity: I realized why I was compelled to hurt my friends by snitching on them. I didn't do it, after all, for their own good; I didn't really do it for the money. But when you're always being kicked in the guts by life, the only people you hate more than the ones above you are the ones below you, those even more wretched and debased. A poor illegal sonofabitch in a Gremlin despises a man on an old Schwinn much more than he despises one in a Benz.

Music videos were playing on the TV set over the bar, superquick montage flashes of bucking slippery jittering perfect oversexed bodies, entities of the distant Realm of Perpetual Coitus. 'Do you ever feel like just fucking somebody up?' I asked Junior. 'Climbing a tower with a rifle and a scope?'

'You're not a violent drunk, Benny. I've never even seen you swing on anyone.'

'I walk around wanting to hit people, and I can't, and I think it's giving me cancer.'

'What can I do about it?'

'I'll give you a hundred bucks to seduce my wife.'

He'd heard the proposition before – at least once a week for a year – and as always he smiled. He was a professional barkeep, and knew when to play along. 'Why would you want to do a thing like that?'

'So I can split.'

'Why not just split and save the hundred bucks?'

'What would she do without me?'

'I'll consider it for five hundred,' he said and went down the bar to serve someone's drink, leaving me alone with a sudden sense of shame. The night was young, and I'd already betrayed Donna, and for a stale laugh at that.

'Mass murder's no way to relieve stress, Benny,' Junior said when he returned. 'Try a *Playboy*.'

'I'm more a *Hustler* man,' I said. No need to mention *The Fantastic Four* and *She-Hulk*.

'Hef's girls are much classier. They hold a little back, make you use your imagination. And the interviews are in-depth.'

'Sure, you learn her favorite color, you learn her sign,' I said. 'I'm gonna abuse myself, I'm gonna use *Hustler*. *Playboy*'s too dangerous. You're flipping between chicks with one hand, your johnson's in your other, all of a sudden there's a Q&A with Colin Powell or Tom Clancy. What then? You have to read it.'

'No, you come back to it when you're done.'

'Works for you, fine,' I said. 'Me, I have to read it. Your wife walks in, she thinks you're jerking off to Colin Powell. That's a dangerous situation, Jack. Pour me a couple more fingers, and I'll tell you the kind of day Charles Whitman must have had.'

Junior complied. I gave him the run-down on the day's torments, the dangerous misunderstanding at the Coast Highway gas station, the full sorry story.

Junior feigned interest expertly, nodding and saying 'Hmm, hmmm' or 'Sonofabitch!' at intervals – he was a professional barkeep – but he was really only half listening. He was busy monitoring the bar, eyes sweeping the room continually, scanning for brewing violence and empty glasses and bowls of Goldfish and Chex Mix to refill.

'One thing I can't get out of my mind is that terrier,' I said. 'It must have had laryngitis.'

'What was the sound it made?'

'Sort of like a cough or a whisper.'

'Surgical devocalization,' Junior said. 'They hack right into the vocal cords and snip 'em. Keeps it friendly and quiet in the million-dollar blocks. Otherwise neighbors wanna sue each other's asses. You hadn't heard?'

The glass paused at my chin. 'That's horrible. Really?'

'Remember a few years ago down in South County, the lady who got whacked with a crossbow in the home invasion? She'd taken out her dog's pipes. Yapped too much. Funny thing, because it might have warned her of the guy with the crossbow.'

I grunted and pounded my drink, thinking gloomily of mute dogs: the poor bastards, inarticulate even at their best, deprived now even of the pure expression of their howl.

CHAPTER 8

Late for work the next day, my head brick-piled under a hangover, I got the expected tongue-lashing when I arrived at Zapata! Zapata!, and took it without flinching. My boss, Aristotle Scabronis, a demonic little Greek in cufflinks and gleaming finger-jewelry, was a shouter and a frequently terrifying man. He owned high-end Mexican food joints around Los Angeles and Orange Counties and he was worth at least a few million dollars. He tried selling Greek food, but Californians wanted Mexican. In his sixties he still worked 80-hour weeks – mostly here, at his ritzy flagship restaurant – charming important diners, browbeating his staff, watching for thieves in our ranks. He had one manner for his customers (gracious, avuncular, expansive) and another for his employees (paternalistic, suspicious, exasperated). He had hair on all his fingers and on his neck, and served as the brunt of many gleeful goatfucking jokes among his kitchen staff.

Scabronis was always going on about the American Dream, and how his kids were in the Ivy League, and how everything was possible here if you worked hard, and how his Mexicans, having no honor, were always stealing from him. What I wanted to tell Scabronis was, 'Here you are, a Greek dude, running Mexican joints with wetback cooks and dishwashers, pillaging another culture's culinary genius, stealing their terrific tacos, their wonderful *flautas*, their voluptuous *huevos rancheros*, and feeling so superior. Who's the thief here?' I longed to tell him his version of the American Dream sucked, even apart from this thievery, because who wanted to sweat off his balls for 30 years only so that he could work 80-hour weeks in his sixties?

Right now Scabronis was scowling at me and jabbing a finger at his watch. I was a half-hour late. The lunch rush started 15 minutes ago. Tables needed to be bused. Dishes were piling up. As I slipped into my apron, he followed me through the grill-hissing, pan-clanging kitchen with its thousand mingling smells of cheese and meat and tortillas: 'Twice this week! You have no pride, no honor! Shit-ass thief! You stole thirty minutes from me! From my family! My children! How will you ever succeed? How do you expect anyone to respect you?'

Having no answer to these questions, I put my head down and headed silently for my place at the sink, cheeks hot with shame, aware the rest of the kitchen staff were witnessing my humiliation with sweet pleasure. The boss usually picked one person per day as the target of his fury; this meant the others were off the hook. As I hunkered down to work, I lit imaginary fires throughout the restaurant. I torched the tony tablecloths and fine silverware and the walls with their beautiful fake bullet-holes and the framed Mexican revolutionary pictures above every table (Zapata with bandoliers; phrases like *Better to die on your feet than live on your knees!* to inspire the diners). I poured jet fuel on the Prada handbags and Salvatore Ferragamo suits of the patrons. I watched all the Ermenegildo Zegna silk ties curl and blacken up their owners' throats. I ignited Scabronis's bushy black mustache and, one by one, the curly black wires all over his fingers. I couldn't even afford to eat in his restaurant; I'd never even get past the hostess; and yet here I slaved.

Rick and Alfonse, the other dishwashers, were working busily to keep up with the growing stack of dirty pans and pots. They were not happy with me, either. They muttered something to each other in Spanglish. Often they spent an entire shift trading what sounded like gibberish. I rarely knew what they were saying, but I was pretty sure most of it was obscene. A lot of the time I suspected they were talking smack about me, but I had no proof.

'*Lo siento*,' I said in a weak voice, pulling on my latex gloves and squirting great gobs of liquid detergent into the superpans crusted with oil and grease and food. Grunting furiously, I tried to scour away my humiliation in the soap-foamy muck of sloshing pinto beans, *mole*, clumped rice, Mexican meatballs, *salsa verde*, and *menudo*. It splattered my arms and apron and face.

'Look at whiteboy go,' Rick said.

'Go, whiteboy, go,' Alfonse said. 'Get that *coño*.'

That broke both of them up. Said Rick: 'Gotta get that *coño*, *holmes*.'

'*El dinero*,' Alfonse said, '*y el coño*.'

They riffed that way for a few minutes, nodding at me with smiling hostility. I had no idea what they were talking about. They were insulting me, somehow. I was sure of this. Then I remembered a *coño* is a pussy. But they didn't seem to be calling me a pussy. They seemed to be suggesting something else, maybe that a sexual encounter was responsible for my tardiness and/or my unusual vigor at the sink. Maybe they meant to say that I was desperate to keep my job because it permitted me to afford prostitutes. Or maybe they were making the broad philosophical point that whatever was wrong with me must be attributable, one way or another, to *coño*. *Coño* was the pox of many a man. *Coño* hobbled you. *Coño* corrupted. There was really no arguing with this. At any rate, Rick and Alfonse were not necessarily insulting me. They might even have been expressing some kind of solidarity with me, extending an invitation to friendship. Being as lonely as I was, I took it, though *coño* was not what happened to be bothering me at the moment.

'Shit, *amigos*,' I said. 'It's all about *el coño*.'

Rick slapped me on the back with one hot sauce-slathered glove, and Alfonse nodded with surprising sobriety, as if a point of deep importance had been confirmed. For once I felt close to them. I knew these men only vaguely. They were tough bastards who never missed a shift, not even when they were dog-sick, and who didn't even flinch when they picked up stove burns. They both wore peeling sneakers embedded with grass clumps from marathon weekend games of *futbol*. Now and then I went to Pomona Park – the very place I met Detective Munoz – to catch these games, mostly for the fistfights that erupted with almost ritual regularity and played out according to certain interesting rules. The players formed a wide circle around the fighters and watched with a quiet, neutral connoisseurship as the men exchanged fists, heels, elbows, and knees to settle some point. It could last for 15 or 20 minutes. Then the fighters mopped up their faces and embraced, and with a round of applause, the game resumed. It was all thrilling and admirable and good. These were men who didn't go around seething and wanting to hit other men, bile burning holes in their digestive plumbing; they hit and then got on with their day. I'd seen both Rick and Alfonse take guys apart, without art, but with plenty of passion. Once I even saw them fight each other. Beyond these things I knew almost nothing about these men, and I was not sure why I craved their approval, much less their friendship, but I did, I did.

Sometime near the tag-end of the lunch rush, as I bused tables, I saw a stunning, slim-shouldered blonde at table 17. She was in the company of an unsettlingly pretty dude with torn jeans and a grungy T-shirt. He had high cheekbones, a goatee, stringy Jesus hair, and petulant lips. The girl, who wore a plunging V-neck top, could have been a model in an ad for perfume or a fine brand of heroin, one of those pale, untouchable 60-foot billboard faces. And yet there was an unexpectedly homey touch that rendered her human. She wore a black hair band, one of those Hillary Clinton deals, an accessory I'd always found winning, and which endeared even the icy First Lady to me. It gave the girl a high, intelligent forehead. Unconsciously, I began filling in her

Playboy questionnaire for her. Despite her designer-drug looks, she was a chick who liked solitary time in libraries, romantic walks on the beach, barefoot seashell-hunting. She abhorred rudeness and pretension. She would love to solve world hunger. She liked cozy sweaters and fireplaces, and her favorite novel was *The Catcher in the Rye*. She sympathized with outcasts and secretly longed to save them. She wondered why she was with this shallow, cocky, inappropriately dressed dickhead. She knew she was way too good for him. She'd already tired of his selfishness, his empty soul, his womanizing. She kind of hated herself (she had to admit) for being with him.

Poison bled from my heart as I watched them from across the room. He was on his cell phone, ignoring her, chatting importantly, making some appointment. He held up a finger, making the waitress wait for him to finish his call. Then he ordered for both of them, ordered in Spanish and mispronounced even the words I know, calling chicken 'polo,' like the game. He was in my restaurant – an upscale restaurant!; a place where important, well-groomed people dined!; a place people respected! – and he came dressed for the goddamn garage and mispronouncing words. Not to mention the chick, way too good for him. Especially the chick. He was in my house, pissing on my leg. It was more than I could take.

Passing through the kitchen, I dissolved six squares of Ex-Lax in his plate of *mole con pollo*. I hustled back to the sink before I was caught by one of the chefs or, worse, by Scabronis. Regretting that I wouldn't be able to witness the dude's face as it registered the onset of gastrointestinal horror, as he lost his coolness, as he scrambled flatulently to the door that read '*Caballeros*,' I plowed through a stack of dishes, buzzing in the clench of nervous, nasty satisfaction. Twenty or thirty minutes later, I heard, 'Benny! You, you shit-ass, Benny!'

Scabronis stood in the doorway, scowling like a terrifying demon.

'Stop skulking there by the sink! We have an emergency.'

'I'm not skulking, Mr. Scabronis.'

'Grab the plunger from the supply closet. A mop, a bucket! Put the "Out of Order" sign on the *Caballeros*' room. There's shit everywhere. Make it unshitty. Ten minutes!'

'Why me? I'm a dishwasher.'

'Because I don't have anyone on the payroll called"shit boy"!'

'Why can't the Mexicans do it?'

'Don't argue with me!'

Emergency, it turned out, was close to the right word for the situation. Turds were hanging in inch-deep water all over the floor, like some strange breed of shrimp. I waded cursing into the turdscape, wishing earthquakes and dengue fever on everyone. The tidal disruption created by my step jostled the turds, which rotated sluggishly in their places and sloshed up against my shoes. At the toilet I found the source of the problem.

Now, Zapata! Zapata! is a classy place, as I've said, and customers shouldn't need a sign that says 'Don't Cram Paper Towels In the Bowl.' Nevertheless some self-centered patron had done exactly that, despite the availability of two rolls of high-quality ass paper in this very stall. It could only have been Table 17.

Steeped in feces, raising the plunger over the stopped bowl like some kind of Excalibur-liberating Arthur in humiliating reverse, I knew my degradation was complete and that my attempt at balancing the scales of justice in the universe were forever doomed to backfire.

At this moment, however, a vision visited me. The blonde with the V-neck reminded me of someone. I thought of the enchanting way she kept her hair, pinned demurely under that hair band . . . like someone . . . like *her* . . . exactly like *her*. Go ahead, say the name. It hurts, but say it: Gwen Stacy. Oh, Jesus. Gwen! Gwendolyn! Yes, you were the blonde I sought amid this morning's cacophony of dream-trains. It was you I was supposed to leave with.

I never talked about it to anyone, but I was not ashamed to admit you were the first woman I loved. I believed I was over you, and then here you came, ambushing me, reminding me that it was your shape gaping in the center of my heart, like a Wile E. Coyote silhouette punched in a rock. You were my missing piece. My poor, sweet Gwendy.

You weren't my girlfriend. You should have been. But you were Peter Parker's, a guy often as lonely and confused as I, a guy, like me, who trafficked in secret identities. I admired how you treated him, adored him, sassed him just enough. An all-around terrific lady: sweet, compassionate, busty, pert-nosed, prone to floods of sudden tears, a lover of mini-skirts and tall leather boots and snug sweaters, which you somehow wore with total innocence, a worrier, a sweet ruminator by windows, a girl possessed of incredibly long, elegant eyelashes, and of course more flawlessly managed hair than a salonful of average girls could ever grow. Your style was urban hip, and your soul was *Little House on the Prairie*; your body a porn star's, and your smile pure *Sesame Street* sunshine. You could have been a centerfold superbitch, considering how fine you looked, but you weren't, you weren't! You didn't quite know what everyone else saw in you, which only made us love you more, love you to the point of unbearability.

You died when I was 12 years old. They assassinated you in *Amazing Spider-Man* no. 121, in June 1973. For exactly 20 cents spent at a Van Nuys drugstore, I bought a broken heart, an awareness of human evil, and an adult's sense of death's finality and indiscriminate reach.

The writer–artist team of Gerry Conway and Gil Kane did you in via the Green Goblin. The Goblin: a reptilian freak in ghoul-face and green tights who zipped around Manhattan on a bat-shaped glider, hurling exploding pumpkins. Who could take him seriously? Who would expect he'd bring death to the Silver Age Marvel universe, where entire city blocks could be annihilated in superhero clashes without a single casualty, where the characters you loved – particularly the hero's sweet, statuesque girlfriend, who existed mostly to be put in peril and rescued, *particularly her* – could always be expected to come through alive? Where the dead inevitably returned a few issues later, with the explanation that only an android simulacrum or alternate-universe impostor had bought it? Nobody was trained to expect the real thing, death of the no-take-back variety. But the Goblin, crazed with hatred, snatched you up on his glider and carried you to the top of the Brooklyn Bridge and, while your boyfriend watched helplessly in his bright action leotard, sent you plunging into the abyss with all of your beautiful hair soaring behind you. By some miracle Mr. S was able to catch you before you hit the water – a cable of webbing snagging one of your stunningly tall leather boots, SWIK! – but the sudden jolt broke your neck. And in case anyone missed the point, there it was, the sickening sound effect, diligently incorporated into the panel: SNAP! Thank you, Gerry Conway! Thank you, Gil Kane! They never found the usual pretexts to resurrect you. There you were in Spidey's arms, gorgeous in death. Unmarked. Perfect cheekbones and full lips. Amazingly, the fall did not even dislodge your hair band. But forever dead. And while the webslinger went on to Mary Jane Watson, the sweet, statuesque brunette who has sustained the hero through many adventures, who continued to be put in peril and rescued, I stayed with you, the original Cool Chick – achingly. It felt disloyal, to try to get over you, and I was nothing if not loyal. But it still felt slightly morbid, to brandish the Lubriderm with your picture in my lap. I mean, you were dead. For one, it was kind of sick; for another, my feelings were too complicated. So for self-abuse sessions I usually stuck to Sue Storm, the Invisible Woman; Storm, goddess of the elements; or She-Hulk, the big, green, chick hulk. But I had to admit there was very little love in it with those ladies.

I'm getting off track. Sorry, Goins.

When I finished mopping up the *Caballeros*' room, I headed

back to the kitchen, sunk in gloomy brooding, wishing I hadn't remembered the dream. True Love was the train I was missing, and it had long since left the station.

At the sink it was clear I'd lost my mojo. My movements were arthritically slow. I didn't care anymore. I didn't even care if Scabronis came in and fired me. It would be the third job I'd lost this year. Rick and Alfonse noticed the ferocity had gone out of my dishwashing. Rick said, '*Holmes*? You okay, *holmes*? *Coño*?'

The Gwen Stacy story wasn't the kind of thing you wanted to share with Rick and Alfonse, despite their philosophical nature. So I said, 'I saw this *puta* out there who reminded me of this other *puta* I knew who died.'

They nodded. They let me be for the rest of my shift, respecting that. They understood these things. They had been there too, probably. But I was immediately ashamed of myself for having sold out my goddess, just to be one of them.

Because you were anything but a *puta*, Gwen.

I decided I wouldn't call you that again, no matter what the circumstances.

Scabronis waited till my shift was over – till I had mopped up all the shit and washed all the dishes – before coming in to sack me. Someone had seen me sabotage the *mole con pollo*; someone had ratted. Scabronis screamed something in Greek, and every muscle in his face seemed to twitch with anger. He peeled off a few fives and tens, the last of my pay, and thrust them at me. Sneering, I balled up my filthy apron and surrendered it with a shrug to the goatfucker's hairy hands. Rick and Alfonse looked sorry for me, but kept turning away nervously.

As I pedaled away, I realized how relieved I was, that I'd probably asked for it. But soon another feeling overtook me, a sick feeling of cowardice, and I cursed myself for not telling Scabronis exactly what I thought of him. Then I decided I should have tried lying my way out of trouble – blaming the Mexicans if I had to – because now I'd have to scrounge for another job. And tell my wife.

CHAPTER 9

As I came down the hall toward our apartment I could already hear the canned laughter from Donna's sitcom.

A big girl, roomy hips, ample all around, Donna sat smoking Virginia Slims on the couch in purple sweats, her bare feet propped on our mini-trampoline, which collected junk like every other available surface: piles of clothes, my heaps of *Fate* magazine and Marvel comics, her heaps of *People* and *Cosmo*, my shoeboxes overflowing with leaves of old *Build a Brobdingnagian Vocabulary!* and *William F. Buckley Word-A-Day* calendars.

'Scabronis sacked me,' I said.

'What you do?'

'Somebody put some laxatives in a dude's food, and it's me who gets it.'

'Why'd you mess with some dude's food?'

'I didn't say it was me.'

'Genius, Benny! Because we're not broke enough!'

She shook her head slowly and seethed, refusing to look at me until I had promised six or seven times that I'd find another job soon. But her mood was permanently soured. Finally she said, 'Did you get my thing?'

For a few days, she'd been asking me to pick up a pink inhaler at the Thrifty pharmacy. Again I'd forgotten.

She said, 'What am I gonna do now, I have an attack?'

'Use the orange inhaler.'

'Orange is medium-strength. What if it's a maximum-strength attack?'

'Maybe you can use the orange one twice.'

Now she glared. She'd explained this to me before and couldn't believe I'd forget again. My selective memory infuriated her. I could remember Rod Carew's year-by-year batting averages, but not a thing as important as her medication. All evidence, she believed, of how I didn't love her like I should.

'You want me to be a sitting duck when the big one comes?' she said. 'You'd be happy if I up and died, wouldn't you?'

'I'm sorry.'

'I'm in no condition to run there myself, or I would.'

It's true that for years I had allowed myself to entertain fantasies of life after her demise, of all the sympathy that would come my way: *There goes Benny Bunt. Know his story? Poor man lost his missus. Deserves a drink. Look at that sorry-ass bike he gets around on. Smart guy, too: knows stuff. 'Course he never did zilch with himself. Wife like that . . .*

'I'm sorry,' I said again, grabbing a Coors and plonking sore-footed onto the couch. Grudgingly she heated up a couple of Hungry Man salisbury steaks and carried them over on TV trays. We ate while the tube gibbered, one sitcom rerun bleeding into another. This show, like the one before it, involved a dysfunctional family whose members spent their time insulting each other wittily. The canned laughers loved it. They loved every joke, right on cue.

Canned laughter always made me think of suicide, the logic of it, even the inevitability of it. Maybe the laughers were suicides themselves. Maybe that's their punishment: banishment to a place where you have to laugh at everything, like a rat leg twitching obediently under the kiss of electricity.

Donna surfed to a syndicated courthouse drama and said, 'Look at that skinny bitch pretending to be a lawyer. You can see the ribs sticking through her dress, like some kind of Ethiopian.

That's what's supposed to be hot these days. Would you like a piece of that?'

'No.'

'Of course you would, if you could snag someone in that league. You'd have to be able to hang on to a job first.'

'I'm not attracted to her.'

'Win the lotto, get a Vette: you'd be porking Lady Skeletor in a New York minute. Because if a woman doesn't have petite little titties, and nibble two pieces of iceberg lettuce a day, and sneak off and puke it up so her teeth rot out of her head, and no fun in life at all, well, nobody wants her.' She scowled at me. 'Benny, you make me so – so insecure.'

'I'm sorry.'

Despite her raft of meds, Donna was always phlegmy, her nostrils miserably red-rimmed and leaking snot. Our apartment was full of things that made her sneeze and choke: molds in the ceiling, dust mites, roaches. Me? I couldn't spend 20 minutes at home without a constriction of the lungs, for reasons having nothing to do with molds and mites. Yes, as I sat here in my own home, my castle, my sanctuary, the smoke-choked tightness of the Greasy Tuesday loomed in my mind like a big gulp of ocean oxygen.

After an hour on the couch I stood and said, 'I need a drink.'

'You've *had* a drink. A couple of drinks! And I haven't seen you all day.'

'My day's been about as kind as cancer. I really need—'

'Jesus! What kind of husband are you?'

'I don't know.'

'But I know. I know what kind.'

'I'm sorry.'

'What's gonna happen when you drink yourself to death?'

I sat down. She produced a magazine and insisted we take a psychology quiz. Stupidly I submitted to the trap. I tried to answer the questions in a way that wouldn't get me in trouble. She would read a word, and I was supposed to say the first thing that came to mind. When she said 'Sea,' I answered, 'Drown.' When she said 'Coffee,' I said, 'First you're nervous, then you shit.'

We got through those two questions before she threw the magazine at me. '"Sea" is what you think of your marriage,' she snarled. '"Coffee" is what you think of your sex life.' She concluded that I didn't love her, that in fact I wanted to push her under a bus and fuck a lot of skinny TV bitches, and she cried. I couldn't leave while she was crying, so I decided to wait out the waterworks. When her face seemed to be drying I said, 'I really need a drink.'

'Take me to Target, baby,' she pleaded.

'I thought you were in no condition to go—'

'Target is therapy. It's different.'

'You can't drink at Target. You go. I'll go to the bar.'

'I thought we were a couple. Couples do things together.'

'A drink is all I can think of after a day like today.'

'Take me to the bar then.'

'It's no place for ladies. All those creeps eyefucking you.'

'Maybe I like being eyefucked. Maybe it makes me feel desired.'

'I'd get stabbed, defending your honor.'

'You're a liar. You're just ashamed to be seen with me. We have no quality time.'

'Fucking is quality time. Why don't we have more of that kind of quality time instead of Target quality time?'

She looked aghast, like I'd just slapped her. And I was immediately ashamed I'd said it; I hurt her. But I couldn't always mask my fury at the state of things. The last time it looked like we might enjoy conjugal relations was three or four months ago. I'd just applied some ointment to my hemorrhoids and climbed into bed when Donna, in a rare good mood, announced, 'We should try to do it.' Suddenly her tongue was slurping at my eardrum and her hand tugging at my joint, and I thought: *Yes! Terrific! Here we go. Why a man marries!* I put a few of my fingers in her mouth to suck.

She gagged and seized them, holding them under her nose. Her expression was savage. 'Preparation H goes on with a Q-tip, you stupid shit! You just don't care at all about trying to make it nice for me!' I spent the rest of the night trying to coax a sobbing Donna out of the bathroom.

The tear-tap was open again now, gushing hot streamlets down her cheeks to pool in the adipose folds of her neck. No pleasure in that for me, none at all. 'I'm your wife, and you speak to me like a hooker!'

'You just said – eyefuc—'

'You'd be happy if my arteries just up and quit and killed me, wouldn't you? Well, one day they will, and then you'll see. I'm a waste of space anyway, if you ask me how my husband makes me feel.'

'Why do we – I mean, why do—'

Why do we keep on like this? is what I wanted to ask.

'You know the problem with our relationship?' she screamed. 'You're only half here emotionally, Benny! You're married to your comics and your pot and your booze! You don't know a fucking thing about love and commitment! About making a person feel special! Not the first basic principle!'

I felt the urge to do something dramatic. Upend that stupid trampoline, for instance, send junk flying across the room. Smash a plate or two against the wall, to make the point that I could only be pushed so far. Some kind of primal Ed-Harris-as-Jackson-Pollock scene is what I had in mind. But I was not the kind of man who did those sorts of things. Donna knew this. I couldn't pull it off. And besides, I worried too much about her condition to risk that kind of gesture. But I needed to get out. Out! Into the cool tobacco dark and encompassing gin fumes of my favorite dive.

'I really have to go, sweetheart,' I said.

I heard her orange inhaler clatter against the door as I fled.

CHAPTER 10

You want to know how a man finds himself in such a cage, don't you, Goins? Alright, I'll rewind. We met at the movie theater, Donna and I. She worked in the ticket-booth at the old Mesa Grand and I came every Tuesday night for the $1 feature. I loved that old theater, even with its wobbly uneven seats and springs jutting through the upholstery and the floor sticky with Pepsi; I felt comfortable there, at one with its blue-collar scrappiness. You got an entire row to yourself, nobody was better than you, and the audience appreciated it when you told an actor what you thought of him.

On the night I saw *Leaving Las Vegas*, Donna slipped me a ticket and said, 'This movie sucks, but there's a couple hot sex scenes in it,' and I have to admit, it was the first time I really noticed her. I had been seeing her for months and not really seeing her, the way people can stand next to a certain kind of wallpaper forever without the pattern ever registering. I loved her frankness and vulgarity. It was just my speed. And her smile, wide, generous, and toothy: there seemed to be something lusty and personal in it for me. I kept thinking of the roomy dimensions of her mouth. That week I came back to the theater five times, to see everything on the marquee. Afterward I'd drop by the booth to hear her tell me in her sassy, cheerful voice how much what I'd just seen sucked.

Even then she was complaining of her health and edging

toward the heavy side, her thighs swelling against her tight polyester uniform. Management kept her planted in the ticket booth because she insisted she didn't have the energy to stand at the popcorn counter or sweep the aisles, and she threatened to sue if they didn't accommodate her. 'I'm a special-needs employee,' she told me. 'The others hate me.' One afternoon, between features, I heard a pair of aisle-sweepers maligning her in the nastiest way. It included a cruel impression of her bratty manner of speech, and remarks about her weight. It was clear from the way they carried on that she was a running joke at the theater.

This cut me, and I fled. Then I realized it was a good thing, in fact a godsend, because it finally gave me the courage to ask her out. She seemed surprised when I did. We shared an oily pizza and root beer and then hit a karaoke bar, and I sang 'What a Fool Believes' to her. I kept sneaking mints in case the kiss came. We drank all night, and I was so glad to have a woman's company. Neither of us had been on a date in years. We shared lists of our top-10 favorite things in all the important categories, including movies, rock songs, sitcoms, and cop shows. We agreed Led Zeppelin was the greatest band of all time; that *Homicide*'s Andre Braugher was the greatest actor; that boy bands should be systematically gassed. We traded our Top 10 People We Despised in High School lists – all the beautiful, clear-skinned people whose adequacy tormented us – and she said, 'How much did the *prom* suck? No one asks fat girls to dance.' So when someone started doing Lionel Ritchie on the karaoke machine, I pulled her to her feet and got my arms around her and we swayed from side to side, real slow. It was the first time I noticed the difference in size between us; my arms didn't quite reach around her waist to her back, and my head came up no higher than her bosom. I heard someone say, 'Play some swing so she can flip him,' and there were snickers, but I pretended not to hear. If she heard, she didn't let on either; she just kept swaying with her eyes closed.

In the lobby of her building we kissed, and then, all nerves, I followed her inside to her cramped, musty apartment and we fumbled with each other in the dark. It was over too fast – I really wanted to please her – and I kept apologizing until she said, 'Jesus, dude, shut up. We can do it again.' And maybe that's the moment I fell in love with her. She was so crass and sassy. She told me there was alcoholism and diabetes and high blood pressure in her family and she would probably be dead by 40. She wondered if those assholes at the theater might be a little nicer if they only knew all the horrible shit she'd been through, watching her mom dropped by a stroke in the meat aisle at Vons and her dad lose both legs to diabetes. I told her not to worry, there were a lot of shits out there, yes, but things balanced. Every bastard got his comeuppance someday, and every lowly sufferer got his moment.

She tugged at all my protective instincts, my sense of justice, my guilt: I wanted to do right by her. I thought maybe I could save someone.

I told Donna all about me. Stuff I hadn't really told anyone. About how my father, Benjamin Bunt Sr., was a conductor on Amtrak's West Coast line. He was supposed to be a little guy like me, but I didn't have any memories of him because he split when I was two, and my mother's only explanation was that I squalled a lot as a baby and my dad loved quiet. I think Mom said it just to shut me up, because she didn't want to talk about the real reasons for his splitting. Maybe he fell in love with another woman, and it was the kind of love you can't do anything about except follow it; maybe the company made him take a job on the Eastern lines and he tried to send for us and couldn't; maybe he died and word never got back. I liked to think it was something like that. But all Mom would say is, 'You squalled. Benny, you were a real squaller.' I remember always asking about the old man. Was he tough? Was he smart? Was he good at stuff? What baseball team did he like? Didn't he love us?

Mom refused to talk about him though, especially after she married Big Hal, because mention of Dad might earn her a beating. Square-jawed and husky, Big Hal drove a concrete truck and read a lot of rifle magazines and said the Holocaust was made up. When he was drunk enough, he spoke of how the State of Israel was engineering the apocalypse. Big Hal lived in our house on Sepulveda Boulevard in Van Nuys for 10 years and said maybe 50 words to me a year. Usually the words were 'dumb-ass,' because I was clumsy and couldn't do anything worthwhile like hammer a nail, or 'faggot,' because I read a lot of comics and magazines, and he thought it was a faggoty way to spend time. Ignoring me was some kind of principle with Big Hal. He had to punish me for being someone else's kid. He'd say to Mom, 'Your brat has weird eyes and he gives me the creeps. Can't you give him to someone? Can't you find a doorstep?' She'd reply that she couldn't blame him for feeling that way, since she knew I was odd, but who would take a kid who looked like me and walked into furniture all the time? I think she said it to protect me. Maybe she half believed it, but I still think it came from love.

For a while I wanted Big Hal to love me. I memorized chunks of *Mein Kampf* to impress him. Once I made him a ceramic mug and painted 'BIG HAL' on the side, along with a swastika and my best effort at a concrete truck, and I brought him his Coors in it. He threw it into a wall and said, 'Big Hal drinks from a can.' He pushed me into a coffee table and my scalp bled. He wanted me to understand how wrong it was, trying something like that: a gift like that. It was sneaky and low of me. Because I wasn't his, and he wasn't mine, and you had to face fundamental facts. You couldn't pretend you were something you weren't. I took the lesson.

After that I thought a lot about killing Big Hal. I didn't know how to go about it, without getting caught. In the seventh grade I tried to do it with black magic. That was the year I worshipped Satan, or pretended to. I took refuge where I could find it. I disfigured walls with pentagrams and 666s, flashed the devil sign in greeting schoolmates, and decorated my Pee-Chee folder with quotes from 'The Satanic Bible.' It's really the same impulse that makes a kid wave around a stick covered with dogshit, looking for screams. In this case I had turned myself into the repugnance on display. I *was* the dogshit. Girls were horrified of me. For a while people knew me at Van Nuys Junior High as 'the Satan dude,' which I liked a lot, because even a stupid rep was better than no rep. Eventually some Christians on the wrestling team put my head in a urinal and took turns pissing on me, and it wasn't fun anymore. And when my spells failed to bring an embolism or freak electrocution down on Big Hal, as I begged the masters of darkness to do, I renounced Satan-worship as not only dangerous but useless.

Big Hal left cigarette burns on me and bruises on Mom, and for a whole week, after one beating, her head looked like a pumpkin. One day a surgeon fucked up his back during an operation – so he insisted – and then he was home all the time, drinking and going crazy. His pride took a hit, because Mom had to pay the bills, working double-shifts at Denny's. So he started hating her as much as he hated me.

There were days you could feel the violence on him throbbing for an outlet, throbbing off his belly and the backs of his hands, like heat rising off a pavement. One night Mom made a sharp remark about how tired she was, and could a man who sat home all day maybe fix his own goddamn grilled cheese for once? He sprang out of his recliner and pushed her head into the wall, and I watched her sag to the floor. I was 17, small but stocky, with strong legs and biceps that I built with weights in the garage; by then Big Hal was fat and weak, with that gimpy back. I don't remember how it happened exactly, but I found myself on top of him, pinning him to the floor, whaling on him, whump, whump, whump, whump. It wasn't me doing it, really. Some reptile part of my brain had seized the controls. We were all alone, myself and my thrashing, suddenly helpless stepfather: the world had contracted to this blindingly bright tunnel in which there were just our two bodies, his meat and my meat, and even my mother's screams in my ear belonged to some dream.

I must have known that if I hit him one more time, I wouldn't quit until I killed him.

There was no choice after that: I had to leave. Mom gave me what she had – 65 bucks, three days' tips – and told me to call when I could, and to come by the restaurant when I needed a meal. She was crying, but there was really nothing she could do. She loved Big Hal.

For weeks I slept in Laundromats or movie houses and by night I roamed Sepulveda Boulevard, keeping company with winos and tweakers at bottle clubs and all-night donut joints. For a while the tweakers were my family: an ever-changing succession of drop-outs and runaways and lost kids like me who snorted or swallowed anything on hand. They taught me to turn a $50 brick of pot into $200, to cook up meth in a Motel 6 sink, to scale the ladders behind strip malls for a patch of roof to crash on. At Thrifty Drugs I slipped Marvel and DC comics into my cargo pants, gravitating mostly to lone-wolf heroes like Batman and Wolverine and Conan the Barbarian, the noble bad asses who smote the evil and protected the weak and didn't need anybody. Certain superhero teams like the Fantastic Four and the Avengers fascinated me in a different way, the ones who loved to gather family-like around big tables in their mansions and deluxe secret lairs. Like all families, these heroes had their feuds, their ego-clashes, their sibling spats. Big, bright-clad shoulders chock-a-block across the page: heat rippling off the close bodies so I could almost feel the family warmth of the room, even as I huddled alone against the wind on top of a Burger King or Dunkin' Donuts. I ruined a lot of comics, crying on them. After a while it was just my gut heaving up and down, and nothing at all coming out of my eyes.

Daytime was easier. I killed afternoons in the library at Van Nuys Community College, passing myself off as a student, hustling a few bucks off kids at the upstairs chess table. Through the window I watched bleach-blond surf boys and tanktopped girls with fine copper fur growing all over their legs kicking around hackey sacks in the grass quad – an idiotic game – while the California sun worshipfully came on their golden heads. To make my fake identity convincing, I memorized all kinds of random data: geographical facts, precipitation rates, lengths of archipelagos, dates of wars and assassinations, endless vocabulary lists – particularly those. The world is full of people who like to make you feel like an ignorant motherfucker. They love to whip out words like 'lagniappe' or 'canard' on you, watch your face fill with panic and bewilderment. It's the petty pride of the tollbooth lady who refuses to let you pass if you're a nickel short: she *lives* for it. I decided not to give this breed a second's satisfaction at my expense. If some college cocksucker tried to drop the hammer on me with 'lagniappe,' I'd fire back with 'epistemological,' and if he hit me with 'canard,' I might unleash 'anaphora' or poleaxe him with 'perspicacious,' to demonstrate that I was not his punk. Of course I suspected that all the 'knowledge' I crammed into what I was already calling my Memory Palace didn't add up to any kind of education, just as the fragments of a man's personality, when you try to fit them together, never really seem to add up to a whole person. But I learned to fake being educated, the way a world of amalgam-men fake being real people.

At the library I met and befriended a man named Ray Castle. He was a retired ancient-history professor from Kentucky, divorced, graying; he was beanpole-skinny with large, bony, liver-spotted hands. I called him the Professor. He wore V-neck sweaters that reeked richly (and, I thought, wonderfully) of menthol cigarettes. He kept taking me to Beef Bowl and Arby's for lunch, and I couldn't afford to say no to such a kindness. Voice trembling with emotion, he told fabulous stories of Greeks hacking up other Greeks, of the Spartans at the Hot Gates, of the love between Achilles and Patroclus, and particularly of the bravery of the 300-man Theban Sacred Band, the most feared of warriors, undefeated until they died to the last man – here tears always shone on the Professor's sunken cheeks – at Chaeronea in 338 B.C. At museums he flew into red-faced rages at the sight of fig-leafs on statuary; it was an unforgivable affront to decency, he explained, to blight beauty. He offered to let me crash on the couch of his small, dusty, book-cluttered apartment until I figured out my next move. I read to him after dinner, though I didn't grasp most of the stuff he liked: Plato's *Symposium*, Mann's *Death in Venice*. He called me a seedling that had been stunted by the rocky soil of my upbringing; all I needed were some cultural nutrients, the water and sunshine of mentorship, and I would blossom. I came to love him. At night he drank bourbon, and I'd wake on the couch to see his shadow framed in the doorway of his bedroom, his hair wild and his cigarette-scarred robe hanging slightly crooked off his gaunt shoulders. He'd watch me while I pretended to sleep; sometimes noises came from his chest that sounded like whimpering. Neither of us would mention this the next day. One night, after I'd been on his couch two or three months, he couldn't stand it anymore: I woke with his whiskey breath on my cheek and a bony, shaking hand suspended an inch from my thigh, trying to close the final distance. I reached into his robe and pumped my fist a few times. He grimaced at the ceiling, as if asking God for forgiveness, while mewling-dog noises came out of his throat. Afterward he didn't say anything, just shuffled back to his room. Next morning I was gone. The last time I saw him, he looked like a very old man, stooped and pouch-eyed and utterly defeated as he stood before his violated Buick, where I'd put rocks through the windshield and spray-painted '*FAGGOT!*' across the hood. I loved that old man.

Soon after I got unbearably lonely and I walked four or five miles to Denny's, where Mom worked. It was a chilly night, late. I stood across the street and watched her seating people through the restaurant window. Finally I went inside and saw her sweeping around a corner with three plates in each hand, headed to a booth full of boisterous men. She didn't notice me. I sat by the pie case until she did. She took me to a booth and brought me a plate of scrambled eggs, bacon and biscuits, and when she got a break she came and sat across from me and stroked my hand and cried. She told me Big Hal had been going out nights looking for me with his .22, and she couldn't make him listen to reason. Otherwise, their relationship had really improved since I'd been gone. It had become clear to her that I had been a lot of the problem.

She brought me an old leather suitcase full of my clothes and comics, which she'd been keeping at the restaurant in case I dropped by. My throat was thick as I took that suitcase on my lap. It was like being handed my own coffin. Entombed inside were 17 years of my life: my boyhood, my home, my innocence, what little I'd ever had of family.

I wouldn't cry, though. I'd be goddamned if I did.

I told Mom not to worry about me. I was doing fine. I was going to be a police officer and I was going to do a lot of important things and help a lot of people and have a lot of adventures. I'd wear a uniform and badge, and I'd have a squad car and a utility belt and a radio, and they were going to teach me all the special codes. I said I'd already been accepted at the LAPD Academy. 'How in hell did you swing that one?' she said. She just couldn't believe I was bright or coordinated enough for such a job. I said I had a guy on the inside I'd paid off. She smiled, proud. The smile said, *An idiot like you might just survive in the world. Maybe you've picked up a thing or two about how it works.* She brought another waitress over to share the good news. Her boy had snuck his way into cop school!

So I went out into the night, carrying that suitcase full of my dead youth, leaving my mother with that lie. Until she died she thought I was LAPD.

I fled south to Orange County, where the rent was cheap and there was a lot of beach and restaurant work and I knew Big Hal wouldn't find me. I got my GED and washed dishes and dealt some pot and crystal on the side and lived with five or six other guys in someone's basement. *Starsky and Hutch* reruns made me cry, reminding me that I had wanted to be a cop for as long as I could remember. As a kid I had lugged the hardware everywhere – that grab-bag of cheap cuffs, painted wafer badge and plastic gun; the walkie-talkie with the decorative knobs I adjusted feverishly in conversations with imaginary fellow eight-year-old cops. (At times the trusted partner I imagined on the other end, working some other sector of the city, calling me 'buddy,' was my father, a wise, faceless, older cop named Sgt. Bunt.) I loved the way people looked at cops when they walked into a room, like: *As long as the boys are here, nothing too bad can happen.* And how everybody wanted to buy them a cup of coffee. And how they could tell chicks, 'You're safe now – you're with *me*,' and it wouldn't be a con, it'd be true. A thousand hours of TV had implanted indelible notions of cop camaraderie. At the heart of the coolest shows were always two men, riding toward action, two capable men who knew each other's measure, who loved each other and would die for each other, but would never, ever betray the understanding between them by saying so: Starsky and Hutch, Ponch and John, Crockett and Tubbs, later Bayliss and Pembleton and Kelly and Sipowicz. (If any of them had wives, I can't remember. On the job I bet *they* couldn't, either: a man's real life, any of it that was worth recording anyway, happened with the dude riding shotgun. They were only 'cop dramas' in name, actually. It took me years to realize it, but the good ones were always love stories.)

I was not fit material for police work. They didn't even want me as a dispatcher or a clerk. Not the LAPD, not the Los Angeles County Sheriff's Office, not the Orange County Sheriff's Office, not the California Highway Patrol, not the FBI, not the Newport Beach or Costa Mesa PD. The shrink screeners found me an unstable, deceptive personality with issues of unresolved rage. The polygraph machine didn't like me, either, especially when I was asked if I'd broken any laws.

Now and then I'd see some sorry-looking cop, and felt myself go sick with bile, thinking, *How could those scamps think I couldn't carry a badge better than that?*

I was in my early thirties when liver failure killed Big Hal, and Mom moved into an apartment in Santa Ana. She was sick by then and couldn't work. I was happy to have a family again, even though Mom was very bitter and prematurely old. She raved and said she'd never have sex again, the way she looked now: they may as well freeze her privates off. She made impossible demands. She could barely contain her resentment toward me. I had been an accident, a curse; I'd driven away the first man she loved, and drove the second to drink himself to death. She screamed day and night, and I never screamed back. She begged me not to put her into a nursing home, which she feared more than dying. We played a lot of checkers and pick-up sticks, and I let her win most of the time. She spent six years dying.

I told Donna all of this – or most of it, anyway – in the few weeks after our first date, some of the words catching in my throat as I said them. Some of it was shameful. At the end with my mother, for instance, I couldn't wait for her to die and I was relieved when she did, because I figured I'd be free, it meant my life could really start. But, I told Donna, it still felt like it hadn't started. In fact I was lonelier than I could ever have imagined. I was still in some kind of indefinite holding pattern, waiting for something I couldn't name.

We were married a few months later: a quick ceremony at the Santa Ana courthouse and then a poolside room at the Holiday Inn with cable, spicy buffalo wings, and a bottle of champagne. All night my bride cried with happiness and told me she loved me and she was so happy she'd never be alone again. I was all hers, and she was all mine. I watched my joint disappear in that super-roomy mouth and felt my whole life going with it. After a while there was a puny spasm, a paltry dribble down her esophagus, and again her smiling, tearful, loving face, pressed against my stubbly cheek on the hotel pillow, and the depths of her throat emitting pleased, purring little sounds. I couldn't sleep. Vacationing Midwesterners splashed in the pool outside, too loud. My forehead was sweating, despite the hotel chill. I was thinking of Gwen Stacy, her tragic end, her long silky hair, getting lost in it. I was thinking how I wasn't amounting to much. I realized I'd always secretly hoped my life was building toward some big event, some trip, some wild *Easy Rider* or *Lawrence of Arabia* adventure that would put me right in my own head and drown the persistent feeling that wherever life was going on was somewhere I wasn't. But I had no idea where I wanted to go and so I'd never even left California. And now I felt the dreadful certainty that I'd never do anything, lashed to love like this. And maybe that's when I quit loving Donna. Or maybe love bled out of me by invisible cuts over the next five years. I don't know. After a while there were no more midnight love-tears and pillow-purrs from her, and I'm pretty sure I bore the blame for the loveless cage our marriage had become.

That's not exactly right. As I mentioned before, I felt a version of love, a remnant of it, when she was sleeping.

CHAPTER 11

The fights decreased at the bar after Gus Miller moved in, which was a disappointment to those of us who enjoyed watching and wagering on them. But it saved Junior some beatings, which put him in a better mood than he normally was, more likely to let you have one or two on the house.

Gus didn't have to raise his voice or lay his hands on people. He just lumbered up and smiled and spoke in a low voice, saying, 'My gut's sending me the message you're a dickhead, but I'm thinking my gut must be lying, since this ain't a dickhead bar. It's a friendly neighborhood bar. Now, you gonna be a dickhead in a friendly neighborhood bar?'

'No, sir.'

After cleaning the bar once or twice, Gus Miller decided the janitorial part of his job didn't suit him. A few times Junior passive-aggressively reminded him that the place needed tidying. Gus ignored him, or grumbled about his sore 54-year-old joints and the shrapnel in his leg. Junior bit his lip. The bar sank back comfortably into its original ooze.

Gus didn't let his new responsibilities impede his alcohol consumption, of course. Sometimes a night's drinking made him very quiet, and he leaned forward, resting his fat tattooed forearms on the bar, watching nothing through his crooked glasses, emitting no sound all night beyond a grunt, and rising only to visit the shitcan or to slip a few quarters into the jukebox, playing anything by Springsteen or Johnny Cash or the Eagles. In these moods he liked songs that told stories and were heavy on misery, songs like 'Ly'n Eyes' and 'Highway Patrolman,' and there was a kind of tearless weeping in the sagging lines of his face, as he listened with half-closed eyes.

Other times, binging on what he called 'fuck-you music,' Sabbath and Scorpions and the Stones and AC/DC, he became a juggernaut of manic energy, a blustering, back-slapping, bellowing circus bear. He insisted on these occasions that you called him Iceman or Mad Dog. His voice would interrupt yours and blast you off your stool. There was no sense trying to talk while he told a story, because no one could hear you while he was at it anyhow. He was competitive about it too, perceiving conversation as a Monster Truck rally with room in the dirt for only one set of jacked-up wheels at a time, his own, and always ready to barrel over any smaller vessels in the way.

I was a pretty good man with a joke or a story myself – better than most – but Gus insisted on winning. If you saw Fernando Valenzuela throw a shutout, back when Fernando Valenzuela threw shutouts – well, Gus saw him back when he was just a promising wetback on a spick sandlot. If you'd done a few months in county lockup, Gus had done hard years. If you saw the famous pit fighter Tank Abbott in a Huntington Beach bar, Gus actually served as his sparring partner a few years before he became a star. If you had a cardiac murmur, Gus had a golfball-sized hole in his heart that could kill him at any moment. Once Sal mentioned getting jostled in the chaos of a Lynyrd Skynyrd concert back in the Seventies, and Gus jumped in with, 'Chaos! You don't know the concept till you've been a bouncer at a Rick Springfield concert! Savaged by the claws of twenty thousand screaming girls is chaos! And I've got the scars!' Up came the shirt over his big, white belly, and there were the Rick Springfield scars, mingled among the pungi-stick scars, and the switchblade-fight-in-Tijuana scars, though it was always impossible to tell which ones he was pointing to. The whole butcher-block mess of them was enlisted to buttress the credibility of whatever story he happened to be telling at the moment. I couldn't blame him; I'd been there.

It was unclear how seriously he expected people to take his stories; he sometimes concluded one with a mighty guffaw and the expression, 'I'm just fucking with you, stupid.'

In any bar in America, you can safely expect the breakdown between sheer bullshit and stone-righteous veracity to be about 60–40, maybe 70–30. And in the bars I frequented it was considered bad manners, laziness, even a show of contempt for your listeners, if you didn't attempt to embellish. Even worse manners, however, was calling a man a liar. Gus quickly developed a reputation as a bullshit king, but no one possessed the stones to challenge him.

Telly's resentment toward him, I noticed, continued unabated; often he would rise with an ugly expression and move to the other side of the bar when Gus was holding court. It was not Gus's bullshit that irritated him, I surmised: it was Gus's habit of preventing other men from contributing their rightful share. When he was drunk enough, Telly lost his fear and mocked Gus's throaty theatrical growl: 'Fuck you, flower lady! You'd deny a job to a man who spent two years in a bamboo cage in the Mekong Delta? Deny a job to a man who can disassemble an M-16, lubricate the component parts, and put it back together in fifteen seconds? Deny a job to a man who had his cock blown off in Kai-San, humped ten miles with the stump of his bleeding dingus, and ordered it sewn back on at gunpoint? Deny a job to—' He was never drunk enough to do the impression in Gus's presence.

Myself? I was Gus's best listener, listening being what I do best. People want to tell me things. And as I said, I've always been a sucker for stories. I'm easily moved.

While all around me men slouched on the frontier of alcoholic comas, I presented an ideal audience, gaping, bugging my eyes, lighting up like a plugged-in bulb, exclaiming 'No!' or 'Jesus

Christ!' I asked intelligent questions. I conveyed absolute credulity. And Gus responded. Quickly he came to trust me. A few weeks after he arrived, he told me in a confidential tone that when he got back from Nam, he might or might not have done a few jobs as a freelance hit-man. He might or might not have had an international reputation.

'Christ,' I said. 'A buttonman? Really?'

'I don't wanna incriminate myself, but I could tell you some stories,' Gus said.

And he did, naturally, rambling over half a dozen states and murder contracts: death by gun, death by knife, death by defenestration, death by garrote, and all the amusing hijinks that attended these adventures. The names and dates bled together in his mind, he explained, but the quirky incidents stuck. He told these stories in the third person, referring to the hero as Iceman, who, he explained, might or might not have been him.

Once, a rich wife on the Jersey Shore wanted her husband whacked. Equipped with a key, Iceman climbed the winding stairs of their mansion, traversed acres of plush carpet, and found the man soaking himself in a jacuzzi-tub upstairs. The man looked up, seemingly not at all surprised to see his assassin hulking in the doorway with his leather gloves and .357. It was as if he had been waiting for him. 'I wondered what you'd look like,' said the man, and added: 'Look, there's some pearls behind the painting in the living room she doesn't know about. I don't want the bitch to have them. Go ahead, take them. They're yours.'

'Thanks.'

'Sure. I'm . . . very tired.'

'What of?'

'Arguing.'

For a long time the doomed man looked at his toes, emerging pink, fat, and wrinkled above the line of bubbles. He sighed with deep weariness and said, 'Well, I guess you better go ahead.' So, grimly, Iceman put one in his head and one in his heart and watched him sink underwater to his sudsy sleep. Then he went down and found the pearls just where the man said they would be.

'He fenced them for twenty large,' Gus bellowed, eyes popping with mirth and remembered astonishment, 'five times more than the contract itself!'

'I don't understand,' I said. 'He gives him these pearls so he won't whack him and he whacks him anyway?'

'No, no, no! The pearls he gave in a spirit of kindness, because our man was doing *him* a kindness. It wasn't Iceman that took the life out of that man. It was the institution of marriage. It was in his face. The bitch had the hex on him and he couldn't get out.'

'Well,' I said. 'I suppose getting whacked can be a terrific service.'

'Sure . . .'

Which reminded Gus of an even more bizarre incident. A cowboy strip mall developer in Houston decided his brother was running their company into the ground, looting the accounts to pay track debts. Naturally he had to go. All stealth, Iceman jimmied the lock to the guy's office one night and crept inside, roscoe at the ready, to discover the miserable gambler slouching at his desk with a handgun in his mouth. Plastered on the wall behind him was a riot of cranial pigments. And his coffee mug was still hot.

'Maybe the taste of the coffee depressed him,' I said.

'Our man thinks, "What miserable, shitty luck – the cowboy won't even want to pay me now." And he starts feeling sorry for himself. I mean, he must have eaten his gun five minutes before he arrived.'

'He didn't even need Iceman's kindness at all that time,' I said.

'Well, so Iceman has an idea, which is that he'll say, "I planned it to look like he ate his gun. I planned it." And guess what? The cowboy buys it. Couldn't have been happier. It made everything easier, really, because there wasn't even a murder case, just a man with plenty of reason to snuff himself.'

He ran a hand over his beard thoughtfully. 'But our man knew what happened, and he got to pondering, thinking, "Here I am, supposedly breaking the law, and the law makes no fucking sense. I get Old Sparky if I put a bullet into him at ten p.m., but if he puts the bullet in himself at nine fifty-five, there ain't even a crime!"'

Gus shook his head and drank. 'They don't take these details into account when they make up our so-called laws, Benny. I say so-called because I don't recognize their authority over me, since I'm an Outlaw. Outlaw's a state of mind, brother. Saying, "No one controls me." You didn't know I was a philosopher too. My master's Mr. F. Nietzsche, the Kraut. He invented a lot of this shit. He's the second-greatest Outlaw of all time.'

'Who's the first?'

'Jesus Christ. I'm Roman Catholic from way back.'

'Jesus Christ?'

'He was the original Outlaw, and he hated the rich, and he fucked up their shit, which is why they had to kill him. A man who makes up his own rules is too dangerous to keep around. Same deal with Satan, who if you ask me always got a bad rap.'

Listening, I began to grasp the appeal of a headcase like Charlie Manson. Say a thing with enough fire and conviction, add a few fistfuls of Svengali charisma, and just about anything sounds true. Gus Miller's mind, it occurred to me, was as chaotically cluttered as his van. He had been picking up things for years that he couldn't bring himself to throw away. So his brainpan swarmed with wild notions snatched from a book half-read in 1972, a conversation with a street-corner prophet in Detroit, maybe a 10-year-old LSD-induced revelation or two: anything he touched went into the bitch's brew of his philosophy.

He seemed to know a lot of unusual things, things I filed away in the rooms in my head. Like how a man locked in a cage can, if he's desperate for alcohol, make his pruno by fermenting orange juice with sugar packs smuggled from the mess-line. How knives could be made from bench struts and toothbrushes, and how prison stabbings almost always happened in the morning, because a man's head is foggy and his guard is down. How an inmate with a toothpick and urine can inscribe a secret message between innocent lines of ink, the piss-letters invisible till you wave a flame under the paper or press an iron to it. How longtime prisoners spoke a rhyme language called Carnie, so 'Caesar's life, struggle and strife' was how you said *knife*, 'I'd like to meet the Lady from Bristol' meant *get me a pistol*, and 'Happy Easter the nail and plank' meant *keister the shank* (and if the occasion called for you to thus sequester your jerrybuilt weapon, you best sheathe the sharp edge with a pen-cap and swaddle it with Saran Wrap before launching it into your ass). He taught me how a man without cigarettes can mix coffee grounds with lettuce to make a smoke, tamping it nicely in a page from the Gideon Bible. He knew these things from first-hand experience. He smoked Genesis through Revelation at San Quentin, he explained, smoked up the Serpent in the Garden and Jesus and the Virgin Mary and the Beast from the End-Times, smoked up the Hebrews wandering in the desert and Judgment Day and all the minor prophets. Most of his reading he did while serving time. There was a book on comparative mythology that he found in the prison library and read cover-to-cover three times. He particularly admired the Norse way of looking at the world. Dying of old age was a pussy's death. You had to make your exit young, and by battle-axe, to be rewarded in the afterlife with . . . more fighting. In Valhalla you hacked and clawed all day, your limbs magically reattached themselves at sunset, and you retired to the Great Hall with your friends for the Norse equivalent of a Coors. He liked some American Indian notions, too. Skinwalkers. Shamans. Vision quests. The Great Spirit who loved warriors and rewarded them with teepees full of virgins in the afterlife. I wondered if he might be mixing up his mythologies.

For years now, he explained, he had been having a peculiar

dream that he imagined might be a vision of heaven. The dream revolved around sex with small-bodied Indian girls with long braids and tiny moccasined feet, girls who spoke only in brief sentences, praising him in sweet bad English. He didn't know why his notions of the afterlife should take this form. Probably a man he shared a cell with once, an Indian or someone pretending to be an Indian, planted it in his head, and he found it so beautiful it stayed with him. Yeah, the Indians had the right ideas. In death Apache warriors went to the front of the line, with their loincloths and moccasins and bodies marked with arrowheads and spear-gashes, elbowed right up with the scalps of a lot of white motherfuckers and said, 'I believe I'm first.' And then all those sweet little Pocahontases were there to bathe your gashes clean with their little brown hands in the eternal cool porno shade of a teepee.

'Isn't that kind of entry-level stuff?' I said. 'I mean, it couldn't be right. Because a man gets tired of fucking girls after a while.'

'Well,' he said. 'Religion's never solved that one.'

'Heaven's got nothing to do with your dick,' I said. 'A righteous man's reward in the afterlife is he loses his need to use it. That's if they even let him keep it, and I doubt they do.'

He frowned. The Indian girls receded, left him, an abrupt pattering of tiny moccasins. He decided it was something to consider. Yeah: lurching after your joint for 45 years left it ensconced with so much bad meat that you barely recognized it. It picked up tags, like an old suitcase. You could read the trajectory of its travels in the scars and sores. Nothing to put your faith in. Before the war had shellshocked his dick, he explained, he had misused it badly. 'Drink up, brother,' said Gus, a charming madman, an inexhaustible source of half-anxious amusement. 'Just wish mine worked again. World's best poon could be right there, I wouldn't give up my stool.'

CHAPTER 12

We had grown tight. There was a fast brotherliness between us based (I suspected) on nothing more complicated than his desire to tell stories and my desire to hear them.

It turned out his handyman gig at the bar did not even cover his drinking tab, so he'd disappear now and then to fix roofs or lay tile or install decks. He also had another kind of 'job,' which was more lucrative, but proved very dangerous. Knowing I was out of work and hurting for cash, he invited me along. On corners in the nicer Newport Beach neighborhoods he lurked, whistling, glasses carefully pocketed, waiting for Jags and Benzes and Porsches to roll up at a red light. While they were still moving, he gave the hood a terrific thwack with his head, howled like a maimed bear, and, writhing under the stopped bumper like a South American soccer player with a pulverized limb, squeezed the bright crimson of a Halloween dye-pack over his forehead. There was good money to be made in this. The drivers emptied their wallets when he suggested (after unleashing some terrifying verbal abuse) that he saw no need to involve the insurance vultures, provided his needs could be taken care of quickly. My job was to pose as an independent witness corroborating that he, a poor pedestrian, had the right of way when the recklessly negligent driver barreled into him. He gave me a third of the take, which helped tide me over while I was out of steady work, and afterward, back at the bar, we laughed for hours replaying every detail. Human nature being what it is, however, the scam was not always successful. There was a sunburned man in a Polo shirt who, even after jumping out of his Lexus to glimpse the bleeding giant under his fender, sped away without a word, much less a cash offering. Springing to his feet, Gus shook a fist into the air and yelled after him: 'Heartless cocksucker! Get me a goddamn icepack, Benny . . .' Sometimes there was as much real blood on him as fake blood, and he complained of terrible headaches for days afterward, wearing a stunned, cross-eyed expression.

Entering a room, Gus instantly altered the energy in it. There was a great collective clenching of sphincters. You were never sure what kind of mood he was in or what kind of drugs he was on; I had seen him ingest coke, pot, ecstasy, crystal, Percocet, Viagra, and rainbow handfuls of capsules I couldn't identify, but which I suspected were psychotropic medications. Nor could you predict how he might try to humiliate you. He was good for lots of laughs, provided you were not the one singled out for treatment.

He nearly killed Sal Chamusco, for instance. As part of his secret Special Forces training, Gus explained, he learned to inflict death with his bare hands in such a way that permitted him to escape before the victim even suspected anything amiss. This was useful when the target was a heavily guarded foreign dignitary or military leader who could only be approached, say, over hors d'oeuvres at an embassy function. It was achieved by the legendary Dim Mak 'delayed death-touch' technique, which could be mastered only after exotic Shaolin training, requiring a great deal of meditation and, to preserve the all-important chi, a full year's excruciating abstinence from ejaculation. With no more than a brush of the palm, the killer wreaked havoc with the flow of the victim's yin/yang circuits, inducing fibrillation, uncontrolled sweating, and violent trembling. Death followed hours or even days later. It was all very scientific, as Gus put it, involving electrical impulses and complicated 'circadian and topological' equations.

'Hey, Sal,' Gus said, having caught the skepticism in Sal's pinched, frowning face. 'You got a guinea name. Come be my guinea pig.'

'That's alright.'

'You think it's bullshit, what're you scared of?'

'I ain't scared. Do Benny. You never do Benny.'

'But I'm asking you.'

'It just ain't funny, Gus. You can't fuck with people all the time.'

'Okay,' Gus said, spreading his hands pacifically. 'You're right. I'm an asshole. I'm sorry. I'll buy you one.'

'No sweat.'

'I push it too far sometimes, asshole that I am.'

A few drinks later, rising to claim the ashtray in front of Sal, Gus bumped him from the side so that startled Sal slipped from his stool. Gus braced him, and they stood facing each other. Sal looked down in horror at the fat hands pressed flat against his ribs, like a man suddenly realizing his tango partner had the Black Death. He flinched away. Gus sat down, and, a few drags into his cigarette, casually said, 'You just been Dim Makked, brother.'

Sal went pale. His attempt to smile, through all the perspiration suddenly slicking his face, including the bare pale spot over his lip where his mustache refused to meet, was a painful sight. He spilled his lighter into the sawdust and spent about a minute trying to pick it up. By now the whole bar was laughing. Hand against his chest, he emitted a high-pitched croak of surrender: 'Am I gonna buy it?' Whereupon gracious Gus, with a series of brisk acupressure manipulations, reversed the fatal process and bought Sal another drink. Cheers!

Gus spared me this treatment. Benefits of being the class bully's best friend. I suppose I validated his self-image. I treated him as he wanted to be treated – as a great, dangerous, tragically ruined man whom the world had sorely screwed and who was justified in whatever rage he harbored against it. At the library I found an art book with a reproduction of *The Dying Gaul* and photocopied it. I gave it to Gus and told him it was how I saw him. His scummed fingertip traced the lines of the soldier's rippled, Olympically tendoned body through which death invisibly stole, and Gus began to nod slowly. 'You're right,' Gus said. 'That's me. A battlefield casualty. Sent by his masters to fight and die because he knows nothing else. Yes. I'm Greek fucking statuary.' Within the week he had commissioned a small tattoo of *The Dying Gaul* on his lower back.

As a show of friendship, one night, he peeled off his cammie jacket, the raveled one with the Airborne patches, and said, 'I want you to wear my bad-ass jacket, Benny.'

'Are you sure?'

'Now you're an honorary PTSD-crazed tripwire combat vet.'

So I started wearing it around. I liked the respectful looks I got in it. I walked into all the bars on 19th and Harbor, bars like the Biker Pit and El Cholo's and Stooge City that I was normally afraid to enter, and just sat there in it, drinking silently, a quiet, troubled bad-ass who looked like he had killed some people and could probably kill some more if he was given any shit.

On weekends Gus and I frequented the beach dives and, blind drunk, headed out onto the sand in the dark with an ignitable log, singing and drinking ourselves unconscious like a couple of pirates. We hit a lot of Saturday afternoon flea markets, prowling for treasure. For me it was old comics, model trains, Hot Wheels and action figures. For him it was Time Life war books, commando novels, battle memorabilia, and materials with which to make birdhouses, mostly wood planks and sheets of corrugated tin.

Through the night he built these birdhouses in his room, one or two a month, with hammer, nails, and a little miter saw, patiently smoothing the edges with a square of sandpaper in the palm of his lumpy hand, his Sony AM/FM tuned to talk radio. Sometimes he gave them away. Once he got drunk and worked up enough courage to haul a few to Home Depot. He walked up to the manager with three hanging from each hand and asked for 10 bucks apiece – they could be easily marked up double or triple, he explained – but the store couldn't use them, even after he lowered the asking price to five. Then Gus tried to get Telly Grimes to unload a few, since he had connections, but Telly told him there was no real market for black-market birdhouses in Orange County. It was the first time I heard Telly say there wasn't a market for something. Besides, Telly said, examining one of the birdhouses, pretending not to know who made it, the workmanship wasn't so hot: you could tell the guy that made it was drunk. 'Tell whoever did it he should try something he's good at,' Telly told Gus. Gus told him to fuck himself and, his bottle swinging at his hip, stumbled back to the solitude of his broom-closet.

So the birdhouses just collected in Gus's van and cluttered his room. Once he spoke of finding a big back yard where he could put out 50 or 60 of them and spend all day watching the thrashers and waxwings, the robins and bluebirds, the sparrows and goldfinches and grosbeaks alight like broken-off pieces of a rainbow. 'Girl of mine,' he drunkenly replied, when somebody asked for whom he was building them. People figured he must have a lady somewhere, though he never talked about her. They were okay-looking birdhouses, too. Respectable. Telly was wrong: you really couldn't tell the guy that made them was drunk.

Once or twice a week, with Jesse James asleep back at the Greasy Tuesday, Gus and I hit the cineplexes. Aside from the sounds of his aggressive mastication – Gus went through three heavily slathered hotdogs in the course of a 90-minute feature – he observed great decorum at the movies, harshly shushing gabbers like myself. It was a holy place, he said. It was church. It didn't matter if it was a comedy or a cop drama or a war movie: Shut up. Before long I too found myself seriously irritated with the gabbers, shushing them and scowling threateningly in my Army jacket.

We caught old movies at the revival house in Corona del Mar. He knew the Nam flicks backward and forward, of course. He emerged always with the same complaint: the filmmaker had shown a deficiency of ball-sack, of first-hand experience, in depicting the horrors of that war. He admired *Full Metal Jacket* and *Platoon* and *Apocalypse Now* for technical reasons, but they were essentially 'soft-and-pink chick flicks' that did not capture even one-millionth of the misery he had seen. At times he fantasized about making the ultimate Nam movie, one so raw it was conceivable viewers would have to be hospitalized. He'd call it *The Devil's Asshole*, because it had been the worst place on earth.

Donna acquired the habit of assaulting me with airborne appliances whenever I was home – she disapproved of all the nights I was out with my mysterious new 'asshole buddy,' a phrase that made me twitch with rage – and found excuses to berate me. Consequently I returned home as little as possible; the thought of being there brought a terrible tightness to my chest, as of a hundred hair-choked drains. I didn't tell Donna much about Gus Miller, and I took pains to hide the jacket from her. I harbored the guilty feeling that I was cheating on her. After a while I began to half-forget I was married.

For a couple of years now, I told Gus, I had fantasized about getting on my bike and going wherever the road took me, in any direction that didn't lead home – beginning again somewhere else, as someone else.

Gus told me I was a coward trying to live the life everyone else wanted me to live rather than the one I wanted to live. He said it was perfectly clear that when my mom died, I went looking for another crazy bitch's troubles to saddle myself with. As was the case with most men, my true, free, outlaw nature terrified me. 'Which is why you're so lucky to have found me,' Gus said. 'I'm here to school you in Life 101. Your problem is you tolerate boredom. Me? I gotta real low threshold for it. Boredom's violence. Boredom's tyranny. Makes me wanna hit back. Maybe I'll take you on the road with me one day, show you some *real* shit.'

He didn't elaborate on what he meant by 'real shit,' but I had vivid buddy-flick visions of long open highways and sweet sage-brush deserts sailing past, the tough big guy and the trusty little guy heading toward some Vegas kingdom of neon and wickedness; I pictured us holding up Brinks trucks and stagecoaches and trains and equally ridiculous things, and dying spectacularly in a shootout with the authorities, as in *Butch Cassidy and the Sundance Kid*.

At the Newport jetty, one sunset, we shared a spliff while a guy played with his little boy in the sand nearby. The kid kept hurling handfuls of sand into the wind, and wailing in shock when it blew back into his face, which got me laughing. Gus didn't laugh. He was silent for a long time, looking off with those crooked glasses, and it was as if I could see a darkness stealing over him. 'Really too good for this goddamn sewer,' he said. 'You know what it's like when your kid puts her arms around you? Game over, man. You're ruined.' He pulled up his shirt, over his familiar showcase of scars, up above his gigantic man-tits, to reveal a tattoo I hadn't seen before. Over his heart, framed by a border of roses, was the face of a pretty young girl with golden curls, no more than two or three years old.

'I got this inked on me from the one picture I had, 'cause I was afraid I'd lose it, 'cause I mislay things, which is just what I fuckin' did. Somewhere in Austin. Mislaid it, I mean, just like I mislaid my family.'

Being stoned, I feared I was missing the tenor of what he was saying, missing the subtext, missing what he wanted from me. The big man's pain made me very uncomfortable. It seemed of a different order than the suffering he usually gassed on about, something too dreadful even to utter. It was a story he actually did *not* want to tell.

I offered the joint; he declined it. Waves built, crashed,

foamed; built, crashed, foamed; and Gus seemed to sink deeper into the darkness that had come over him, way out of reach of anything I could say.

He and the girl's mom had a doublewide outside Tampa, he explained after a while. He had steady roofing work. He had a family. What he'd dreamed of, all that time in lockup. 'The first time – the only time – I had my shit together enough to be mistook for an ordinary, non-substance-abusing American,' he said. 'Put my ear against that little girl's heart and told myself, "This is just the ultimate." You know? "There's no way I'm gonna fuck *this* up."'

He would carry the girl to the park and point out the birds to her, and the songs from the trees transfixed her. He bought her bright books of bird pictures. He imagined she might grow up to be a scientist. He built her birdhouses, to attract finches.

After a brutal workday he had come home, stepped inside the door, and felt his heart pounding in panic. The stacks of diapers, the ranks of bottles, the piles of baby-food jars, the smell of sour regurgitated milk, the supermarket coupons, the clutter of toys, the riot of hair-curlers, the mounds of laundry, the ironing board, the day's iron-ruined dress, the kid screaming, his wife screaming, the whole place a berserk, boisterous, womanly mess: it all conspired to frighten him, all melded into the shape of banal confinement no less terrifying than a bamboo cage. He looked into the life he was building and saw a strange, pinkish prison pod where he would grow flabbier and squishier, where his hard body would grow tits, his balls would shrivel and drop off like a poor penned bull's, where his prison-guards would yell 'Fetch the Kotex, hon!' and he would jump – *Right away, hon!* – and over the years he'd turn into a shapeless, sinewless jelly-thing like something washed up on a beach. And Jesus, if the day had been a little kinder, if the sun had been just a little less punishing on the roof where he'd been spreading tar all afternoon, he might not have needed a little air just then, he might not have needed a drink. Two full years sober, the two best years of his life, and – just like that – nothing mattered but finding that drink. His wife calling from the kitchen, 'Is that you, hon? Can you give me a hand over here? Are you there?' And Jesus Christ, if he hadn't just turned around, walked right to the nearest pub, and before he knew it – he didn't even remember how – he was three states away, getting blown by a teenage Cajun hooker. A week later, still drunk enough to forget who he was, he was in love with her and trying to rescue her from her pimp, offering to kill him for her if she'd run away with him to California. He couldn't even remember her name now. By the time he sobered up enough to long for home, he was already in lockup, and, having violated his probation, facing state time. In the woodshop at Starke he built his daughter birdhouses. A car hit her sometime in the third or fourth year. Her mom had been at the stove, distracted for just a minute, a minute or two, and the girl was supposed to be in front of the TV, *'Sit right there,'* she'd told her, and then from the sidewalk there were screams, and a neighborhood kid who'd been gunning his Camaro was carrying her body to the sidewalk. Gus couldn't really blame him. No reason to expect a toddler in the road. Yeah, plus Gus knew – no doubt at all in his mind, not a shadow – that the girl's daddy had put her in the car's path. They didn't let him out for the funeral, and had to shove him in the hole for his rage.

She never got the birdhouses. When they let him back in the woodshop he just kept building them.

CHAPTER 13

One night, about six weeks after Gus Miller moved into the Greasy Tuesday, the talk along the bar turned to a story that had been all over the newspapers. A roofer named Chick Perrino was on trial for abducting a 21-year-old UC Irvine girl whose Acura broke down on the 405 freeway a couple of miles up the road. Perrino garroted her, dismembered her, and scattered her parts around Orange County. He must have wanted to get caught, because he left her parts in boxes bearing his company logo. Everyone agreed it was a seriously fucked-up business, and Perrino should die in a much nastier way than the law would allow. Gus said he'd like to disembowel him personally and feed him his own guts for doing such a thing. He should have done it, in fact, when he had the chance: he once met Perrino on a roofing job and found him a creepy, shifty-eyed piece of snot who looked just like the sick twist he turned out to be. Jesse James, ever sensitive to a man's true nature, had wanted to chew off the man's nuts, and Gus wished now he'd let the dog follow his instincts, because that poor girl might still be alive. Then, shifting from moral indignation to professional disdain, Gus said, 'His own company's boxes! Why not leave your wallet too, shitbird? Fucking amateur. I respect this guy on *no* level. I mean, go back to school, asshole. The only reason cops nail anyone, ever, is because people do stupid, irrational shit like this.'

'If he was smart, he would've dropped her off the pier,' Sal Chamusco offered.

'Well, except the gas fills you up after a couple days, and you float,' Gus said. 'Way to get rid of your mess, you find a patch of woods. Between here and San Francisco there's plenty of it. You've got your lime and your hole, maybe three to four feet deep, and that lets the critters scatter what's left in a hundred directions.'

'But the water's quicker,' said stubborn Sal. 'Put some concrete blocks on the feet—'

'Then you've gotta *carry* the concrete blocks. You ever try that? And people hear the splash. The splash is what did in the guy in Atlanta, whatshisname – in the Eighties – did in all those people—'

'Wayne Williams,' I said.

'Right,' Gus said. 'Benny's the Trivia King. Company boxes are no way to go either, if you're not an amateur and you're not trying to get caught.' Thinking, shaking his head, he added in sympathy: 'Not to mention, shit, what happened to that poor girl. Can you imagine her folks sitting through that trial like they are, and keeping their hands off him?'

'You know,' Sal said later, when Gus disappeared to run some errand, 'that he's a hit-man?'

'He told you that?' I asked.

'He confided it in me,' Sal replied.

'He confided it in me too, and I don't even like him,' Telly said.

'I guess it's a confidence he's proud of sharing,' I said. 'Why don't you like him?'

'Bullshit king. He's always gotta be right,' Telly replied. He squinted at my Army jacket. 'And who do you think you are in that?'

'It's a cool jacket,' I said, stiffening my back in it, soldierlike.

'Yeah? What's *your* kill-count?' Telly said.

I decided I would have to put him in jail again soon.

The burning source of Telly's animosity toward Gus remained obscure to me – and to everyone else – until several nights later. That night, Gus was feeling sorry for himself and was muttering about how the world had never stopped pissing on him, even after all he'd given. No, the world was short on love for Gus Miller. Always had been, but that was okay. Because he'd learned to make do with the love he got from his dog, and the special love he got from the people who listened to his stories (which love lasted exactly as long as he had their attention). In a tremulous, quiet tone, he said, 'You know, Benny, I've always felt like the world's nigger. I never had the advantages.'

'The world has niggers of all colors it kicks around.'

'That's what I'm saying. Look, you – uh—' He pounded back his beer and tried to look at me, but his eyelids fluttered involuntarily in a series of quick blinks; he couldn't quite hold my face. 'What I said that day at the beach, I don't tell nobody. I, uh, it means, you know, a lot, having a buddy.'

'Sure, Gus.'

Then neither of us could think of anything to say. A minute stretched into two minutes, and it became excruciating. Finally Gus alighted on the idea of taking out the bowie knife he kept strapped to his boot. Saying, 'Watch this shit!' he spread his right hand on the bar and began tapping the blade lightly in the spaces between his fat splayed fingers. It looked particularly dangerous, considering there was very little bar between the lumpy meat prongs. Half a dozen people came over to watch as he sped up, the blade moving in a blur over his knuckles and going wick-whack! wick-whack! wick-whack! He knicked himself slightly, but managed to remove his hand before anyone noticed but me, leaving the wobbling blade standing in the knicked wood. A modest round of applause followed, and he said, 'This show ain't gratis! I'm accepting drinks now!'

Someone cried, 'Whatever he wants,' and Gus touched the bill of his Yankees cap in gratitude and asked for something called

Blue Fire. It was a whiskey shot you set on fire and drank blazing – a favorite, Gus said, of the hardluck bastards like himself who had to endure those long sweltering nights at Bien Hoa Air Base in Southeast Asia. He made a little ceremony of it now, touching his lighter to the alcohol and smiling as the blue flame ignited. Always nostalgic, he recalled that the first time he and the boys in the 173rd tried it, the Stones were doing 'Honky Tonk Woman' on the radio. By great good fortune, it happened to be one of the three Stones songs on the jukebox here; carrying his incandescent drink across the room, he dropped a quarter into the box and, as the music cranked, started assaulting the air with an invisible drumstick wielded in his free hand. Then, tilting his head back, he upended the flaming shot over his gaping gullet, slammed the glass down on the counter and exclaimed, 'Ooaaaaaahhh.' A curl of flame had attached itself to his whiskers an inch below the chin. It began smoking. He didn't notice, he just sat there, his skull split by a satyr's stupid grin, running his tongue along his lips to catch the last drops of goodness, saying, 'Ooaaaaaahhh, ooaaaaaahhh, sergeant . . .' and unleashing those annihilating drum riffs. As our poor barkeep knew so bitterly, the Greasy Tuesday was not teeming with men who rushed to render aid in a pinch. In a generous state of mind I attributed this immobility to an almost Hinduistic respect for fate, a feeling that misfortunes must run their course without interference; but the more likely reason was the pure reptile joy of seeing other people fucked up. And in Gus's case there was the added pleasure of seeing the barroom bully-braggart fucked up, to which even I, his friend, was not immune. So Gus burned and burned for a good 10 seconds, fire eating his goatish gray thatch, climbing and crackling up to his jaw line, illuminating the passive faces of the men ranged around the bar, who with flames flickering in their staring gimlet eyes resembled a cabal of rats at an unholy bonfire. It fell to me to save Gus. Reaching over the bar, I snatched up the water hose and fired three quick jets at the conflagration. Amid a great hissing and rising of smoke, Gus jumped to his feet, startled and angry, his hands waving and batting at the air. After a marathon coughing jag he sat down, water dripping from the chewed remains of his beard, and, with the awful stench of 10,000 incinerated bristles impregnating the air around him, grunted, 'Which is why it ain't for pussies. Gimme another!' So he downed one more, to prove he could. Good enough as come-backs went, I suppose, but as poor Gus sat there, pretending to ignore that ashy swath of blowtorched beaver hanging off his face, with those crooked glasses on his nose, he looked shrunken, humbled, and ridiculous. He looked . . . vulnerable.

A very drunk Telly Grimes, who had been watching Gus's near-immolation with barely concealed glee, left his stool and walked over to the jukebox, squinting against the convex glass at the Rolodex of songs. He returned without having inserted any coins and said into his drink, with a tense little smile, 'Funny, that song wasn't out till '69.'

Gus, gazing slack-eyed into the smoke, seemed to realize that the remark was directed toward him, but gave in response only an indifferent grunt.

'You were with the 173rd, right?' Telly said.

'I said I was, didn't I?' Gus replied.

'Bien Hoa Air Base, right?'

'Yup.'

'You heard "Honky Tonk Woman" there?'

'I guess that's what I said.'

Telly's bloodsucker smile widening to its capacity, his gapped and forward-slanting fangs on full, insolent display, he said, 'Well, that's pretty funny.'

'Why's that funny, *amigo*?'

'Because the Stones didn't come out with it till '69. Check the jukebox if you don't believe me.'

'Why do I give a shit?'

'Because the 173rd had moved on to II Corps by then, *amigo*,'

Telly said. 'They left Bien Hoa in '67. I know because my cousin was there.'

A silence extended itself over the bar like death-bringing biblical fog; my barmates suddenly found themselves fascinated by the ice cubes in their gin and the Surgeon General's fine-print advisories on their bottles about beer consumption during pregnancy. Gus walked slowly and heavily to the jukebox, peering in for a long moment. Then he came back and said, 'That date's a misprint. Ask Benny. He's Mr. Memory.'

'Well . . .' I said, weighing my loyalties, calculating the risks, beginning to perspire. And before I could think of the smart answer, I said, 'Actually, it was a '69 song.'

'Sonofabitch!' Gus bellowed, slapping the bar with his palm and turning to Telly. 'You gotta mind like a steel trap, brother. But if you knew anything at all about PTSD, you would know that memory loss is one of the classic symptoms. Classic! I've got all of 'em: amnesia, insomnia, fear of intimacy, substance abuse' – swigging a longneck – 'sudden feelings of fear and anxiety traceable to no external source, feelings of worthlessness, impotency . . .'

'Shellshock, right?' Telly said.

'It's called PTS-fucking-D!' thundered Gus, an ugly vein standing forth on his forehead. 'It's an American Psychiatric Association-recognized condition! It's legit! And I'm legitimately fucked-up!'

'Shut up, Telly,' panted a sweating Sal.

He seemed to be thinking of that bowie knife, hilt-up on the bar top before Gus.

'Sure,' slurred Telly, his smile frozen humorlessly on his face, like some dentist had applied painful invisible clamps to the sides of his mouth to get at his molars. 'Sure . . .'

'Every man in this bar has seen my scars, motherfucker.'

'But you know what?' said courage-crazed Telly, addressing the whole bar now, in thrall to some principle he'd perhaps just discovered he possessed. 'You know what? My cousin Teddy was there in The Shit. And I know other guys that were there in The Shit. And what they have in common is, you can know them for ten years without ever knowing they'd been in The Shit. Because what The Shit is all about is, no one who's been in it wants to talk about it all the fucking time.'

'Maybe you need to call it a night, Telly,' Junior said, discreetly removing the bowie knife from the bar top. 'You're talking bull-shit now. Everyone knows that's not true. Otherwise where do all those movies come from? And Gus may take it as an insult.'

'Yeah,' Telly said, 'our badboy war-hero hit-man communist-killing *janitor* might feed my ears to his farting old pooch . . .'

Telly flattened his money against the bar and stood up. Putting one snakeskin boot in front of the other, he made his way slowly and coolly toward the back door, even pausing to take a drag from someone's cigarette, just to show he was in no hurry. Whether by dint of guts or lunacy or alcohol, he pulled it off so it looked like victory; I had to admit it was impressive.

Gus didn't turn to watch him leave.

He waited a full 20 seconds before following Telly out the back door.

The bar emptied fast. People spilled their drinks trying to get outside.

In the parking lot Gus was engaged in a tug-of-war with Telly's brown DeVille over the Chupacabra's wriggling, kicking body. Grunting Gus was pulling one way – trying to haul Telly by the armpits through the half-open driver's side window – and the car was stubbornly refusing to surrender him. Telly's body was four feet off the ground and nearly horizontal, like a magician writhing on invisible strings in some trick that had gone hideously awry. Only the snakeskin boot on his left foot, tenaciously lodged under the roof, kept him attached to the car. For a good 10 or 15 seconds, everything hinged on that piece of scaly footwear, Gus glowering at it like an unexpected curse, while a yelping, terrified Telly eyeballed it like his last hope; despair filled his face as, inch by inch, he watched it peeling off his heel. Then *whoosh!* – the boot was tenantless, Gus and Telly sailing backward as a pair. Slamming into a Pontiac, Gus lost hold of his victim, and all the pounds that comprised him translated into a titanically messy topple over the right fender and onto the hood and then straight into the cracked blacktop. It seemed to happen in slow motion, so that at every stage in his ass-over-teakettle trajectory toward the pavement you could witness another humiliating defeat to gravity, his inky meatslab arms flailing to brace his off-kilter mass, fat hands scrabbling every-which-way to avert that nasty asphalt terminus, but clutching only air. Gravity was not his friend, not at all; give it an inch against him and it owned him, that hypertrophied upper half and those spindly supporting pegs transformed into a 300-pound earthbound missile.

By the time Gus climbed to his feet, raising himself with a hand on the bumper of the car that had betrayed him, Telly had scrambled back into his DeVille and rolled the window up tight. He fired the ignition and, as in every horror movie you ever saw, it coughed and sputtered a few times before catching. Telly looked up to see Gus looming over the hood with his fists cocked above his head, howling. Down came the fists, sledgehammering brick-sized dents in the hood and shattering the left headlight and making the car lurch up and down like a quarter-activated supermarket pony. Watching this with stupefied disbelief, Telly, the man with the steel-trap memory, remembered that he probably ought to drive away. He dumped the DeVille into reverse and jerked backward. Gus, hands affixed to the fender, refused to let go; he held on for a full couple of seconds before sprawling to the pavement again, this time with face-first finality. The DeVille careened into the street while Gus sat up, ashen, panting, the broken skin of his forehead embedded with asphalt pebbles, while sweat poured in violent runnels down his face and glistened in the patches of his fire-mutilated beard.

Someone handed him the orphaned snakeskin boot, and Gus held it in his lap like some kind of prize, some kind of validation, though to me he looked like an oversized retarded kid gaping at a toy he'd broken, trying to grasp why it came apart in his hands.

'Benny,' Gus said. 'Nitro. Need my fucking n-n-nitro. A little overwrought here. My t-ticker . . .'

'Where are they?'

'S-shitwagon . . . g-glove box,' Gus said, handing me the keys to his Dodge.

Johnny-on-the-spot, I rummaged through the glove box and came back with the pill-bottle labeled 'Miller, Gustavo.' He sucked one down with saliva and sat gasping for another minute, then his breathing grew slow and steady and controlled and the color returned to his face. Jesse James, again the last to join the scene, trotted out on his shaky old limbs to lick his master's martyred face, with age-weary but ardent affection.

It took two or three of us to help Gus to his feet and back into the bar. His face was full of shame and hatred. Junior brought him gauze bandages and rubbing alcohol and gave him back his bowie knife, saying, 'I took it for your own good.'

Junior seemed to want to say something more, something harsher, something critical, like *Don't bring this shit in here*.

'You know,' Gus said, holding the blade up for a moment before slipping it back in its ankle-sheath, 'back in The Shit, I once saw your pops use one of these to open up a pregnant village girl. Those were some tough times for all involved.'

The blood drained out of Junior's face.

For the next couple of hours my barmates took turns buying Gus longnecks and putting pieces of the DeVille's broken headlight in front of him like jewels, goodwill offerings. The boys said things like 'Way to go' and 'He had it coming' and 'He needed a beating.' It was understood that Telly had been way out of line. You didn't piss on a man's pride, whatever your passion for historical accuracy; you allowed a man his embellishments or memory mix-ups.

But Sal, Telly's best friend, sat watching grimly from a far corner of the bar, flicking his lighter until the gas ran out and there was no flame, but only the tiny sound of incessant scraping.

Gus drank quietly and stared forlornly at the snakeskin boot that stood before him on the bar top, the boot's spine broken midway so that its top half sagged, and Gus staring as if seeing his entire personal tragedy embodied in it. A lifetime of battles, and only this bent reptilian trophy to show for it.

'Johnny Cash could write the song,' I said with a nudge to Junior, but Junior just stood there looking sick, gazing at the photograph of his father on the wall.

CHAPTER 14

Gus disappeared the next day, with his van and his dog, leaving behind his mattress and his books and his padlocked freezer and his cigar box full of medals and ears. For three days, no one heard from him, and it would be a lie to say he was much missed. Then word got to me that he was on some kind of marathon bender, crawling between beach bars down on Balboa Island and raising a lot of hell. Whether I worried about what might happen to him, or found myself angry that he didn't invite me for the party, I couldn't say; but some impulse I should have ignored sent me looking for him.

I had picked up some under-the-counter scutwork on the Island, a few hours a day peeling shrimp and scrubbing floors for a fish shack. After a morning shift, pedaling around the beach strip in the cruel, blinding heat of a cloudless late-summer afternoon, I found myself on a wavering, heat-distorted expanse of bleached parking lot pavement, and in the distance, marooned there like some monstrous prehistoric crab carcass, its shell protected by punishing disks of daylight, sat Gus's dusty Dodge. As I approached I found a parking ticket with yesterday's date stuck under the windshield wiper. The hood was hot as a stovetop. With my palm I rubbed off a circle of dust and peered through the back window. Nobody inside: just those flea market towers of packrat treasure slouching against each other in fantastic gravity-defying shapes, like those mortarless interlocking Inca stones you see on the History Channel that not only manage to hold together, but also outlast all conquerors and earthquakes.

Chaining my bike, I kicked off my Converse All-Stars and walked out onto the white, hot beach in my sweat socks. That kind of sun's no good for you, and if you ever had some cancer spots, like me, and if you read up on the statistics, like me, you would dress like I did for the beach: feet covered, long sleeves, collar up, big floppy fisherman's cap pulled down tight.

My eyes followed the diminishing line of quadrupedal wood-plank lifeguard towers that rose out of the pitted sand every few hundred feet. Passing under their slanting legs, I discovered they were empty all the way down the line. I found myself thinking that on the day the dead rose from the ocean for the final war against the living (and this afternoon's parched, brooding desolation gave a hint of that day's weather), these sea-towers would prove terrific sniper-posts for mankind's resistance fighters; perhaps some George A. Romero-inspired official even had such a secret use in mind in building them. Underneath were little oases of cool shadow in which I paused to rest, squatting and breathing.

No one was swimming in the Pacific today, and there was no wind. Miles out, minute, windless white sail-flecks hung dead in the water. There were just a few bodies on the beach, each alone in its own empire of empty sand: indistinct shapes quivering in the distance on blankets and beach chairs with hundreds of yards separating one from another. And above, the heat glaring down like the lunatic eye of a flower, and breeding cancers in their skin.

Gulls screamed in the rolling gray sea foam. I saw a dog wandering in the haze along the edge of the water up ahead, nosing clumps of seaweed. As I approached, it began moving toward me uncertainly, limping, its back legs trailing bandages in the wet sand.

'Hey, old boy,' I said, recognizing Jesse James.

Abruptly the dog stopped and began growling hatefully at me, staring with those cruel, clouded eyes and dripping saliva from an open lip.

'Hey. Hey, where's Gus? Take me to your master, alright?'

After a few moments the dog turned, and, lowering his head, loped away down the beach. I followed for a hundred yards until we reached a rock jetty. There I found Gus Miller asleep in a wedge of rock, face-up in his sleeveless chihuahua T-shirt, fleas crawling on his sunburned face and flecks of vomit in his recovering beard. He smelled of shit, sweat, salt sea, and vodka. Lacking his glasses, he looked like a different man – quieter somehow, more introspective, naked. He was caught in some nightmare that, I judged from his mumbling, seemed to involve old men beating him with canes. My shadow fell over his glistening red face, and, groaning and spluttering, he blinked up at me.

'You here to punch my ticket, Bonehand?' Gus croaked, eyes working with confusion and fear.

'It's me, Benny.'

His mouth twisted skeptically. 'I can't see your face. Where's my specs?'

After a minute's searching I retrieved them from a nearby rock and slid them on his fat, heat-sticky face, which lay so rigidly sunward that he might have been the victim of some Apache severed-eyelid torture meant to burn out his retinas. He studied me through the lopsided slant of his lenses and said, with a dry voice leached of all emotion, 'I thought you were fuckin' death, come to make me answer. But you're just my boy Benny. Hey, Benny.'

'Why you out here?'

'I guess maybe I was hoping to snuff myself.'

'Snuff yourself?'

'I was thinking the crabs could carry me away. Work me through their crab guts and crap me all over the ocean floor. Little meal for the bottom feeders. Next I'm a thirty-buck shellfish plate on the pier. Great cycle of life. But I'm rescued. It's a sign.'

The prospect of survival seemed infinitely wearying to him. He sat up slowly and placed his back against a rock, his knees bent in front of him. He patted the pockets of his jeans and from one of them freed a thick wad of soggy, sand-covered bills wrapped in a rubber band. Holding up the bills, he thumbed them, studying them as if to reassure himself of their reality. They were all hundreds; there might be a few thousand dollars there.

'Fact is, I hit a payday and decided to celebrate and got a little carried away and then decided I may as well snuff myself,' Gus said. 'I got pretty you might say depressed.'

'You could've reached out.'

He grunted ambiguously and said, 'It ain't really dying I'm scared of. It's the all-alone part that kills me. A good death would be you're gnawed apart by vultures live on national television. Or going like one of those crackhead basketball players that drop in front of fifty thousand people . . .'

Mumbling, he added, 'The rich are very strange. Stranger than me, and I'm brain-damaged. Except if you're rich you're allowed to be as fucked-up as you want, and they just call it "eccentric" and "colorful." Hey, boy, hey . . .'

Jesse James had come up to lick his face; Gus enveloped the dog in his arms, smiling wanly as the dog offered languid old-dog kisses. Then he said, 'Help me up. My foot's hurt and I've got metal spikes going in behind my eyeballs.'

With the dog trotting a few paces ahead, Gus limped alongside me over acres of sand back to the van, where he stripped off his soiled clothes and, upending a Hefty bag plucked from his astounding masonry of interlocking junk, found another pair of worn jeans and another faded T-shirt to put on. He neatened the dog's bandages and muttered something vague about an accident. I filled an Arrowhead jug with sink water from a nearby bathroom, and he tipped it over the dog's throat and then chugged the rest himself, his throat pumping.

Twenty minutes later we were sitting in the cool of a Harbor Boulevard taco joint – Jesse James fed and resting on a slab of shaded pavement outside – and Gus, hydrated and glutted with Tylenol, was fumblingly unwrapping his fifth fat burrito.

'I've, uh – hit a geyser,' Gus said slowly around a mouthful of beef, in a tone that suggested he couldn't quite believe his luck and yet wasn't sure luck was the right word for it. 'I'm sitting on what you call a heavy-sugar proposition. This bulge next to my dick? Payment for services to be rendered. If I'm not going to snuff it, and it looks now like I ain't, it's a real tough proposition for me to turn down. In fact, shit, it's maybe just what I need. Bar crawling is really no life for an aging outlaw troubadour. I've always thought Tehachapi would be a good place to shift into quiet gear. Beautiful desert up there. I don't need a shitload of acreage, just enough. A garden for Jesse, a shed to fuck around in, a place for a lot of beautiful birds. No more begging for old Gus, and no more Salvation Army horsemeat, and no more handouts from that Australian who runs that bar. What an idiot *he* is.' He gazed out the window, puzzling over something, every year of his life visible in the cracks of his forehead. 'Look, I put stock in signs. I'm a Venice boy. Born the day they dropped the A-bomb on Bikini Atoll, and I always felt that ought to mean something. "Son of the bomb," you know? What did it mean? I never could figure out what. Anyway, my whole shitty childhood I spent here in California, then a lot of the rest of my life I spent anywhere else I could think of. And now they led me out here again.'

'Who's "they"?'

'Signs. Don't ask what kind. But I'd been asking for one, and passing through Arizona I got a motherfucker of one, and it said, "Go to Orange County, go to the Greasy Tuesday." And I just been waiting and waiting for something to happen since I got here, thinking after a while, "The universe's fucking with me again.

Pulling a nasty trick on a sucker who won't learn. There's nothing out here, nothing behind the curtain at all." And now, finally . . .' Putting his elbows on the table, leaning his bulky shoulders toward me, he added: 'I think you know what I'm telling you here. I'd like to bring you in.'

'I'm not sure I know what you mean.'

He looked at me with opaque squinting eyes, as if surprised at my denseness and suddenly uncertain how far he could trust me. 'What I'm saying, if I needed help with a thing . . .'

'A thing? You mean a *thing*?'

'Right. I'm saying. You understand?'

'I think so.'

'Well, that's the kind of thing I'm talking about.'

'You mean . . .'

'Look, Gus Miller has been bent over the barrel before. A man's dog, he knows he can trust. But people are a different animal.'

'Well,' I said, 'you've just gotta be careful who you confide in.'

'The main thing is, it's like that song that goes "Something something, loose the fatal lightning, bla bla bla, whatever, the terrible swift sword . . ."'

'Glory, glory, hallelujah . . .'

'Right, right.' His eyes widened in blustery emphasis. 'Brother, Gus Miller *is* that lightning. And it's about to fall. There's a mission to be done, one last balls-to-the-wall road trip to be taken, and I need some ordnance and some backup.'

'Why me?'

In a softer tone, he said, 'Look, I'm stupid on a lot of things in this world. I never finished tenth grade, my brain don't work right anymore, and some would say I ought to be institutionalized. But one thing I know, and that's this . . .' Leaning across the table between us, he poked a finger tenderly into my chest. 'I'm an Einstein of the human heart. I've got credentials out the asshole on it. Character! I've survived this long by being able to read it. And you, Benny, are a stand-up individual. I mean, you might have saved my worthless life out there. No one else gave enough of a shit to come find me. All my old road dogs are dead or locked up. So you're the only one I trust with a job like this. It's only a couple days' work, good pay, adventure, invaluable life experience . . .'

'You mean—'

'Stop with that stupid look. You're not as dumb as you pretend to be. I'm talking your basic All-American contract hit.'

Back in the van he searched under the dashboard until he found a Maxell tape labeled 'C's Recital.' He didn't say where he got it. Sliding it into the deck, he said, 'You wanna hear something beautiful? The chick that did this was fifteen.'

Into the musty air of the cab poured the sound of a single trembling violin. I couldn't name the piece, nor the notes, nor even the key; I don't know classical music. But it was a sound like an extinct Andean bird trying to climb the steps of the wind, something alternately plaintive, wistful, and brave. Very beautiful. The music rose and expanded and filled the filthy van. I looked over and Gus had his eyes closed and his chin uptilted like a sleeping Buddha. We just sat there until it was over, the hit-man and I, listening in our separate places. That bird kept going.

PART II

THE COWBOY

CHAPTER 15

It's three days before my prelim, and Goins is late for this morning's session. I've been waiting in the interview room for 40 minutes, my hands manacled to the table, by the time he shuffles in with sweat-stains in his pits, looking tired and not at all apologetic. His battered old suitcase bears faded stickers that say 'VOTE GREEN' and 'BROWN FOR GOVERNOR.'

'Counselor Groins!' I say. 'My pubic defender. My public pretender.'

'Benny,' he grunts, sitting down heavily and opening his brief-case. 'I had three other clients to see.'

The Three Stooges are making stupid faces on his tie. I glare at it sullenly and refuse to speak until he gets the point that I disapprove, I disapprove with the utmost kind of serious disap-proval.

'My protest against the greasy pole,' he says finally, catching on. 'My way of saying "No thanks" to the rat-race.'

'Isn't there a dress code?'

'Nobody gets less respect than a free lawyer. My whole office turns over every three years. I'm there going on twenty. Two hundred felony trials under my belt. They're not about to sack me.'

Overworked, underloved, and pale as a dead fish's distended gut, Goins exudes ill health, incipient stroke, or cardiac arrest. I wish I could afford a real lawyer. I heard of a defendant who slugged his public defender and the court had to give him a free private defense attorney. But they might just give me another PD. Plus I'm not a violent man, and I have come to like Goins; I identify with his misfitness.

'How come you never went private,' I say, 'go for the bucks?'

He doesn't say anything for a few moments, and I can tell he's debating what it would mean to answer the question, whether he wants to permit a personal fissure in the strict lawyer–client wall. Giving up anything personal to a potential sociopath is dangerous. Yet he knows it's unfair to ask me to divulge all the heartmeat stuff without a dollop of good-faith reciprocity from him – or at least a show of it.

'I hung out a shingle a while back,' he says finally. 'I decided I liked to eat too much.'

'You didn't have the chops?'

His expression is strained. 'I found I didn't have the appetite for all the hustling. Shaking hands, self-promotion, all of that. I found it all extremely wearying.'

'What brought you out here to Bumfuck, Egypt?' I say.

'My wife's folks are here. Believe me, I didn't think I'd wind up in Mojave. Ever heard of a lawyer named Barry Groutmanstein?'

'The one who's always on Larry King?'

'Law-school buddy of mine,' says Goins. 'He wasn't always a prick. He even had ideals.'

I smile conspiratorially, to encourage gossip. I can tell he wants very badly to dump on the famous Groutmanstein. I'm a good audience. I welcome it. He tells me that Groutmanstein once dropped a murder defendant – one with a winnable case – because the guy ran out of money. Goins finds this despicable, beneath contempt. I shake my head grimly, agreeing. Beneath contempt! Goins still sees Groutmanstein every few years, on trips to LA. He seems to have memorized every detail of Groutmanstein's 35th-floor office, as if he's measured it mentally for himself a hundred times. 'Obscene,' Goins says with a snort.

'Wraparound windows, fumed-oak bookcases, Corinthian leather armchairs. And this whole over-the-top predator theme: brass eagle busts, pictures of Alaskan bears, a stuffed white wolf. How he sees himself. Ridiculous! And of course, he puts every story ever written about him on the wall. Lawyer-of-the-Year stuff. Funny thing, back in the day? Exam time, he always came to *me* for help. The professors knew, too. Who was smarter. Two roads diverged, et cetera. Whatever . . .'

His voice trails away. He seems to be making himself depressed.

'I've never understood how it is you guys do what you do,' I say. 'Defending guys you know are guilty all the time and pretending they're not.'

'I get that at barbecues,' Goins answers with a touch of irritation. 'Particularly from the in-laws, who are John Birchers. And what I say is, it's not so much the individual I'm defending as the integrity of the system. Because God help the little guy – guys like you – who get sucked into it.'

'Still, a murderer is a murderer, and a murderer deserves to be punished.'

'You realize that if every defendant exercised his right to trial, the system would collapse? You know why? They expect you to get scared and plead, save them the trouble of proving it. Say you shoplift a Hershey bar, and you knock a guard's hand off your shoulder. Boom! That's assault during the commission of a theft. Say you happen to have a whittling knife in your pocket. Boom! Assault while in possession of a deadly weapon. Prior record? Boom! They can send you away forever. And they will. I'm here to make sure they play by the rules.'

'What about a baby rapist? You'd stand up for one of them?'

'I'd stand up for anyone,' says Goins. 'That's my pride, Benny. Few years ago, I had a guy accused of strangling his wife with a Mr. Coffee cord. A junkie, and they made him sweat through withdrawal while they interrogated him for two days straight.'

'I've detoxed. You'd want a bullet in your head first.'

'Exactly – torture. The cops tortured him to get their confession. Did he kill her? Probably. But I worked up some motions, blistering stuff, top form, and I got the confession thrown out, and he walked. The PD's Association gave me a plaque. Last year, the guy's back. He stomped his kid and put her in a coma. Do I take that stuff home? Do I dream about it? Do I wish for someone else's life once in a while? Sure I do. Do I do my job anyway? You bet I do – like a professional. I don't get to pick and choose. I don't get to say, "I only represent the nice guys, or the totally innocent ones."'

Goins studies the tip of his pen. By his expression I can tell he said a little more than he wanted. Clients usually don't give enough of a shit to ask him personal questions, so maybe I caught him off-guard.

'You ever get one?' I say.

'Get one what?'

'An innocent guy. Saved his life. Have you?'

He rubs his temples in slow, semicircular motions. 'Factually innocent versus technically? I dunno,' he says. 'It'd be a nice thing to hang your hat on, at the end of the day. But like I said, for what I do, innocent and guilty are really irrelevant categories.'

There is something wrong about his voice when he says this, something tinny and mechanical and disembodied, as if he's reciting a prayer memorized a long time ago, from a religion he's no longer sure he believes in. Not deep down, not at a cellular level.

'Well,' I say, 'I'd like to be able to make you believe that I'm one of them.'

'One what?'

'An innocent man.'

He nods slowly, looking me over, and gives me a small, noncommittal smile. It's clear from his eyes how badly he longs to believe in the slumped, desperate little man sitting across from him. Longs to believe, in spite of himself, that Benny Bunt is not just another name in the gallery of monsters he has been charged with defending. I suspect my lawyer is sick with himself. I think of a thin, fresh-faced young Goins, a bright law student carrying his law books to class, propelled by phosphor-dot Perry Mason fantasies as deep-seated as my own Steven Bochco dreams. But in the real world his clients are pond scum, and he could say 'I'm defending the integrity of the system' all day long – he could even keep going for a while on the pure juice of courtroom competition – but at the end of the day, he doesn't dream about his victories. He dreams about the kid in the coma with the kicked-in head.

As I look at Goins, sitting across from me, waiting for me to tell the rest, his face different now from the cold mask he wore when I first met him, I understand that he longs for some unambiguous injustice to correct, something even the John Bircher in-laws could not write off. He's been auditioning me for this role. He's wondering whether I will be the newspaper clipping he keeps in his wallet as an old man and fishes out to show strangers in the park. The one he sends to Groutmanstein with the note, 'I saved a good man's life. What have you done with your millions lately? Cheers.'

He wants so badly to believe in me, and I want so badly not to let him down.

Now he says, 'Just keep building me the bridge, Benny. Between Orange County and the Mojave Desert. Plank by plank. Leave nothing out, however minor it seems. Gus Miller has a contract. What happens next?'

'I do what any responsible citizen would do. I sell out my best friend to the law.'

CHAPTER 16

Detective Munoz met me at our normal spot, in an alley behind the evangelical bookstore on Harbor Boulevard, and whisked me in his chocolate '89 Porsche Carrera to the garage at John Wayne Airport. We sat behind the dark-tinted windows listening to the planes come and go.

'Not the worst little measly tip you'll ever get,' I said. 'A 187 is not too shabby, huh?'

His jaw pumped silently and rhythmically. Since he quit smoking a couple of years ago he chewed three sticks of Big Red at a time. When he spoke I inhaled the sharp cinnamon of his breath and glimpsed the wolfish glint of his immaculate choppers. Again I was reminded of all the fucking I was missing; he was that kind of guy.

'Who is this fat-ass *cabron*, Cowboy?' Munoz said.

His tone of voice suggested he was less excited about the story than I thought he might be. On a certain level this came as a relief to me, since I believed I may have loved Gus Miller. At the same time I didn't want to disappoint my man Munoz, who was a busy guy with important and interesting crimes to solve, a guy with whom I had a friendship based on mutual respect.

'We're dealing with an unpredictable and dangerous dude,' I said, realizing as I gave the description that Gus Miller himself would proudly be tagged with it. 'He's supposed to be a war hero who slaughtered half of Vietnam. Also a prolific professional assassin, hand-to-hand combat expert, torture survivor, manic-depressive, suicidal, chemically dependent berserker Rambo. So he's supposed to be alla that, but underneath he's all squishy and pink. Sentimental. That's our perp profile.'

Munoz was not impressed by this, either. He'd been at cop-work too long to get excited easily. Still, he took it down dutifully in a small lined notebook that he flipped open over the steering wheel.

Sighing, he said, 'I know you dig the brothers-in-blue parlance, partner, but he ain't a "perp" till he's done something. We're looking at a maybe/might-be/probably-not perpetrator. Hate to deflate your sails, but how do you know he ain't just a lard-ass liar, like every asshole in every bar that ever was?'

Considering this for a minute, I felt a little trickle of desperate sweat roll from my hairline into an eyebrow. 'I guess I don't know. But he's got medals and everything. And scars and prison tats and stuff. And he's flashing a big wad of money he says he got for this hit.'

'You overheard this remark?'

'Shit, man, he wants my help. He wants me to drum up a piece of ordnance for him and tag along.'

'A hit-man without a gun. Does he kill with his wit?'

'He's got two strikes on his record already. Too risky to be packing with guys like you out there. He says it's just another excuse for the man to burn him.'

'And this hit? Details?'

'He won't say much about it, on account of it's against assassin protocol to divulge more than is absolutely necessary. Need-to-know status and all that. I think he got that stuff from a book.'

Munoz gave an amused and disdainful little snort, saying, '*Cabron.*'

'He says every assassin worth his salt operates that way.'

'He won't tell you anything?'

'Only that we're going after some gecko guy.'

'Gecko guy?'

'Yeah. He let it slip and he seemed angry at himself that he did.'

'What's Mr. Gecko's first name?'

'I don't know. He's just some dude up in Northern California who did someone dirty.'

He blinked at me, shaking his head. He wrote it down. 'Anything else? Like who wants this guy taken out? Like who's paying for it? Like why?'

'I don't know.'

'It's an unusual situation,' Munoz said, nodding slowly and opening his teeth to accommodate the tip of his pen. 'Why did shitbird approach you?'

'He considers me a friend. We drink together.'

'You still drinking at that shitty little dive with the sawdust on Harbor? The "Greasy Asshole" or "Greasy Forehead"—'

'Greasy Tuesday. It's a landmark.'

'I never heard a stupider name for a bar. But go on.'

'Well, he lives in the back room with this sorry old German shepherd and does chores here and there, when he's sober, which isn't a lot of the time. He gets drunk and tells these stories and nobody's really sure whether he's full of shit, but everybody's afraid of him. Even Junior – he's the proprietor – even he's afraid to say, "Hit the bricks," and I know he'd like to. Look, am I doing the right thing, coming to you?'

'Why not?'

I shrugged, thinking: Because Gus Miller's my friend and, however this shakes out, he's going to be in a world of trouble.

Then: If I consider him such, why would I have called a cop in the first place?

Answer: Because I'm trying to save the poor bastard from himself.

And: We're on different sides of the game, me and Gus. Simple as that. Really sorry, man.

'Some genius,' Munoz said with a warm smile, 'picking *you* for this.'

'He's supposed to get five grand for it, and promises me a cut,' I said. 'He made me make out a budget for him.' I handed Munoz a soiled cardboard Anheuser-Busch coaster scrawled diagonally with my handwriting:

THE HIT
Expenses:
Gas $50
Food & snacks $80
Sundries $50
Dog treats $15
Ordnance $150
Benny's cut $1,000
= $1,345

A little bullet of Big Red hit the dashboard as Munoz pitched forward laughing. When he stopped, he retrieved the gum with a napkin, saying, 'Oh shit, that is good . . .'

'He's not so confident in his math skills, so I, you know, helped him out.'

'Exhibit number one, your honor! The official budget. Every hit-man worth his salt insists on one, right down to the – *Dios mio* – canine rations . . . "ordnance" . . .'

'He wants to leave by this weekend, so he told me to have him a piece by today or tomorrow. "Doesn't need to be high style," he says. "Don't worry about the bells and whistles. Something blue-collar and reliable," he says.'

'What'd you tell him?' Munoz asked, mirth glinting in his eyes.

'I told him I'd score one for him. I thought about just taking the money he gave me and disappearing, but then I thought, "Someone could get hurt. He could hurt someone." I don't want any blood on my hands.'

'That's very admirable, my man – the act of a responsible citizen.'

I gave Munoz the make and model of Gus's Dodge, along with the Arizona plate, all of which I'd committed to memory. I could tell this impressed him. He wrote it down, then put the notebook in his jacket pocket along with the beer coaster. He took a PowerBar from the glove box and chewed, all business now, thinking. After a few minutes he gunned the Porsche and we purred out of the garage to join the snarl of traffic leaving the airport.

'Isn't this where I get paid and slink back to my rat-hole?' I said.

'I hate to hear you put yourself down, Benny. Some advice? Chicks find that self-deprecating, Woody Allen bullshit a major turn-off, like bad breath. You need to work on your self-image.'

'I don't have a lot to work with.'

'One of these days, you and me, we'll hit the racks. Maybe cross-train. You run?'

'No.'

'Well, we'll hit the racks. Get you fighting trim and improve your confidence a little bit. You climb?'

'No.'

'Some weekend, we'll hit Joshua Tree. I'll introduce you to some climbing buddies. I bet you're a cowboy up there.'

'Your buddies – like, a bunch of cops?'

'Cops and ex-cops, sure – you'll fit right in. In a way, you know, you're one of us. We're all on the same side here.'

'I guess working out together would be kind of fun.'

'I just hate to see a guy like you – a guy as good as you – put himself down all the time.'

As we merged onto the 405 I asked where we were going.

'The station,' Munoz said, 'to work out a game plan.'

On the way there I thought more about being Detective Al Munoz's workout partner than anything else. Pictures kept filling my head. Me spotting him on a bench-press, leaning over him with two fingers extended under a thick-stacked bar that he strains to work off his chest. Gym-suited Benny urging him on in that rough way rack-partners do. Munoz's inverted face grimacing mightily below me and the veins bulging in his biceps. 'Your turn, partner,' he says. People thinking, 'They're friends.' Afterward: showering unselfconsciously, toweling off in the steam, going for a PowerBar. Buddies. And the desert rocks: sheer cliffs and clinking carabiners, my life in his hands and his in mine. All of this going through my head, as I said, on the way to the Costa Mesa Police Department.

'How's life on the mean streets?' I said.

'Truth? I'm looking at retirement next year. Fifteen years is plenty, and they're making it impossible to do real police work. Goddamn lawyers telling you what you can and can't do, driving out the real cops. If you're any kind of hard-charger, they'll sic the IA jackals all over your carcass.'

'Internal Affairs?'

'Some scumbag dope-dealer complains you put his cuffs on a little tight, you get written up. I got more use-of-force complaints in my file than any cowboy out here, and you know what? Badge of honor. Because it means I'm not on my ass, avoiding trouble. But someone leaked my IA file to the *Daily Pilot* a while back, so they've held up my promotion, even though I scored first in the department on the captain's test. So I figure, next year, I'm in Aruba. Let someone else save the city.'

We were stopped at a red light. As it turned green, his Porsche stalled out. Cars were lining up behind us. Munoz worked the key, over and over, rage and humiliation contorting his forehead. The transmission wheezed. We weren't going anywhere. '*Hija de puta!*' he cried. '*Hija de la chingada!*' Finally it started, just as the light was turning red again, and he gunned it angrily through the intersection.

'Captain's rank is a twenty-grand pay bump,' he said. 'And they won't do it, even though I took a *bullet*.'

We rode the rest of the way to the police station in silence.

Soon I was sitting in a small interview room with pink pastel walls and Munoz was handing me vending-machine coffee in a plastic cup decorated with poker-card queens and jacks. It was hot and bitter. Munoz said, 'Cool your heels,' and disappeared, leaving me a copy of *Ultimate Climber* magazine. When I finished looking at the pictures (so frightening they instantly banished any rock-climbing fantasies I had) I found myself staring at the walls and wondering why they were Easter-egg pink, as in a nursery or a ward for crippled kids. I remembered reading somewhere that they didn't paint prison walls bright red because that particular color acts on an inmate's rage like kerosene. Not without a little twitch of pleasure at my perceptivity, I decided the pink walls were intended to swaddle the jittery nerves of whoever might be in this room, which nevertheless only ratcheted up my jitteriness because it reminded me that I had reason to be jittery if I was in this room. This is where they must bring rape victims and other people who'd been seriously fucked-up when they needed to talk to them. Psychology! On the wall in front of me was a framed oil painting of ducks flying against a pretty cloud-flecked sky. More psychology! Aren't they soothing! They had the ducks in their corner too. The great minds of law enforcement had mobilized even the ducks and sent them into battle in the war against crime. Cops were smart that way; they had their angles and knew how to work them. The temperature in here, I noted, hovered around a friendly 70°F. I decided that I appreciated the pink walls and the ducks and the pretty sky and the AC – I appreciated the consideration for my nerves they showed – but I was still twitchy as hell and getting more so by the minute.

It might have been 40 or 50 minutes before the door opened. In came Munoz with Capt. Harvey Wein, Munoz's supervisor in Crimes Against Persons, he of the prehistorically protuberant jaw and indented forehead. 'I understand we have a potential situation,' Wein said unsmilingly.

'Benny's gonna help us get to the bottom of it,' said genial gum-chewing Munoz. 'It could be pretty bitchin'.'

'We've got some basics to clear up first, like who we're dealing with,' Wein said in a flat, commanding voice. He had buzz-cut gray hair and the stiff manner of an ex-Marine. 'We ran the name through the state booking database. It's a pretty common one. Look at these.'

He set out 10 or 15 mug shots on the table in front of me. It looked like a random sampling of criminal faces – a bleary-eyed Mexican, an Irish guy with red eyebrows, a somber black dude, a pimpled, bewildered-looking white teenager – all caught in the unhappy flash of a squad-room camera somewhere. And under them, the names: Augustus Miller, Gus Miller Jr., Gus V. Miller, J. Gustafson Miller, and so on.

'I don't see him,' I said. 'Maybe he doesn't have a California record.'

'The Dodge tag linked up to a Phoenix address,' Munoz said. 'A few years ago it was registered to a Gustavo E. Miller at 139 East Fischbach Court. D.O.B. July first, 1946. Is *this* our man?'

Now Munoz slid a piece of paper in front of me. It was a grainy, faxed photocopy of an Arizona driver's license. It only took a glance to tell that Gus Miller of Fischbach Court (mid-fifties, hard-looking face, long jaw, hooded eyes, broken Roman nose, thick, luxuriant hair) was not the Gus Miller of the Greasy Tuesday.

'That's not him either,' I said.

Munoz and Wein looked at each other.

'What?' I said.

'Well,' Munoz said, 'for the last two months this particular Gus Miller has been receiving VA disability checks at 11,520½ Harbor Boulevard, which he lists as his primary residence.'

'That's the bar,' I said.

'Yes,' Wein agreed. 'Which raises some interesting questions. Like, "What happened to the *real* Gus Miller, if your guy is driving his motor vehicle and cashing his checks?"'

'You think he whacked him?' I asked.

'Could be,' Munoz said.

'Well, whoever this individual is, we're not ready to bring him in just yet,' Wein said. 'It would be a tactical mistake at this stage of the operation. We need to know whether he seriously means to hurt someone, we need to know who and why, and if we haul him in now, the whole thing is as good as shot.'

'We're short on leverage,' Munoz said.

'Yes,' Wein agreed, thoughtfully stroking that monster mandible. 'If this really is a righteous contract hit – and it does happen – we've got nothing so far to compel him to divulge the identity of the person, or persons, putting him up to it. Which means, even if we bring him in, the intended target is still waiting out there with a bull's-eye on him, whoever he is – this Mr. Gecko. Whoever wants this person dead will simply turn to someone else.'

'So what's the strategy?' I asked.

'You're the strategy, Cowboy,' Munoz said.

'Excuse me? Beg pardon? Come again?'

My forehead was suddenly moist, despite the companionable 70°F of the thermometer.

'We're gonna have to wire you up,' Munoz said.

'I have to say my comfort level with that is not real high.'

'I've been telling Captain Wein here, "Benny's a friend of mine, not like these other low-lifes we have to deal with. He knows right from wrong—"'

'I'm just your eyes and ears out there,' I said. 'I'm good for a phone call. I make it, I get paid, I'm in, I'm out, I don't linger, I don't walk around with electronic bugs in my asshole. I never wore one of those things.'

'Don't make a fool of me in front of my boss,' Munoz said. 'I told him, "Benny here will play ball. Benny's a cowboy. We have an understanding. You watch."'

'Maybe you dudes remember Brian De Palma's *Blow Out*, with

John Travolta?' I said. 'Or maybe Big Pussy from *The Sopranos*. I seem to remember fatal things happening to people who wear wires.'

'Well, of course those Hollywood hacks gotta *dramatize* it,' Munoz said, as if explaining to a child that the pretty square pegs go in the pretty square slots. 'In my fifteen years on the force I've never seen it happen, and Captain Wein's got nineteen—'

'It never happens,' Wein said.

'That's thirty-four years in law enforcement between us, and it hasn't happened,' Munoz said. 'And that's the voice of experience. We use wires all the time.'

'If he finds out I'm snitching—'

'No!' Munoz cried, slapping his palm on the table. 'Don't ever use the s-word in my presence again. You understand? You're not an s-dash-dash-dash-dash-dash, okay? That's their word. A despicable word. The same way they try to hurt us by calling us pigs. They're worthless human germs and need to demean their betters. But we don't internalize their hatred. We don't let them define for us who we are. We're not pigs, we're law-enforcement officers. And *you* are a confidential police informant. We're equal partners here. Alright?'

'Okay.'

'Now look,' Munoz said. 'We're gonna PowerPoint you on what we need.'

'Point One,' Wein said, seemingly impatient with anything but business, stabbing a long index finger into his opposite palm, 'we need his prints, and we need them in such a way that it doesn't alert him to our interest in him. We'll run them through AFIS – that's a national database – and look for hits. Get a sense of whether this is a bona fide killer or just another schmuck running his jaws . . .'

Wein's mouth continued to move, but suddenly his words were coming from a long way away; on the pink wall behind the cops, directly between their forward-thrust heads, I saw the carefree ducks, the police ducks, angling as a family into their serene, cloud-flecked sky.

'... anything he lays mitts on ... keys, wallet, glass of beer ...'

The birds didn't know (their bosses hadn't told them) about the men in the bushes below with the shotguns; didn't know that in a moment they'd all drop from the perfect sky like stones.

'... try not to smudge ... not doing anything without a few more concretes ... information is ...'

They were dispensable. They were fucking birds. They were easily manipulated, having birdbrains. But they should have suspected this.

'... you there?' The gash deepening between Wein's eyes, dark and harsh. 'I'm not telling you this for my edification, mister. Repeat PowerPoint Number Two.'

'Prints ... intelligence ...'

'Intelligence!' Wein said. 'We need it. Flatter, wheedle, cajole, buy him drinks, whatever you need to do, but get him talking.'

'My man here is a professional elicitor of intelligence,' Munoz said. 'His ass has a bag a tricks like Felix the Cat! That's you, right, Benny?'

I heard myself grunting in assent. Then there was a pen in my hand and I was putting my signature on the bottom of a form that said: 'CONSENT TO INTERCEPT COMMUNICATION WITHOUT WARRANT.'

'You just got the part in the school play, bro,' Munoz said. 'Cinch if you think of it like that. Didn't you always wanna be in the school play?'

'Who-what-where-when-why,' Wein said, holding his palm toward me with outsplayed fingers that he peeled down one by one, counting five. 'The five Ws.'

'I'm supposed to get him a gun. He gave me a hundred and fifty dollars.'

'Tell him you're working on it, you need more time, whatever,' Wein said. 'Delay.'

Somehow I managed to ask for money. Wein was on his feet.

'We'll need something a little harder before we tap the hard-working taxpayers of this city,' he said. On the way through the door he added, 'Details to nail.'

Munoz peeled four twenties from his wallet and clasped them in my moist palm.

'From my own pocket,' he said. 'There's no guarantee yet there's even a for-real crime being planned, and I don't get paid back unless we get some usable intel. So this speaks to the reservoir of goodwill between us.'

'I didn't know that's how it worked. Thank you, Detective.'

'Call me Al, Cowboy.'

'Look, I don't wanna let you down, but . . . I don't know if I'm made for this.'

'Sure you are. You're like me. You're a goddamn pistolero. A pistolero in the school play.'

CHAPTER 17

It wasn't a part I was ready to play, however, not a role supportable by the little nerve I possessed. Already I regretted going to Munoz with what Gus had told me. Somehow, a line had been crossed. Snitchwise, I had suddenly been pitched out of the kiddie-pool shallows where I dwelled comfortably into barracuda water, with no current home save cooperation. Exhausted, I found a bench in Pomona Park and closed my eyes and tried to get my head straight, and suddenly I was caught in a terrifying dream.

In it, flames rose around Gus Miller's fat and smiling face. His beard burning and crackling, but not consumed, not diminished. Flames climbing in long tongues around his cheeks, tips wriggling toward his smiling eyes.

– When are you gonna fix those fucking glasses?

His lenses tilted so far to one side they were falling off his face. As his head burned, he toasted me with a flaming shot-glass.

– It ain't the glasses that's crooked, Gus said. It's my head.

– You shouldn't have done Gwen that way. True love doesn't come around that often. Do you understand about true love?

He drank fire from a flaming pumpkin, saying:

– A boy loves his dog. It's in a story.

Jesse James stood over me with his bad, cataract-occluded eyes. His teeth were tearing off steaming gobbets of my torso while I watched with a detached, nerveless horror. My innards turning into sausage-links as they disappeared down his maw.

The dog licking me, his spit glistening all over my body. Didn't I hear somewhere that certain dogs' saliva is poisonous? I burned all over, soaked in venom, aflame with napalm jelly, screaming . . .

Jolt awake. I lay slumped on the park bench. My heart was hammering. *I'm so tired. I'm so tired. My mind is going to kill me.* I needed something. I needed help. I couldn't do this thing without help. Make me fearless. Make me supercool.

Being a frightened Benny, a cowardly and unsteely Benny, I did a stupid thing. I went looking for Moe Shanks, the man who supplied me with meth (and employed me) during my blurry, eye-twitching, teeth-grinding stint as a committed tweaker during the Reagan Era.

Ninety-eight hours without sleep: my proud personal best, back in the day. Not so impressive for some of the career speed freaks I knew, who could binge two weeks straight minus a wink. But nevertheless an experience frightening enough to make me realize no sleep was the quickest route to the mind's unraveling. Sleeplessness spaded up the brain's buried maggots and amplified them to lurid Creature Feature dimensions.

Moe Shanks ran a landscaping company in Newport and paid half his staff in speed. Shrewd Moe winning both ways: he got a fleet of tireless lawn boys *and* he got to keep the cash proceeds of their labor. Naturally the first few lines he gave you free, along with his reassurances: 'Don't worry, kiddo. The only mind game is shadow people.'

A half-assed *caveat emptor*, to say the least. Apart from seeing malevolent conspirators in random shadows, which is a constant, the real hallucinations start squirming out on day two. The truly scary ones commence thereafter. Postmen follow you like KGB agents. Claws reach for your ankles from the gutters. Wigshop windows become a gallery of maniacally chatty severed heads. It doesn't stop you from wanting to extend the binge, though. Crystal meth is *still* the closest you ever get to feeling like Spider-Man.

Not that you do anything heroic. Oh, no. Mostly you sit in your room with your shades pulled (*they* are out there). Shave off a line. Incline conveniently ventilated skull. Line up those custom-made twin cranial delivery slits. Find the runway. Nasty napalm burn. Toxic drain-cleaner/lye cocktail raping your throat. Find the next. Now you're alright. Bulletproof, in fact. Adamantine skin and a Lamborghini Spyder engine gunning in your chest. Time to color! Get out the fucking Crayolas. Attack your Thrifty's paint-by-the-numbers kits. Technicolor sword-and-sorcery scenes lining up all along the wall. Then the real treat, the main event: your special jar of nuts and bolts. Pour them out on the coffee table. Fabulous toys for a meth monster. No happiness like laying siege to a fat pile of nuttage and boltage. Screw all the nuts onto all the bolts. Unscrew them and start over. Screw, unscrew, screw, unscrew . . .

Five hours gone. Three a.m. and time for another couple of lines. Feel that blast. Time for some cleaning! A meth freak must clean: he can't help himself. Do the toilets, the sinks, the floors, the dishes. Find some lingering dirt and do it all again. Take apart the toaster piece by piece. Dismantle the coffee maker. Read some cheap sci-fi. Weep buckets over the death of a benevolent, gerbil-like alien. Dig up some old *Hustlers*. Reacquaint yourself with all the girls. You're the king of marathon masturbators. Shave off another line . . .

The closest you come to feeling like Spider-Man, sure . . . until you don't anymore. The downside commences. Wander for a week, looking for a broken bottle with which to slash your wrists. Listen to the ocean roar in your ears threatening to drown you in its fathoms. Don't worry, that's just your blood pressure screaming toward stroke levels.

You're smart enough not to try the needle, because you know you'll never come back from a feeling that good. That decision saves your life.

But you wake up a couple of years later to find your teeth are ground down a quarter inch from the gums, and you look 10 years older than you should look and people who pay attention can tell something is wrong with your eyes. All you have to show for it is a worthless stack of acrylic dragons and broadsword-swinging barbarians in your closet and a kitchen cluttered with the component parts of violated appliances. Worst of all, your brain is different. You fear you have used up all the high you're allotted in life. Happy people seem exotic, implausible, unfathomable. You watch them edge away from you in elevators. Your clothes are weird. You seek the dark. You're a mole man.

A few hours after I parted company with Munoz and Wein, my Schwinn found the strip mall on the Balboa peninsula where Moe Shanks kept his shop. I say the Schwinn found it (you've got to believe me) because I was not conscious of having anything to do with it. The Lawnmower Man could get me to supercool and fearless, if anybody could.

'Hi, Fabulous Moe.'

'Welcome, Benny,' said Moe, tinkering with a weedwhacker as he watched me approach through neat ranks of used mowers and edgers. 'What can I do for you?'

I used to run on one of his West Newport crews, and in one blurry three-day stretch I did 132 lawns for him. We hadn't seen each other for five or six years. His face seemed much older than I remembered it, and the awful auburn rug on his head made him look older still. Moe used to be some kind of an actor. On the walls hung faded headshots of obscure performers with personal salutations to Moe.

'Moe,' I said, 'I have an important project coming up for which I'll need some serious, serious . . .'

'Yes?'

'Some pep. Some go.'

'Pep and go, those toe-tapping twins!' Moe said. 'Matter of fact, those lovely coozes just dropped by with their manager, Mr. Chutzpah. Come back and say hi. They've missed you.' And back Benny went.

CHAPTER 18

That night I was gnawing my lips at the Greasy Tuesday and listening to the scrape-scrape-scrape of molars in my skull, waiting for Gus to show. Here I was, second stool from the right on the far curve of the bar facing the front entrance. Sal Chamusco eyefucking me from across the room. One of his fingers in his cheek, applying cream to a canker sore. Telly the Chupacabra nowhere in sight. Look around the bar: a clutch of regulars. The typical Friday-night crowd. *No one knows.* Every expression familiar. Lassitude and vague menace. I was a fixture here, like the sawdust and Sal and Old Larry. Benny Bunt, one of the indigenous trolls, a mushroom as native to this dank piss-smelling cellar as any of the other human molds and fungi. Right where everyone expected me to be. Not to worry, Benny. It's just the speed. No one knows about the police-issue brown paper bag in your pocket. No one knows about the wire strapped against the barbered swath of your sweating chest, or the men in the truck listening down the block. Just the speed. There's no such thing as shadow people.

Make some small-talk. Sports, current events. 'Something eating you, Benny?' Junior said. 'You're sweating. Have a napkin.'

'Why the fuck should anything be eating me?' I said. 'I'm a regular, aren't I? I'm here where I always am, drinking what I'm always drinking.'

I watched Junior frowning and walking over to Sal; the two

exchanging words, glancing over at me. More people eyefucking me now. I wore Gus's bad-ass cammie jacket. But what everyone saw was the snitch jacket. I felt fear spreading between my shoulder blades. It was written back there, as clear and loud as the gaudy cursive on a bowling jacket: Benny the Snitch. In lock-up, the snitch jacket put you on a moral plane with rapists and pedophiles. It made you Typhoid Mary. It was a death-mark, a bull's-eye for any sharpened soup ladle or razor-tipped toothbrush. No: *no one knows*.

'A helluva production,' said a man with a combover down the bar, 'to get over a bitch.'

The TV glowed on his uptilted face. The screen flashed people making masks. Crazy, vivid tribal masks, beast-and-demon masks. All around California, a TV voice explained, they were ramping up for some kind of festival in the desert. The screen flashed ugly ass-naked bodies running through the sand with their hands in the air. Pixilated black dots floated over their pubes and titties. Glimpses of fires burning; a bunch of Christers protesting; a big wicker sculpture exploding like a great flaming skull; some guy saying it's a beautiful epiphany that he circles his calendar for every year.

'How do you mean,' I said, 'a bitch?'

'How that party started,' combover said. 'Some schlub goes into the desert to burn his ex-girlfriend's furniture and scream his head off over how she fucked him over, right? And now it's ten years later and ten thousand other morons are out there with him.'

Here was Gus. Large, incoherent beard-mumbling mass to my left reeking of liquor. Nobody eyefucking him. And now, owing to him, nobody eyefucking me. With quick, smooth motions of his lumpy fingers he started rolling smokes on the bar top, expertly pinching lines of tobacco into the rolling paper, packing them so tight and even and flat at each tip they could be mistaken for machine-made. Passing them horizontally in front of his beard with a dart of his tongue, moistening, sealing. One by one he lined them up; two spawned four; four spawned eight; a family forming. Career convict's easy expertise at work. A task so familiar to Gus he could do it perfectly 10,000 times dead-drunk. He handed me one still moist with his saliva and I put it in my mouth.

Turning his eyes red-rimmed and bloodshot toward me, he said, 'You secure that thing?'

'I'm meeting a guy tomorrow about it. It's all arranged.'

'Good, because the shit's time-sensitive. We need to leave first thing the day after. There's a narrow window here.'

'You figure maybe you'll clue me in as to what it's all about?'

He seemed offended by the question. His voice grew sharp and focused.

'You're not looking at some bush-league candy-ass humper with a popgun and a pipedream,' Gus growled, gesturing with a wave of his palm to the coterie of decayed regulars. 'I'm not one of these. This ain't some nigger-rigged raft going down the Mississippi, but a dreadnought, a dreadnought called the USS *Fucking Miller*. Black Ops! Don't you know anything about how Black Ops works?'

'Well, if we put our heads together—'

'Not how it works! I say too much, I violate the protocols and prerogatives of the chain of command. You think in Nam they told you what the hell you were doing? You've gotta trust the commander. What if the enemy captures you and tortures you? When they sent Martin Sheen up the river to get Colonel Kurtz, did every asshole on the boat know what for?'

'But we're not in Vietnam, and besides—'

'You never read up on the Gambinos? The Don never goes out and dirties his hands. He has his captains talk to the soldiers, and the soldiers talk to their underlings, and so on down the line. Buffers! So it doesn't get traced back. See?'

'But I don't understand why—'

'Less you know, the better. I've made mistakes before. I've told my confederates too much. They brag to some bitch, they talk in their sleep, whatever – it comes back on you, bites your ass. I'm not doing any more time because of someone else's blunders. A professional's always a little paranoid.'

'Don't you think I deserve—'

'I've killed forty-two men, eight women and three children,' Gus said. 'I know what the fuck I'm doing. All *you've* gotta do is follow orders.'

'I got a wife. I need to know, at least I need to know how long we'll be gone.'

'A day, two tops.' He ordered a Bud longneck and pulled on it. I watched his thick fingers pressing against the glass of the bottle, smearing invisible fingerprint oil all over it. The enigma of his identity living on that bottle. His real name, his real past, waiting to be dusted into focus sharp and clear.

'C'mon, it'll be fucking cool,' Gus said. 'The road! How many people can look in the mirror and say, "I did a murder for money"? And it's a good deed besides. Needs to be done. Trust me on that.'

'What did this guy do?'

'He's an evil piece of shit, that's what. And that's all you need to know for now.' Gus drank. 'Look, you may think this is about money, but it ain't. It's about helping someone out of an unfixable situation. Think of it as opportunity's knock. A chance to do something you can be proud of. You know that dream you told me about once? About the train you can't quite catch?'

'Yeah . . .'

'It's me, brother, the USS *Miller*. It's in the station.'

Suddenly I felt beautiful, hearing that: felt the scales fall from my eyes, cool electricity kissing me inside and out. Then I remembered I was on a mission. I was here for intel and working for someone else, for the law. *Those* were my friends. Keep your head, Benny. Don't go wiggy. Keep slipping him the questions. Ease them in. Attack from a hundred angles. Coax, manipulate, nudge: Who's Mr. Gecko? Who wants him wasted? Why?

An hour's persistent headwork and I couldn't pry loose another bastard clue. Gus impregnable. Blood from a stone.

His last words: 'Get that cannon. Sunday's the show. You and me and the Lady from Bristol leave at first light.'

Watch him lumber and weave back to his room. Slip out with the beer bottle. Now, while you can. Pay your bill. Say your good-byes. Get the fuck out. Cool stride down the length of the bar. Head for the door.

The sudden pressure of a hand on my wrist. Attached to the hand: surly Sal Chamusco staring at me agate-eyed.

'What?'

'Whaddya got down there?'

Look down. The bottleneck forming a tent in the front of my pants. Look innocent. Take out the bottle, show it to him. Say, 'You get a nickel for 'em down at the supermarket.'

'You that hard-up?'

'It's also good for the environment.'

'I'm a poor, dead-ass broke motherfucker, and I've done just about anything you can name for a buck, but you won't find me stooping to *that*. I got a little bit of pride left.'

'Well, fuck you.'

'Yeah, fuck you too, Woodsy Owl. Hey, Junior, he's stealing your bottles.'

But I was already out the door, striding through the night toward the boxy white van around the corner where the boys sat waiting among the banks of recording machinery. The van said 'Friendly's Flowers' and had a tulip on the side.

'You were fuckin' Kevin Spacey in there, dude,' Munoz said, sliding open the door. 'Give the man an Oscar.' With latex-gloved fingers he took the longneck from me and deposited it in a super-size Ziploc bag. 'Now it's our move. We'll find you tomorrow.'

I watched the piece of glass disappear in the van. Somewhere on it lay my best friend's name.

CHAPTER 19

The prints proved coy on that particular point, however. They told a more complicated story, as I learned from Munoz Saturday afternoon. Run through the national law-enforcement print bank, they yielded four *other* names linked to Gus Miller. They described a 30-year span of shifting identities, incarceration, and wretched felonious bungling. Munoz read me the police reports and nearly choked laughing. His laughter was infectious. I laughed along. But I felt something else: sadness and pity and disbelief.

January 1967: During the daring daylight burglary of a nursing home in Clearwater, Florida, flimsy plywood panels send an intruder plunging from a ceiling crawlspace into the cafeteria, where the lunchtime serving is under way. Showering down with him: all the watches, wallets, bracelets, and valuable family heirlooms he swept into his bag during a raid of the premises. As the police report phrases it, 'The perpetrator sustained two fractured fibulas in the fall and was unable to defend himself against irate residents, who set upon him with canes and cutlery. Perpetrator suffered numerous lacerations to the scalp, abdominal area, and extremities.' When he regains consciousness, he gives arresting officers the name Evel Sanders. His real name is determined to be Gerry Finkel.

December 1976: A young waitress in Denver, Colorado returns home to find, sprawled on the floor of her rear pantry, the helplessly thrashing head and shoulders of a fat man in a ski-mask. The intruder's midsection remains pinned in what the police report called 'the canine ingress,' through which he tried to gain illegal entry. The waitress beats the masked head with a tennis racket until police arrive. On the way to the hospital he gives the alias Quentin W. Cash.

October 1984: An audacious car thief attempts to steal a sports car belonging to Rick Springfield while the rock star dines in a New Jersey restaurant. The intoxicated thief cannot operate the stick shift and is stopped by a mob of 20 or 30 teen and preteen girls. They haul the thief bodily from behind the wheel, tear his clothing to ribbons, and rake his skin with their nails. As he's being sutured, police check his driver's license, which is stolen, belonging to the man whose name he has been living under, Dale Delacroix.

Evel Sanders, Quentin W. Cash, Dale Delacroix, Gus Miller . . . Gerry Finkel.

'Can't be the same guy,' I said, surprised at the defensiveness in my voice. 'I mean, it can't be the one I know.'

But it was, and to clinch the point, here were the mug shots that accompanied those arrests, which Munoz laid out side-by-side: the arc of my barmate's bruised and bleeding life. The evolution of his face. Variations on a theme: studies in American Toughguy *manqué*.

Photo one: a longhaired hippie in his mid-twenties who, despite the cuts and shiners from the recent nursing home pummeling, managed to convey an aura of toughguy arrogance and disdain – squint, sneer, uptilted chin and all – a pose clearly perfected by years of practice in the mirror, in anticipation of important Kodak moments like these.

Photo two: thicker face, sideburns, ample but disheveled Seventies hair, and, even with one swollen-shut eye and a forehead crossed by racket marks, a face alight with defiant bluster and superiority. Already a veteran con's practiced glare.

Photo three: the glint of the gleefully insane. A fat-cheeked, brown-bearded, middle-aged crook with terrifying psychopathic eyes. Having survived the siege by all those vicious teenage claws, he seemed to have crossed some kind of psychological threshold, at one now with the malignant absurdity of the universe. Here he looked like the Gus Miller I knew: the expression was one he'd leveled at me over a hundred beers.

'The *cabron* should've watched his weight, he might've been a master criminal,' Munoz said. 'My favorite part is box seven of the '67 arrest report, where they list his official occupation. "Assistant gym teacher, Clearwater Catholic School for Girls." Of course, he was *really* in Southeast Asia . . .'

'Maybe he got his dates mixed up,' I said. 'I mean, there's still a chance he was there.'

'You can't be in Vietnam if you're in lockup through the war. You ain't picked up by now that he's just blubber and blabber?'

'He wouldn't be the world's first bullshit artist.'

'He's not your friend, Benny. He's a conman, a crook trying to play you – a very shitty, ham-fisted crook, but still a crook. *I'm* your friend. Law enforcement is your friend. Remember that.'

'Does that make the hit bullshit too? Does that mean I can go home and forget about this?'

'I would have said yes to bullshit – until this morning. Just because everything a man says Monday through Saturday is a lie doesn't mean he ain't telling the truth, or at least part of the truth, on Sunday. Cop consensus now is, blubberguts actually means to whack someone.'

'How'd you come to that?'

'We're tenacious detectives. You'd expect us to do some digging, wouldn't you? Last night we stealth-raided that junkheap Dodge of his and found something extremely pertinent.'

With a flourish Munoz produced a piece of paper and slid it before me. It was a photocopied page from a Thomas Bros.' road guide. The area of concentration was Santa Cruz. A section of a road called Peach Terrace was circled three times.

'It was open to this page,' Munoz said. 'Naturally we replaced the map book exactly where we found it. We know exactly where he's going now.'

'There might be a hundred houses on that block,' I said. 'How do you know which one the target's in?'

Flashing a wolfish smile, as if he'd been waiting for that question, Munoz continued: 'How many geckos live on that block, do you think? One! Professor Manfred A. Geikowitz, world-famous but controversial chairman of the English department at UC Santa Cruz. Funny name, but thank God for that. Imagine our headache if it'd been Smith. Your next question will be, "Does anyone actually want a tweed-sucking academic dead?" And I say to you, "Yes, yes, yes."'

'A professor? How are you sure about this?'

'Instinct, Benny. Call it intuition, call it logic – call it Detective Al Munoz's cop brains – but for all we *don't* know at this point, we can say for a certainty that this professor's the one with the bull's-eye on his back.'

'Why?'

A strange story followed. As it turned out, they had tele-conferenced with Professor Geikowitz just a couple of hours ago. To the detectives' question, "Who may want you dead?" there came a long silence from the academic's end. Then they heard him weeping. 'I knew it would come to this,' croaked the professor, confessing that a lesser academic had for years leveled allegations of plagiarism against him.

The work in question involved certain obscure ideas having to do in some way with Karl Marx and William Faulkner. Professor Geikowitz had vaulted to glory on the strength of an essay entitled 'The Snopes Cow and the Dialectical Implications of Bovine Rape,' which I'm not really qualified to talk about, but which sounded like hardcore, breakthrough shit. The thesis stemmed from a series of obscene fingernail doodlings discovered on the walls of Faulkner's Oxford, Mississippi animal barn, scratched into the wood (it was assumed) during one of the Southern writer's legendary drinking bouts. They were now considered the Rosetta Stone to Faulkner's difficult fiction.

The man who claimed to have made this breakthrough, it seemed, was a humble lecturer at tiny Huntington Beach Community College named Norby D. Valentine. This Valentine, a sometime newspaperman, was murderously bitter over what he claimed was Professor Geikowitz's theft of his research. For more than a year he'd been sending Geikowitz anonymous but very threatening limericks. It was really only a matter of time before Valentine worked up the courage to try to murder him. Now Professor Geikowitz was very scared. He insisted he had done nothing wrong. Perhaps (he allowed) he had borrowed certain amorphous *notions* from Valentine's literary cowfucking scholarship, 'But really, Detectives, this Valentine, who has actually worked as a journalist, lacked the theoretical chops to extend the proletarian bovine thesis to *any* kind of rigorous conclusion. Like so many of this world's also-rans and mediocrities, the ex-journalist is full of envy toward its successes, and would like to see me in my grave.'

(Geikowitz, it turned out, still bore a slight limp from a knife attack as a graduate student at Columbia University years earlier. The attack was prompted by his use of the word 'niggardly' at a Harlem bar, where he was trying to impress an undergrad with his vocabulary.)

'Are you gonna arrest Valentine and Gus, or – or whatever his name is?' I asked Munoz.

'Too soon,' Munoz said. 'We don't got enough.'

'You just said you're sure about—'

'*We're* sure, but if we bring this case to the DA right now, he's gonna light a cigarette, kick up his feet and say, "Get outta my office, it's the weakest case I've ever seen." We need our hit-man to set foot in Professor Geikowitz's driveway with a gun. Or we need him to speak the professor's full name, to make the plan to kill him explicit. That would be enough to nail him on attempted murder for hire.'

'I couldn't make him talk,' I said. 'I think maybe he doesn't *know* all the details himself yet. Or he knew them, but lost them already.'

'Maybe, but we figure he'll have to know them by the time you guys leave to do this job.'

'That's supposed to be tomorrow morning.'

'When he leaves, you leave with him.'

'Huh?'

Grinning as he talked, with his bright wad of Big Red pinned between his teeth, Munoz said, 'Chill in that seat and listen. We got together a plan. It's a bitch of a plan, and you're maybe gonna be a little reluctant at first, but it's as close to foolproof as they come. You can bounce a quarter off this plan, it's so tight and so right. And I say this not without a touch of pride in authorship, my man. We've done all the hard work. All we need you to do is tag along with a wire.'

Unease twitching through me, invading my bowels, I found myself suddenly sitting there, fighting to keep from shitting myself. Sick in the presentiment that I was being guided through a glossy, four-color brochure for a room at the leper ward. Jesus Christ, it looked like the Hilton in the picture.

'We'll be watching every step,' said confident Munoz. 'We'll be following you with unmarked units, plus a helicopter and a fixed-wing. And we'll have men planted all over Peach Terrace with Professor Geikowitz. Like I said – bulletproof.'

'You forget that I'm supposed to get him a gun.'

'Taken care of.'

'What?'

He withdrew a heavy object from his waistband and placed it in front of me. It was a black Smith & Wesson .38, old, battered. He pressed the handle into my hand.

'It looks real.'

'It *is* real. Only the firing pin's been shaved down, and the rounds are blanks. This way no one gets hurt. Safe as a squirt gun.'

'What if he wants to test it?'

'Tell him it's an old gun, you got it off the street, best you could do. You musta got ripped off. Be angry.'

'What if something goes wrong?'

'We won't allow anything to go wrong.'

'What if it does?'

'You didn't become the best-respected CI in Orange County because you're not willing to take a few little risks on behalf of what's right.' He took the gun back and put it in his belt. 'You'll get it just before you go.'

I didn't say anything for a minute or two. Munoz leaned back with his arms folded across his chest, frowning.

Ape-jawed Wein walked in. He leaned forward with his elbows on the table and that vicious slash between his eyes trembling angrily about a foot from my face.

'If you back me up against a wall, I can make your life uncomfortable in the worst way,' Wein said. 'I'm capable of fucking you up.'

'I'm trying to take care of you here,' Munoz told me. 'You're not allowing me to take care of you.'

'What does he mean about fucking me up?'

'In the last two years,' Wein said, 'you've been issued exactly one thousand, five hundred and sixty-five dollars and twenty-three cents' worth of citations for unlawful operation of a bicycle on the sidewalks of local municipalities. Not to mention racking up a half-dozen Failure to Appear charges for the court dates you've missed. All of which we have generously been willing to ignore.'

'He's saying we might not be able to accommodate you any longer,' Munoz said in a tone of regret.

'You're staring down the barrel of a prison sentence here, and that's a place an individual like yourself doesn't want to be,' Wein said. 'I've seen it happen, word gets out about the kind of work an individual like you does. And then there's no way we can protect you.'

Munoz reached out to put one of his fine-boned piano player's hands on mine, to stop mine from shaking. 'I'm taking Benny for a ride,' he said. 'He's jumpy.'

Munoz drove me to a hill overlooking the Costa Mesa municipal dump, a place he frequently came, he said, to clear his head, to meditate on life and nature and the state of man. 'I won't let him fuck with you,' he reassured me. 'But we need you to play ball.' He put his arm around me and nodded toward the mountains of refuse stretching before us under a hundred little storms of birds.

'What do you see down there?'

'The world's shit.'

'I see something beautiful,' Munoz said. 'I see the life cycle. All the little creatures that nobody ordinarily pays attention to – the maggots and the fungi and the other decomposers – are busy breaking all that shit down out there, putting nutrients back into the ground so the great cycle of life can continue. Because without them – I saw it on the Nature channel – the world would choke on shit and pile high with carcasses.'

'I don't understand.'

'The real heroes of the criminal justice system aren't guys like me, all flash and profile. Who are the heroes? It's the invisible ones, the unsung, brave little creatures who soldier away in anonymity – the Benjamin Bunts of the world.'

'I feel like I'm being lubed up for an ass-fucking, man.'

'Listen, Benny – I admire the hell out of you, okay? You may not think much of yourself, but *I* think a lot of you. And I'm trying to help you out of a pinch, here.'

I remembered I had leverage. I had a card to play. I blurted, 'Was it Wein who shot you that time behind the Dress for Less? I mean, so you could get that Glock guy?'

The question made him blink; a tremor of uncertainty flashed across his face. The next instant he was all smiles, all brotherliness. 'Why would a cop shoot another cop, *compadre*? What kind of *pendejo* question is that? Let's get back to the station.'

What did I expect to gain, with the remark? Before now I had never conceived of mentioning it, because to do so would tell Munoz I distrusted him, would put him on notice that I constituted a threat. I feared his reaction, the sudden obliteration of our friendship, his fearsome transformation into an enemy. What's more, I didn't *want* to distrust him.

His breezy response left me even more off-balance, more uncertain. As we pulled away from the dump in his dark-windowed Porsche, he told me paternally that for a long time he'd been worried for me, considering the crowd I ran with. I might forget I was on the side of the good guys. 'It's dangerous for your soul. All kinds of temptations to do bad,' he said. 'Bad's a habit, Benny, like booze or coke or anything else. It gets easier and easier.'

He promised that when this was all over he would swing me a guest pass at the cop gym and put me on a six-month workout program. He would be my physical-fitness mentor. He was already working on the details of my high-protein diet. When he finished with me, I wouldn't be a mole man anymore.

'What you need is some ab work, some bench time, bicep-curls, upright rows,' Munoz said. 'We'll build you a nice striation foundation. On alternate days: some military presses, quads, lats, and glutes. I've got an extra juicer and a Foreman's Grill I'll give you. Maybe throw together some pimp-ass threads for you. You're gonna have a whole new glow. You'll be knee-deep in bitches: a whole new man.'

'I'll still just be a snitch.'

Munoz frowned. He removed a piece of paper pinned under the sun-visor and passed it to me. It was a brochure for the Costa Mesa Police Academy. Shiny young-faced recruits – a Mexican chick, an Asian chick, a black guy, a white guy – stood shoulder-to-shoulder in uniform, smiling proudly. 'JOIN OUR FAMILY,' it said.

'We've got twelve openings and a shortage of talent,' Munoz said. 'Lots of guys taking early retirement, so we're thin. And we're aggressively recruiting minority candidates. You've got some American Indian blood, don't you?'

'Not that I know about.'

'I hear that you do. And I'm gonna say so to our recruiter, Captain Hines. Good friend of mine, Dick Hines. That application of yours that's been sitting on his desk for God knows how long shoots to the top of the stack.'

'You mean I could get on that way?'

'I could swing it for you, bro. All you need's a piece of paper shows you got somebody in your line with a few drops of Comanche or Choctaw or whatever. Not hard to get. I could hook you up.'

'But I wouldn't, you know, what about getting in on my own merit?'

'You think the mayor's nephew, who wrapped his cruiser around a tree last week, you think he got in on his merit? Or half these other jokers? The Indian blood gets you in the door. Hines makes his minority quota, he's a happy Hines. He's not gonna fuck that up by asking a lot of questions.'

'What about my record?'

'Little trickier. Takes a court order to get it expunged. But all the convictions are misdemeanors, and I've got some IOUs to call in with the DA, who can make that happen.'

'How naïve do you think I am?'

'Not at all,' he continued, undeterred, sincere, dead serious. 'Which is why you know this is exactly how things work in the real world. You think it's *merit* that gets these assholes on the force? You think they've got a thousandth of what you've got? I've seen the DA's office seal worse records, when it's necessary. And when they say, "What did this Benny Bunt ever do for us?" I'll have an answer. I'll be able to tell them, 'I know Mr. Bunt to be a man of the highest character, bravery, and integrity. He has all the qualities that make for a good cop." And I'll say, "Mr. Bunt was instrumental in helping law enforcement crack a recent murder-for-hire case." I mean, I really want to be able to say that.'

'Alright,' I said, thinking furiously, trying to figure my move, my best move, buying time, knowing only that right now I had to tell him what he wanted to hear. 'I want you to be able to say that, too. I've always wanted to do what you do.'

I went home to pack.

I scoured the apartment, my hands stuffing my jacket pockets with road gear: cigarettes, lighter, gum, comb, deodorant, aftershave, toothpicks, spare change, fortune cookie, loose peppermints, batteries, flashlight, pens. Suddenly I noticed Donna standing in the doorway, watching.

'Going somewhere?' she said. 'Your eyes are funny. What are you on?'

'Nothing.'

'You're lying. Why are your eyes jittery like that?'

'I have to go on a road trip.'

'Somewhere with your asshole buddy, right?'

'Don't call him that.'

'Going to Vermont? Because I hear they'll marry you there. But you have to divorce me first, Benny. *You have to divorce me first!*'

'It's a mission,' I said. 'It's an important government mission, and I can't talk about it. I love you, Donna, but I've gotta go.'

'Mission?'

'Gonna be a whole new world when I'm back. You're gonna see me put on a uniform to work every day. You know what kind?'

'Two days? What takes two days? It's that place in Nevada, right? That whorehouse with the rabbits in the name? The Furry Bunny Pussy Ranch?'

'It's called the Moonlight Bunny Ranch, but that's not where we're going. Guess what kind of uniform.' I hummed the *Miami Vice* theme.

'The lies, Benny, it's the *lies* I can't stand,' she said. 'It wouldn't be so bad if you just came out with it. If you just said, "Donna, sweetheart, I'm going whoring for a couple days at the Skanky Rabbit Snatch Ranch, stick my dick in some whores, maybe blow my boyfriend a few times." If you just said, "Don't worry, Donna, I'm gonna use a condom, so you don't pick up any awful sex germs the next time we do it, maybe six or eight months from now." If you just told the truth—'

I drove my foot through the wall behind the TV, leaving a hole in the plaster. It filled me with nasty satisfaction. I believed I could tear down the walls and rip up the floor with my bare hands. Donna looked horrified, and I said, 'That's your luck. That's so I didn't hit you.'

'You're tweaking! I can't believe you're tweaking again, Benny, you sonofabitch!'

Downstairs, the neighbors were screaming at me to stop the ruckus and banging their broomstick on their ceiling, the sounds thumping up from below. Grunting animal noises, I stomped the floor savagely six or seven times, outdoing their violence. The broomstick stopped. Donna was crying. 'Are you insane?'

'I'm in no mood for people's shit,' I said. 'I have a mission to go on.'

'Did you even consider . . .' Her voice was choked with sobs. 'Did you even consider maybe I'd like to come along and have some fun too?'

As I slammed the door I heard her screaming that she wouldn't be there when I got back.

CHAPTER 20

It was early Sunday morning and we were going to kill someone today. Things were already getting wiggy. I hadn't had a night's sleep in three days and I itched all over as if scales had been grafted to my skin, my nails making a feverish circuit between my arms, legs, midsection, and shoulder blades. I kept thinking of the New Jersey man in the bathtub staring at his toes and waiting to die, the poor bastard just aching to have it over and done with, praying for the doorway to fill with the shadow of the gunman . . .

'Some kind of plague?' Junior said from his place behind the bar as he watched me claw my skin.

'Rats carry plague,' I said. 'Are you saying I'm some kind of rat?'

Junior said, 'There's a resemblance.'

'Well, your friendly neighborhood rat is a highly underrated creature,' I said. 'Centuries of bad PR over that Black Death business. Allegedly played a role in wiping out a third of Europe – as if we need more fucking Europeans anyway – only the truth is, he's as much a victim as anyone else. A victim of the fleas. He trusted the fleas and they used him. He gave them a home on his body and they blackened his name forever. Can't show his face at any of the respectable parties anymore.'

Flying spring-loaded from my mouth came a memorized entry from my one-volume *Complete Webster's Family Encyclopedia*, the one I got for $4.99 in the bargain-bin and kept in the bathroom so I could improve my mind during visits to the bowl. 'The Black Death originated in the Far East and spread through Europe and England in May 1348,' I said. '*Pasteurella pestis*. There are three forms of the disease, the most common of which is bubonic plague, in which fever, vomiting, and headache are accompanied by swollen inflamed lymph nodes – buboes.'

'What are you doing here at six a.m., aside from dying of plague?' Junior asked.

'I'm supposed to meet Gus in half an hour. Not to mention rats make terrific pets.'

'He cleared most of his stuff outta that room last night and hauled it back to his van, but he wouldn't tell me anything. About fifty of those birdhouses. I even helped him carry out that goddamn freezer of his, which must weigh three hundred pounds.' He added with a touch of hopefulness: 'You think he'll be, uh, moving on down the road?'

'I think so. Business opportunity.'

Junior nodded and tried to keep his expression blank, but I could tell he was pleased with this news. He had come to dread his handyman and the reminiscences he shared about Junior's gook-slaughtering dad. The stories were always bloody and the death toll seemed to rise by the day.

Now Junior was making his morning rounds, wiping surfaces and arranging bottles behind the well and brewing coffee, preparing for the early crowd. Through the wall behind him Gus snored like some kind of asthmatic zoo beast, deep, wheezy, stentorian.

Junior listened with an expression of wariness and distaste. 'I've gotta run out for bacon. Keep an eye on things,' he said and vanished.

Now here I was, alone at the bar in a speedfreak fog. The sounds of molars grinding in my skull and badger claws scrabbling at my skin: my own fingernails. Hands twitchy with the compulsion to tear open my shirt and rip loose the electronic snake twisting up between my nipples. *You there, assholes? You listening, Munoz? How about you, Wein? Are you in my brain? Don't wig. Don't wig don't wig don't wig . . .*

After a while I looked over and saw I was not alone at the bar. A man sat three stools down in a soiled lime-green leisure suit. He must have come in without me noticing: a gaunt man with thinning hair and pale skin and hands shaking even more violently than mine. He held a racing form that rustled in his fever-grip. He made quick marks on it with a stubby pencil and I noticed a few of his fingers hung at bad angles, bent backward or sticking straight up from the back of his hands.

An unrecognizable voice croaked from my throat: 'Tony the Money. This is a sighting.'

Preoccupied, he didn't look up. His voice was flat and toneless as he said, 'Nice to be remembered.'

I heard him muttering what sounded like the names of horses and I asked, 'What does the day look like?'

'Privileged information. You'd have to be dead to know.'

I could see the neat black circle where the slug went in at the right temple just beyond the line of his hair. His skin was a bad color – bloodless for 30 years will do that – and I noticed now that his fingernails were long and curved and that his thin hair, while nearly bald on top, hung halfway down his back like an old woman's, and I remembered what people said about the nails and the hair continuing to grow, after.

'I've always wondered,' I said. 'Do the dead gamble?'

'Some can. But suicides get special penalties. The Almighty's penal code. The whole universe is set up like a penal system, in case you didn't know. So every day I get a racing form. Every day I get a pencil. Every day I know how the ponies are gonna finish. Here's the curse . . .'

One by one he pulled out his pockets and made little tongues of them. Every pocket was empty and all these tongues were hanging from his slacks and from his leisure jacket like so many wounds spitting flowers of blood. Then he looked at me with his pale face full of desperate pleading.

'Look. Do a kindness to a poor ghost. Spot me a c-note?'

'I haven't got that kind of bread.'

'Maybe you don't understand. No, you can't possibly understand. I'm guaranteeing a three hundred percent return. No rational man would turn that down. You're a rational man, aren't you?'

'Not really.'

'But you're a smart man.'

'No. I'm a fuck-up. Everybody knows that. And I've only got fifty bucks.'

He ran his tongue over his lips. 'I'll break the rules, this once. I'll tell you what you want to know.'

'I want to know who the smart money is on.'

He studied the racing form and jabbed at it with his trembling pencil and said, 'Well, Latin Sex Brigade is the odds-on favorite, of course. He's won fifty of his last fifty-one races, even took a bullet once without breaking stride. Excellent musculature, and have you seen the dick on that horse? Win or lose, he'll be put out to stud after another few races.

'Hard Luck Bastard hasn't won a race in a long time. These days, the insiders consider his prowess mostly hype, and there's doubt he's even running under his legitimate Christian name. Terrible habits. Bloat apparent. Then again, he knows the stakes: the glue factory if he loses. His last shot, and desperation does remarkable things for a horse.

'The Gecko? An enigmatic horse, that. No one's seen him yet. A wild card. Very exciting.

'As for Snitch Jacket, no one's betting on him. He's pretty much fucked, a Number Thirteen. He'll be lucky to get around the first turn without breaking a leg. It isn't even clear whose race he's running, really.

'What's for sure is it's gonna end disastrously for one, and maybe a couple, of these horses. At least one and possibly more will get put down by the end of it. I mean a real bloodbath. Carnage!

'Those are my predictions. How about that fifty?'

'You haven't told me anything.'

'You think I'm bullshitting you? I've got a gift. I'm a fucking soothsayer.'

'You're just one of those hucksters on late-night TV, man. You're like Miss Cleo or that psychic bitch down the block. You don't tell people anything they don't already know. You dumb dead motherfucker!'

His face became a mask of guilty, pathetic desperation and he told me I just didn't know what it was like, to be where he was. 'Being dead's like a horrible dream. You can't keep stuff straight from one minute to the next. It's all jumbled and tangled and shifty. Man, I really, really need that fifty . . .'

Suddenly I hated this pale guy with his broken fingers and dirty dead-epoch threads. He was trying to do something terrible to me, sent by someone, fucking with my head, maybe planning to kill me. I was not going to let him. I heard myself screaming at him, calling him a liar. 'Hair and nails growing after you're dead is only urban legend, asshole! Dehydration and shrinkage of the corpse create that illusion! I read about it! I know things! So fuck you, man! Fuck you!'

I lined up the last of the gray powder on the bar top and leaned in to take the blast and felt the chemicals strafing my esophagus and nasal cavity, and then I felt alright, I felt okay, brave and bold and Spider-Man-tight and not seeing any dead assholes in leisure suits. Who am I? I'm a secret government agent. I'm Steve Austin, the bubonic man. And the bubonic man always keeps his cool. Scan your surroundings. Impeccable meth logic screamed: this bar needs cleaning. Some serious tidying is in order. How did I fail to notice the condition of this place?

In 30 minutes I had cleaned and spit-shined the bar, scrubbed all the stools, Windexed all the glass, swept all the sawdust off the floor and collected it in two Hefty bags by the door. I was wondering what color to paint the walls and where I could find some paint to do it when Junior returned saying, 'What the hell you doing?'

'Tidying up. I thought—'

'Sawdust is atmosphere, not trash. You're mucking up the atmospheric touches!'

The angry little man upended the garbage bags and shook them out on the floor, cursing, muttering, 'Benny, you tweaking again? I thought you quit.'

The air filled with sawdust. It exploded upward and floated sideways and settled gently about the bar, like so many squalid white-trash snowflakes.

Gus stood in the doorway of his room bleary-eyed and hustling his balls, reeking of liquor even from 10 feet away. Steadying himself with a hand on the doorframe, he said, 'What's all the hoo-ha?'

'Ask him,' Junior said bitterly.

'Let's bail,' I said. 'I hate this place. I always have.'

'I'm clearing out,' Gus said, ducking into his room for a moment and then lumbering out with the last of his belongings, including his mattress and his box of war souvenirs, Jesse James slouching along arthritically at his feet.

'You're going?' Junior said. 'I mean – it's a shame to be losing you. *Mi casa es tu casa.* You're not coming back?'

'I'm headed north,' Gus said. 'I can't say much about the quality of playmates in this sandbox. Find the caliber of character pretty low. I need to be around some real human beings. Hope you understand.'

They didn't shake hands. In a flat voice Junior said, 'Good luck.' He wore no expression on his face as he watched us leave through the back door.

My watch said 6:46 a.m.

'You're jumpy like a maggot,' Gus told me in the van.

'You're totally tanked,' I said, aware that he probably drank all night and crashed at two or three. 'Maybe we should wait till—'

'I hold booze fine. You're with a professional. Plus we're time-pressed, and it's not like I'm letting *you* drive. Got that cannon?'

'Right here.'

I handed him the Smith & Wesson .38 and he turned it around slowly, feeling its weight. He said, 'I guess it'll do, for a ladies' weapon.'

'What?'

'Anything smaller than a forty-five is essentially a chick's gun.'

'It's blue-collar, meat-and-potatoes, just like you said. If you wanted a bazooka . . .'

He popped the revolver, checked the bullets, and, shrugging, tucked the gun carefully into the waistband of his Levis. 'Don't get your asshole tight. I said it'll do.'

He took his necklace of ears out of his souvenir box and draped it around his neck. 'You and me are gonna kill us one motherfucker today,' Gus said. 'How you feelin'?'

'I'm feeling really positive about it,' I said. 'How about you?'

'Real positive. I killed sixty-three children, nine men and twelve women. I'm blood and instinct, brother. I'm what a famous Jew writer from the Sixties called a White Nigger. First, let's get us some snackage.'

With one lumpy fist on the wheel and the other hand hanging loosely at the V of his crotch, bleary Gus directed the rattling, bumping van down Harbor Boulevard. Behind us the wall-to-wall rows of junk thrummed and vibrated.

Beyond the dusty windows, in the chill iron-gray morning, the sea fog hung thick over the streets and shrouded the storefronts and the still-lit lamp posts whose high, malaria-yellow eyes burned blurrily as they followed us.

Watch the side-view mirror: the boxy white flower van

bobbing out of the fog and disappearing into it again, pursuing steadily at a distance of a block or two.

Other cop eyes everywhere, following from the skies and roads, invisible. All those unseen ears: pressed against the mike on my chest.

Jesse James lay on his forepaws in a cleared space just behind the two seats of the cab. Every time I looked back the dog seemed to be looking at me. His wet mouth hung open and his cloudy old eyes studied me with unnerving fixity from that gray face, and I kept looking back and he kept staring.

Then I remembered what Gus said about the dog's preternatural powers and in an instant I was convinced the dog knew everything or strongly suspected: the dog smelled the flopsweat slicking my bones and the constabulary's wire under my clothes, and soon his master would know too and—

When I was a kid, I once lured a squirrel into an empty coffee tin and clapped on the plastic lid. As it fought for life in the airless cage, I found myself unexpectedly terrified by the intensity of its panic. I set it free right away. I remembered it now because my heart felt that way: like something caged and thrashing and trying to claw its way out of my chest.

The demon dog and its Zen powers. I read a science-fiction story once about a boy and a telepathic dog, and it ended with the boy feeding his girlfriend to the mutt and I thought it was a terrific story at the time, very imaginative. But now I was thinking – no, no, I was deadfuckingsure – the writer got it from a true story, there were such dogs, and I could almost feel the foul, hot breath on my neck . . .

I decided to murder the evil motherfucking dog.

Gus pulled into a 24-hour Lucky Chucky's supermarket and I suggested he try to sober up in the van while I went in to stock up on snackage, and he said alright, but don't be long. I bought chips, soda, beef jerky, a couple of hot microwave burritos for Jesse James, and something else: fistfuls of Baker's chocolate.

Which is bursting with something called theobromine, a natural stimulant from the cocoa bean, which happens to be toxic to the canine system. Nine ounces will do in a 50-pound dog: nervousness, pissing, cardiac arrest, death. All of which I had in my head, in one of those rooms. Another stupid piece of knowledge, completely pointless till you need it.

Your glands betray you, Gus once said. *Evil's in a man's sweat, it lives there, and Jesse smells it oozing outta you . . .*

I returned to find Gus snoring, his mouth agape.

I unwrapped the chocolate and fed chunk after chunk into the dog's rotten old craw, and he slurped and chomped and snapped happily until he shuffled into the back of the van behind some junk and fell over and lay on his side twitching, doomed.

I popped in AC/DC and turned it up, loud. I didn't want Gus to hear what was happening back there.

Gus woke up. 'Let's go,' I said.

He took the 55 to the 405 to Interstate 5, heading north toward Los Angeles. *I'm what this famous Jew writer called a White Nigger.* Where had I heard that?

By the time we passed through Anaheim the fog had mostly vanished, but the skies were massing with storm clouds. Directly ahead of us loomed a pair of them, a bloated round one nudging a crooked thin companion: ugly inky blots that reminded me of a pair of upside-down thumbprints pressed on a police file card.

When I looked up again they had bled into surrounding clouds to form an unbroken reef, black as chimney smoke, running across the horizon.

'You see that?' Gus cried over the music, looking up through the windshield.

'What?'

'The clouds. Like a fucking hell-bird up there. A roc or monster crow or something belched outta hell, something from Revelation. Wings two thousand feet end-to-end. You see it?'

'There's nothing up there.'

'It's gone now, but it showed itself. Looked right at us.'

The first raindrops started hammering the windshield, tearing loose little clods of crusted dirt and cutting jagged rivulets down through the dust.

Gus looked bone-white, sick with anxiety. His free hand scrabbled through the cab for a paper bag. He turned his head and puked violently into it. He hit the wipers. They moved sluggishly left-right, left-right, left-right, and the mud followed, smearing and thickening until it covered the windshield and I could barely see the curve of the freeway ahead.

PART III THE POET

CHAPTER 21

From the *Desert Sentinel-Gazette-Intelligencer*:

TWO DEAD IN 'TECHNO-PAGAN' FESTIVAL

Mojave, CA – A 33-year-old Berkeley man was found murdered Sunday night at the annual Howling Head Festival, while an unidentified man burned to death in a grisly but apparently unrelated accident.

Matthew Nastahowsky suffered what authorities called 'homicidal trauma to the upper body' on the culminating night of the controversial three-day event, which has been billed as 'North America's most dangerous underground art festival.'

Nastahowsky, who performed self-written poetry at the festival under the stage name 'Gecko,' was found dead in his tent about 9:35 p.m., and was last seen alive about half an hour earlier. No one has been arrested for the crime, and police acknowledge the difficulty of finding suspects among the 12,000-person crowd in attendance.

'There were just a lot of strange folks around and about, and a lot weren't necessarily in a cognizant state,' said Mojave Police Capt. Ed Trench. 'We haven't found anyone yet who saw anything.'

Nastahowsky's record shows a 1995 arrest for possession of marijuana, and another in 1997 for dousing a San Francisco police memorial with urine. Police would not say if they suspected the motive for his murder.

'He was one of our favorite freaks, a flat-out genius,' said Ian Holt, the festival founder and organizer.

Sobbing uncontrollably at the scene was Cloe Langley, Nastahowsky's 24-year-old girlfriend, who said they had spoken recently of becoming engaged. Langley is the daughter of Dean Wentworth Langley, CEO of Langley Mustard Co. of Newport Beach, a Fortune 500 company.

The 13th annual Howling Head Festival culminated about 9 p.m. Sunday with the traditional burning of a three-story wicker sculpture built in the shape of a screaming head. As festival-goers waited for the sculpture to be lit, an unidentified man in flaming clothes broke through the crowd and ran toward it, screaming and flailing his arms. Fire from the man's body ignited a series of wicks at the base of the sculpture, triggering a chain-reaction of the explosives packed inside, which included magnesium bricks and 16,000 firecrackers. The crowd cheered as the sculpture – and the man – were immolated.

'We all thought it was Mickey the Mylar Monster,' said Holt, the founder. 'Mickey wears this Mylar suit and sets himself on fire and runs up there and kind of twitches around and gyrates. And then he sets the wicks on the Head and rolls in the sand to put himself out.'

By the time people realized the flaming man was not the designated wick-lighter, and that he had not fled the sculpture, it was too late. 'Everybody's screaming, going crazy,' said Holt. 'The Burn is just this big catharsis. People wait all year for that moment. They thought this dude was part of the show.'

The man was burned beyond recognition, and no one has come forward to identify him. While thousands of people witnessed his death, there is no consensus on what he looked like. It was night, and the scene was lit mostly by the torches and glow sticks of festival-goers.

'We've got two thousand different descriptions of him,' said Capt. Trench. 'A lot of our witnesses admit to being under the influence of controlled substances. Some of the stuff we haven't even heard of.'

Camcorder footage of the incident sheds little light. Taken 30 or

40 yards away, at the safety radius where the crowd was kept, it shows the blazing figure running to the sculpture and disappearing in an explosion of flame.

Every year, the Howling Head Festival attracts performance artists, experimental musicians, free-love advocates, and various other alternate-lifestyle enthusiasts to the desert for what organizers call a 'techno-pagan saturnalia of primal rage and transformation.'

Holt said he came up with the idea of torching a model Head in the early 1990s as a means of venting his anger over a failed relationship. 'People come to burn stuff and blow it up,' said Holt. 'It helps them work through their issues. They're torching all the negativity in their lives.'

Politicians, church groups, and public-safety officials have tried repeatedly to shut down the event. Since its founding there have been 12 deaths reported at the festival, mostly the result of accidents involving some combination of fire, drinking, and drugs. Nastahowsky's death is the first reported homicide.

'It's a satanic snake's den of sin and depravity,' said Will Sipple of the California Coalition of Christ. 'It's Babylon all over again. It's the end-product of forty years of run-amok liberalism, starting with bra-burning. Now they're burning people. Next they'll be burning our babies.'

CHAPTER 22

Goins reads the clip over for a dozenth time and, sighing, leaves it on top of the stainless-steel tabletop between us. His tired eyes look up at me. On his tie today is a pattern of cartoonish golden retrievers, dozens of them arrested in identical mid-air leaps. The back of his tie is missing its loop; it flops around. Two days till court.

'I'm working around the clock on this case,' says my fishbelly-hued lawyer. 'Dreaming about it, even. I pulled our investigator off all our other cases to run down some leads. We've got a ways to go. First, I need to understand your motives. They're muddled. Opaque. You're telling me you participated in this sting because you felt threatened—'

'They dragged me into this shitstorm balls-first, Goins. I couldn't figure a way out.'

He gazes at me levelly. 'And your reasoning power is compromised by your drug-addled state,' he says. 'Okay. Maybe that's part of it. But here's my guess. You're being pulled in different directions. One Svengali over here, another over there. Both battling for your soul. You worship Miller, and you worship Munoz. Opposite sides of the law, and each one represents something you want to be. You're a follower by nature. Easily influenced. Malleable. And you're not sure which train to hitch your fate to. That hit close to home?'

'Like I've got no spine at all? Like I'm some gum wrapper blowing around in the wind?'

'We're going to have to explain why you agreed to do this. That's just one avenue we can take. But judges and juries like motives clear-cut. Ambiguity troubles them. It sounds like guilt. So let's say you did this for the snitch money. You lost your job, and your wife was sick with that chronic lung thing. You wanted to take care of her, like a good husband.'

'That makes me look like a stand-up human being, at least. She's wheezing all over me. Begging for the inhaler. There I am, trying to help.'

'The trouble with the money motive is, the state will kick our asses with it. "This man Benny Bunt is jobless and penniless and without prospects, and a cut of five grand sounded real good to him, especially with family medical issues. All he had to do was kill someone."' Goins pauses. 'To tell you the truth, five grand doesn't seem like a lot of money to whack someone.'

'It's not like there's a going union rate written down somewhere.'

'Five grand, you can't even get a good used car.'

'I guess people pay what they think they can get away with.'

'Well, it makes you look even worse, if prosecutors can sell the idea you were involved in the hit. Which is exactly the notion they aim to peddle.'

'That's ridiculous,' I say. 'I'm just a snitch. I go along with the plan. I'm wired up, and they're following, and then—'

'They lose you.'

'Because of what I did to Jesse James. Stupid.'

'How?'

'Because somewhere between Orange County and LA he starts calling for his dog, and no answer, no answer, and then he pulls over and finds the body back there. He insists we go into the hills and bury him. We're barreling around curves in the rain, up in Griffith Park, and the cops must have lost us there.'

'Still, they're supposed to be staking out the location of the hit – waiting for you.'

'You might have guessed by now this Professor Geikowitz and his cowfucking scholarship is a red herring.'

'Peace Terrace in Santa Cruz? The block Gus circled?'

'I figured it out. His ex-wife's up there. I think he wanted to drop by and leave her a cut of his money. Which is how it happens the idiots are waiting for us at the wrong place.'

CHAPTER 23

We sat parked for what might be 10 or 15 minutes while the rain pounded the van, tattooing the hood like steady handfuls of hurled pebbles. Gus's face looked lumpy, sledgehammered, ready to crack with grief. He stared over the steering wheel at the water running down the windshield. The shadows raced down his cheeks in furious wriggling streaks. He said, 'Please close his eyes, Benny. I don't think I can.'

After I did it I said, 'He was suffering. He's out of his misery. Matter of ti—'

His voice was suddenly so terrible I felt the impulse to flee: 'Shut up. You never knew a goddamn thing about friendship.'

We waited for a lull in the storm. He carried the dog in his arms like a sick child. I followed with the shovel. The downpour resumed, drenching us. We crashed forward, sopping, and I thought I could feel the exact moment the wire drowned: the tingle of the electrical short-circuit buzzing through my doomed bones.

I spaded up muddy earth while he waited with the dog wrapped in a Mexican blanket and dripping wet in his arms. Shovelful after shovelful I dug, topsoil and compacted dirt and finally hard crimson clay, until there was a narrow shaft six feet deep. Gus stooped and lowered Jesse James in, and I covered his wrapped shape with dirt.

'One thing you can say for him, he had his share of bitches,' Gus said to the hump of the grave. Rainwater poured from his beard and from the shriveled ears around his neck, like a clutch of weeping gargoyles. As we trudged back to the van I fell behind a few yards, far enough to strip the useless wire from my body and ditch it in the brush.

Back in the van, he said, 'Poor Jesse. I bet it was bad tacos. That's the second evil omen of the day, after the hell-bird. Something ain't right.'

We got on the road and drove in silence for a long time. By the time we reached the edge of the high desert it was mid-afternoon and the rain was gone; instead of a gray thundercloud canopy, the sky was a maddeningly deep and markless blue like the vault of an infinite cathedral; to think about it too long might take your mind around the bend for good. We filled the tank at the last little single-pump gas station and drove past the last little ghost town and into the desert, past dunes, past trackless slopes of sand, past ranges dotted with Joshua trees and impasto clumps of sagebrush and snakeweed, through salt-flat valleys and woven sand ridges, past explosions of wild sunflowers that seemed almost obscene amid their parched surroundings. I could identity some of what I saw from 'Welcome to California' postcards I'd studied in drugstores and felt, then as now, a kind of lonely, resentful panic that the state's rugged coffee-table-book bounty did not feel like mine, that I had never known what exactly to do with nature, how to look at it or pray to it; it had never extended its friendship to me; and now it served as the landscape of an incomparable nightmare. Bugs detonated on the windshield by the thousands, the wipers smearing and thinning their gore. After a long time, the earth flattened completely and everything around us looked dead. We were heading down mile after mile of heat-cracked and signless pavement while in every direction the desert reached away utterly level. We rode forever, the air cooking with dry heat and our brains blistering deep in their chemical furnaces, drunk Gus's fat neck leaking whiskey while I twitched and tweaked in the grip of crystal, both of us pouring sweat and cursing the lack of AC. We kept the windows open until the wind started picking up, sending lateral sprays of sand into our eyes. We might have been in the desert an hour before we saw the sign that said 'THIS WAY TO THE HOWLING HEAD.' We followed the arrow off the pavement, the van bumping over sun-blasted, prehistoric earth, every jolt like the squeeze of a power drill behind my eyeballs. Finally you could see it: the Head. Out of the desert it rose, growing and sharpening through the windshield beyond miles of gusting sand. Even from here you could see the great cave where its mouth opened in a scream, and the angry tendons of the neck snaking like enormous oak trunks into the sand. The sand picked up for a while and whited out the view and then I half believed, as meth clenched the poor sponge of my brain, it must have been a crystal hallucination, that leviathan somehow existing out there in the flat wastes; then the wind died and there it was again, bigger and stranger. The Head, howling at the sky, made me think of some ancient sand-swallowed alien colossus crying for home beyond the stars, or some titan hurled like a thunderbolt to earth for defying its masters, or the enraged cyborg cousin of an Easter Island monolith. I began to think there was a body attached, under the sand, and this god or devil was trying mightily to free itself and do some Godzilla-scale violence, squash the buglike villagers who were trying to kill it. Then I was telling Gus we must have stumbled across some secret burying ground for outcast genetic freaks, all those monsters you read about in the supermarket checkout line and wonder where they go . . .

'Quit with your pie-hole already,' he snapped. 'You're annoying as shit, all that babble. Babble, babble like a bitch, for miles now. I should be shot, bringing a speed freak along.'

'That thing wants to eat us! Lamb to the slaughter! It's like Area 51—'

'They build it every year and set it on fire,' he said tightly, but there was a tremor in his voice. 'Don't ask me why. It's a kind of party for dirt-worshipping hippie heathens. It's like Europe, or something. I have no use for 'em.'

The van curved toward the Head in a long caravan, all around us the big tires of Escalades and Avalanches and Denalis and Sequoias and Humvees and Yukons and Rams kicking up dirt, windblasted sand slicing the air in crazy flurries, and the Head rising and growing with every blink, and all of us like pagan pilgrims converging on an idol, and Gus telling me something, my brain too wiggy to make sense of it.

'At midnight they burn it,' he was saying, 'and in the hubbub we ice the motherfucker.'

'What? Who?'

'The Gecko, like I been saying. The Gecko!'

'Why do they burn the Gecko?'

'They don't burn the Gecko! They burn the Head! And then we ice the Gecko!'

'Who's the Gecko?'

Rolling outward from the Head in a ripple of expanding circles were a thousand wildly colored tents like concentric lines of confetti scattered on the flat-baked desert. As we passed under a big flapping banner that said 'BURN THE HEAD!™' the vehicles fanned out to wait their turn at a bunch of little kiosks that spread across the sand like turnpike tollbooths. A young guy with shaved eyebrows leaned out a kiosk window and said, 'Hi, dudes, welcome to the Head! Standard admission is fifty dollars each. We take Visa MasterCard Discover, cash or check. It's eighty bucks for a Silver Pass, which gets you admission to all events plus a free ticket to tonight's raffle. That makes you eligible to win prizes that include a new fully equipped Ford Expedition, five thousand dollars cash, and a tremendous Boca Raton vacation package. Along with dozens of other exciting prizes! There's also the VIP Gold Pass, which for just a hundred bucks gets you all of that, plus a front-section spot to watch the Burn tonight.'

Gus looking at me in confusion, like: What do we do? Benny

saying, 'The second sounds best.' Gus going, 'You think so?' Benny going, 'The guy said we can win some shit.' Gus forking over a wad of cash. Plastic goodie bags materializing in our laps, crammed with coupon books, programs, souvenirs, sample packs of gum, breath-mints, teeth-whitening strips, analgesics. Then we were in, riding under a gigantic sign that read:

Welcome to Edge City!™
PlumpyBurger Inc.™, ComTekk Cell Systems™
and
Screaming Demon Power Drink™
Proudly Present
The 13th Annual Howling Head Festival™
North America's Edgiest Counterculture Party™
'Where You Can Be An Individual!'™

Parking attendants in little reflective-stripped vests took another 20 bucks from us and waved us past a few football-field lengths of parked trucks and SUVs till we found a spot. Around us people were pouring into the desert in fantastic masks, demons and aliens and insects. They leered suddenly in our windows and pounded and howled and disappeared, Gus flinching every time, looking sick, his hand tight on the gun under his gut.

'We've gone off the end of the world,' he muttered fearfully, his carapace of cool cracking. 'I just remembered a dream I had last night. Skullmen on horses and goats with human heads and rivers of fire. And here it is . . .'

'Christ, we're both gonna buy it, aren't we?'

My cowardice seemed to hit his veins like a hypodermic, injecting him with furious courage, Gus shouting, 'Grow a sack, soldier! You losing your nerve? Are you? Are you?'

'What are we doing here?'

'To find the Gecko, you whimpering polesmoker! And the girl we're gonna save! Don't you listen?'

Gus removed a photograph from his shirt pocket and passed it to me and I studied it, not understanding what I was seeing, studying them and squinting and trying to fit them into the world, wondering from what dream or TV show or epoch of my life I saw these faces before . . .

Skyblue studio backdrop: mom, dad, daughter. Sharp-dressed. Honey light beautiful on their faces. Mother poised, petite, commanding, weighted with jewelry. Benny blinking, remembering. Her hair reddish in an Eighties perm, not the piled-high orange tower she wore when I'd met her at the mini-mart on Pacific Coast Highway. The photo was 10 or 15 years old, but the face belonged to the same lady – those droopy brothel-madam eyes, heavy-lidded, just-ravished. Yeah, definitely, *her*, the same: she of the plastic parts and the mute rasping dog, the one who called me something strange (nigger? white nigger?), who tried to proposition me for – for what? Murder? This murder? Connections being made. *Anthrax spore. Nasty little number. Juilliard daughter. What is it you're packing? A switchblade? Blackjack? Brass knuckles? Gun?*

The lady's hand rested on the left shoulder of a girl, 11 or 12 years old maybe, sitting prettily cross-legged in a floral-print dress. The girl freckled, blond-banged, holding a violin in her lap, smiling sweetly and awkwardly, a shy smile. She inherited Mom's sleepy eyelids, but on her they somehow made an opposite impression – innocence, dreaminess. On her right shoulder: Dad's hand resting. Dad somehow familiar to me too: handsome in a conservative gray suit, with a square jaw, deeply sad eyes, and an apostrophe-shaped port-wine stain above the right one.

'Remember that violin piece I played for you that time?' Gus said, taking the photo back. 'That's who did it. Little Cloe. Little Sunshine.'

'The girl?'

'Ain't she a doll?' Gus rubbed his thick thumb along the photo, petting her hair. His voice was embarrassingly sentimental.

'Good girl. Honor Roll. Played a gumdrop in *Nutcracker*. Hello Kitty. Swim team. Loved her violin. Walked around like it was attached. What you call a prodigy. Parents gave her everything. *Everything*. Little bit sassy, little bit headstrong. Show me a girl that ain't.'

'What do we care about her?'

'She got herself abducted is what,' he said. 'This evil piece of shit – some kind of fucking poetry-writer. First he defiles and despoils her using mental tricks. Then he washes her brain. Like the chinks used to do with POWs? Remember *Manchurian Candidate*? Turn them against everything they hold dear. Poor little Cloe, her folks can barely sleep for worry. Lucky for them, there's remedies in this world, a few people left who care about making a difference . . .'

'With Frank Sinatra? And Angela Lansbury as that scary mom?'

'It's a great flick, but this ain't about that.' Shaking his head, lips downturned in disgust, he returned the photo to his pocket and said, 'It's about an innocent little girl got turned into a whore. He's selling her like chattel out there. All to bankroll his lazy, poem-scribbling lifestyle. Remember Harvey Keitel as that evil pimp pimping out little Jodie Foster in her hot pants? Remember that shit?'

'*Taxi Driver*.'

'And she still loved him. Incredible.' He pounded his heavy fist six or seven times on the dashboard. 'That worthless waste of flesh! That motherfucker! She's someone's kid, you know.'

He let out a few breaths, and it looked like he was struggling to say more. 'My ticker holds out through this, I'll be—' Then his face turned the color of ashes and he was leaning out the door and retching, spitting phlegm and puke and beer. Panting, he closed the door and slumped in his seat. 'I was saying, I hold out through it, I'll be a blessed man.'

Running his forearm over his beard, wiping spittle away, he

turned slowly to face me and added weakly, 'Benny, what would you say if – What if I said—'

'What?'

'What if I told you I ain't genuinely done this shit before?'

Silence hanging between us in the van, Benny scouring his brain for a way to break it, trying to fit his mouth around the right words, and instead just pretending not to hear, saying the safe thing, saying, 'What?'

'What if I told you I ain't done this before? Never genuinely even did someone?'

'Well, I guess—'

'You'd probably call me a goddamn liar, wouldn't you? And I couldn't blame you. Take one look at Big Bad Gus, anybody'd call him a liar for saying that. But what if he said, "I never really did a *good* thing in my life. A noble kind of thing." You'd believe that one no trouble at all, wouldn't you?'

His eyes were full of uncertainty and fear and he wanted to tell me something.

'People are a mixed bag,' I said, but I didn't know if I was having the same conversation he was; we were on different drugs.

'Maybe the Almighty or the Great Spirit or whoever's in charge don't give up on His fuckups like I thought,' he said. I thought I saw moisture fogging up the lenses of his slanted glasses. 'Maybe not totally. Because then why would He give 'em one last thing to do? Why would He give 'em an important mission, if they were lost to Him forever?'

He wanted something from me, I didn't know what, his look imploring me for some kind of words. Finally he muttered, 'Real reason I brought you along, brother? 'Cause you're better than Jack Daniels himself for giving me balls. I don't mean just when you're acting like a pussy, either. And that's the first and *last* time I suck your dick . . .'

Clomping into the back of his van, rummaging among the junk aisles, he emerged moments later changed, his body topped by the bright crimson head and tall cruel ears of an Egyptian jackal-god. In one hand he extended an awful white face, with amoeba-shaped perforations in its eyes and mouth. A Greek stage mask.

'Put it on,' Gus said. 'We're gonna need to fit in.'

I fixed it over my face and tightened the straps behind my skull. Benjamin Bunt (a name I already only vaguely recognized: strange characters on someone's birth certificate, a marriage license, a rap sheet) vanished . . .

Now bodies were jostling us, Gus swaggering half-drunk, his thick inky arms swinging beside me, his body flinching at the screeeeeBLOOMBLOOMscreeee of electric guitars being tortured on a stage somewhere close . . . Air impregnated by smells of burning petrol and sulfur and cordite . . . Liquidy carnival faces surging past us on either side: malignant insects, demonic Rumsfelds and Cheneys and George W. Bushes, wormheads with pulsing gashes in place of mouths, corpse-white swinethings like creatures out of Grimms' Fairy Tales ambling around with sunscreen tubes and Evian bottles . . . Horror-house apparitions: smiling devil clowns stalking the desert on stilts (*were they born that way*?) . . . painted bodies rolling around in gigantic hamster wheels and flinging themselves into the sky off trampolines . . . Sand thick in my throat . . . Mobs blowtorching television sets . . . Revelers bouncing around bare-assed, guys with naked corporate-cubicle guts and heavy swivel-chair asses and flabby hippie chicks flailing their limbs in dance like mustard-gas victims, their arms above their heads flaunting (celebrating!) run-amok armpit thatches, and their nether triangles fuzzing up bellies and snaking mosslike down the insides of legs, pubic hell-thickets fit for ticks and brambles, malevolent mushrooms, colonies of trolls . . . A sign that said 'LEARN TO AUTO-FELLATE WITH THE WEST COAST'S PREMIER YOGA MASTER DEEPAK PRAHUPADA! BLOW YOURSELF THE PRAHUPADA WAY!™' . . . Groans belting from a medical tent where people were getting their feet bandaged, blistered by hours of hot sand and too blitzed to know it . . . A troupe of performance artists lacing up their sneakers for a re-enactment of the Heaven's Gate suicides . . . Wheeling by on castors, the glass-encased corpse of Sixties poet Andy Gibberstein, author of the famous 'YAWP!', dead ten years but looking spry, rebellious, wild-bearded, a jumbo cell phone planted in his taxidermied hands, a digital sign flashing above his waxy head: 'I Yawp!™ for CommTekk's Free Weekend Minutes Anywhere in the Continental United States! Because It's All About Freedom™' . . .

My heart whacked thwam! thwam! thwam! against my chest and I could hear the roar of freighter-crushing sea fathoms in my skull and my breath short and hot and foul in my mask, my face melting like candle wax down into my neck, and there came the sound of someone muttering prayers: 'Forgive me, Father . . . Deliver us not into temptation . . . Though I walk in the valley of the shadow of death I will fear no evil . . . Fear no evil . . . Fear no evil . . .' Whether it was my voice or Gus's, I couldn't be sure . . .

Something went KAPLOOOOM! nearby and Gus staggered back a step or two, and I could see the gray eyes behind his mask move with fear and I could hear his breathing getting shorter and tighter, going into prison-riot mode, incoming-flack mode . . . 'Too much like The Shit,' he muttered, advancing with his hand on the lump of the .38 in his waistband . . .

Howls and cheers erupted from a crowd nearby. In a dirt pit, two remote-control gladiator droids with Bill Gates heads were battering each other into fragments.

Then someone was telling Gus, 'Gecko's right in there,' and pointing us to a 12-foot-tall geodesic dome made of PVC pipe and covered with sheets of Desert Storm-style camouflage tarp. We ducked inside and saw him. He looked like some kind of unhinged trailer-park Jesus or acid-rock prophet – stringy long hair, greasy goatee, soiled clothes, high sharp cheekbones. But it was clear he wore the look to conceal how pretty he was. Sensitive globular eyes, long feminine eyelashes, arrogant bee-stung lips: shaved and scrubbed, you could imagine a fresh-pubed *Teen Beat* coverboy spattered with kisses, a boy-band bad boy. It took me a few minutes to recognize him, from that afternoon in Zapata! Zapata! when something about his mixture of insolence and entitlement and the way he treated the girl he was with had driven me to sabotage his *mole con pollo*. Right now he slouched contemptuously in a wheelchair, a blanket across his lap. Shriveled flippery legs stuck out from under it. His chest was scrawny, his arms long and bony. On his T-shirt President Bush stared knot-browed under the words 'THE GREATEST MIND OF OUR TIME.'

'Some people have called this next one an indictment of the capitalist packaging of the godhead,' said the gimp. His voice – high, thin, almost girlish – supplied another motive for the roughed-up look. 'Some have called it a Marxist take on religion. I consider it a full-frontal assault on the hypocrisies of our time. If it doesn't offend every asshole in this tent, be sure to tell the Gecko, and he guarantees the next one will . . .'

He flashed a fuck-you smile/sneer, bringing narcotized worship-noises from the red-eyed, smoke-fogged audience clustered around him – 10 or 15 half-naked dudes and chicks slumped on their sides or ranged Indian-style with monster bongs, nasty blunts, carved peace pipes, syringes, junk-works – Gus and I trying to keep low, willing ourselves into invisibility.

'Anyway, I think you motherfuckers'll find it pretty subversive,' said the gimp, reading from the PowerBook in his lap:

Freebase Jesus, cook him up in a spoon
Pack Mohammed in a bong, pain dies soon
Put Buddha in a blunt and Vishnu in a pill
Like Yahweh on a mirror, snort Him through a bill

'First taste's on me,' says the man with the vial
Medicine to keep the pain away awhile
Pack Confucius in your pipe, fill it to the brim
Put Jesus in a needle and find a vein for Him . . .

'That's the bomb!' the crowd cried, and 'Awesome!' Gecko the Gimp's face getting redder and angrier as the waves of audience love washed over him.

'What distinguishes a real poet from the rest,' he piped in his high voice, 'is he looks right into the abyss! The rest of you can't do it! You aren't willing to do it! You flinch!'

Applause.

'You comfort yourself with stupid illusions! You brainless lemmings!'

Wild applause.

'I loathe you! I despise you for worshipping me! I'm no one! I'm against mediocrity in all forms! I do not crave the adulation of apes! My work is worthless! And you're worthless for tolerating it!'

Ecstatic applause.

Gus's elbow rammed my ribcage. He pointed to a waifish, sunburned blonde girl propped on her elbow a few feet away in a hemp flower skirt, one hip in the air, smoking an elephantine blunt. Here she was. Same heavy-lidded eyes as before, but everything else different, everything else corrupted, just a few years separated from the girl in the photo, but aged as if by decades; she was not even the heartbreaking heroin-ad Gwen Stacy I'd seen weeks back, but something sadder and less substantial, like a photograph bleaching toward oblivion.

'Look at the whore he made her,' Gus said angrily. 'Stay cool. We have to get his guard down.'

The crowd thinned, people eddying in and out of his geodesic tent in their fantastic masks. Gus and I lingered, pretending to belong, my brain now and then focusing enough to remember why I was here and to ask what I should do. Was there a chance – a slim chance – police had picked up our trail and followed us here? Were they waiting right outside for some signal, some code word they'd given me that I couldn't remember? Was the chameleonic Munoz already in the tent with us hiding behind one of the masks, the bull or demon bear or lunatic clown or Tonto the Indian?

'This used to be a really cool party,' Gecko the Gimp was telling Gus. 'Five, six years ago? No cash allowed here, all barter-system. Radical concept. You packed your own food and traded with everyone else and survived the weekend that way.'

'So what happened?' said Gus, sucking a blunt through the slat of his mask.

'Bad sushi, *E. coli* outbreaks,' said Gecko, shrugging. 'I mean, look, so you shouldn't swap snacks with the feces fetishists. That's a given. That was the problem. But to bring in vendors and sell a bottle of water for eight bucks? There used to be a *point* to this festival.'

'What was the point?' I said, realizing suddenly that my face was naked, my hot mask somehow vanished, my hand going to my face to ensure it was still there, unmelted.

'Just this great big fuck-you, anti-establishment howl, man,' said Gecko. 'It's all just staged rage now. I'm here strictly ironically, and under protest. They're selling this pathetic simulation of experience out there, so shitheads can come and pretend to have an experience and put nothing on the line, and it's all vapor, man, the vanilla Disneyland of the soul. No one believes it anymore, no one goes home changed! It's got as much to do with rebellion as the House of Blues does with blues, or the Hard Rock Café does with rock 'n' roll, or Sea World does with the fucking sea. It's theme-park reality, man. I hate these people, everything they represent. They come for the weekend and get wasted and go back to their corporate climbing and their murder of salmon populations, the economic butt-fucking of indigenous Eskimo populations, the great savage ass-rape of globalization, while Third World populations die in sweatshops so that overpaid American athletes can sell sneakers to ghetto kids who grease each other on the playgrounds, priests diddling choirboys, the hypocrisies! I mean, the fucking hypocrisies!'

'I'm sympathetic to your being a gimp,' said Gus. 'I had brothers in The Shit who lost limbs. Landmines, screaming amputees, bone, blood – I've been there. I mean, they weren't born gimpy, like you, they got that way in Nam. I'm only saying the principle's the same – no legs. You know that if a man's standing between you and a mine when it goes off, his atomized flesh and bone will embed itself in you? Major cause of infection.'

Gecko wore a look of fascinated admiration. 'That's bad-*ass*,' he said. 'That's what I'm talking about. You've really lived life. I love your tats, man. You've done time?'

'Sure, these are my degrees,' Gus said, pointing to a forearm crawling with biker bitches and Norse heroes. 'San Quentin, class of '78, *summa cum laude*. I got a Masters in sarcasm and criticism, brother. You can call me Iceman.'

'I hope I get to do time someday,' said Gecko, swigging bottled water. 'I mean, not a lot, not enough to be raped, just enough for a serious taste of it, you know? Write the prison memoir. Raw incarceration poetry. Same as war. I'd go in a second. Not long enough to get my ass shot up, lose my nuts, fight for some stupid shit the fat old men dictate I should kill and die for. Just to bear witness, you know?'

'I don't think they take the handicapped,' I said.

'My deformity mirrors what's inside me,' said Gecko. 'I know what you're thinking – this guy's grotesque. You're thinking, "Someone shoulda slammed that thing against a wall or left it on a mountain when it was born." I can face the truth about myself. I'm an abomination. Go ahead, say it. Say it!'

'Abomifuckingnation,' I said.

'I'm like that monster in *The Fantastic Four*,' said Gecko. 'The Human Thing? A great big rocky orange dude who got all fucked up falling into a nuclear dump. Now he's just a walking rock, a total misfit. It's a brilliant metaphor for being outside the mainstream, for a poet's alienation, a poet's basic *stance* on things . . .'

'The Thing,' I said.

'And this lumpy guy, he just wants to be like everyone else,' said Gecko. 'Except it's his very freakishness that gives him superpowers. See? His very deformity that leads people to worship him. What'd you say?'

'His name's the Thing, not the Human Thing,' I said. 'And it was space rays that made him that way. Got him on a rocket flight.'

Muscles twitched in Gecko's face. His eyes went about 100 degrees colder, fixing on me. 'That doesn't change what I'm saying one iota, does it?' he said. 'I'm talking about a metaphor. You know what that is? Maybe you've got some observations about the creative process, *from having lived it*, that you can enlighten us with? The fucking cauldron, the fucking demons?'

I didn't know what he was talking about, so I didn't say anything, and I could tell Gus wanted me to shut up anyway, let him do the work. 'My friend here,' Gus said, 'he's got a mouth. Sometimes it needs a smack.'

'Whatever,' said Gecko. 'He's with you, so I respect him.'

'See these?' said Gus, touching one of the ears on his necklace. 'This is what the fat old war pigs reduced me to doing.'

'I heard about that,' said Gecko. 'I mean, total dehumanization. *Total*.'

'That's right. You ever wondered what a human body smells like when it burns?'

'It is horrific?' said Gecko, leaning forward.

'I haven't had a good night's sleep since '69,' said Gus. 'We were on long-range patrol. Monsoon season. VC everywhere . . .'

Gus's voice rose and fell, grunting, bellowing war stories, getting them jumbled, railing on until abruptly he stopped, as if realizing why he was here.

An awkward silence set in until Gecko said, 'Have I introduced you to Cloe?' He nodded toward the girl. 'She's my muse. My queen. My life force. She makes it all possible.'

She wore no expression. She was trading bong hits with a skinny, incredibly handsome cocoa-colored dude.

'This is Marvin, her latest friend,' said Gecko. 'They delight in humiliating me with the spectacle of their passion.'

'He has to put himself into a totally impossible state to write anything,' the girl said in my direction. 'Mostly that means making himself sick with jealousy. No puke, no poems.'

'Well, that's my intensity,' boasted Gecko. 'You have to understand the creative process. No poems ever came out of a soul like a placid lake. I need the churning, I need the turmoil. Suffering is art's crucible.'

Suck up, Benny – here's your chance. 'Like Caruso on *NYPD Blue*,' I said. 'A poet of the screen. Everyone on the set hated him. Why? He was too intense for them. And now? Season One is legendary.'

Gecko ignored me and said, 'Why do you think poets have the shortest life expectancy of any creative type? Studies show: sixty-two years average. Shorter than novelists, way shorter than writers of *non*-fiction.' He said this last word with the disgust of a Presbyterian minister saying 'cunnilingus.'

'Consult the stats, man: I'm doomed. Even though any poet who makes it to sixty is a dead relic anyway, in my eyes.' He added: 'I have no respect for that.'

'You should take your medication, Matt,' the girl told Gecko.

'I hate it. I can't feel anything. It's like I disappear when I'm on it.'

'You're gonna disappear if you're not on it.'

'I need to feel something, even if it fucks me up. As long as it's not numbness. Like the android Arnold Schwarzenegger played in *Blade Runner*. Where he sticks the railroad spike in his hand just so he can feel alive, feel what it is to be human?'

'It wasn't Arnold,' I said. 'It was Rutger Hauer. Arnold was in *The Terminator*. Which was stolen from *The Outer Limits*.'

Gecko sneered in my direction, basilisk-cold, and said, 'Who is this guy?'

'He should shut his trap is who he is,' said Gus. 'Just someone I picked up. A tag-along.'

'I understand,' said Gecko, nodding slowly. 'Sure. Guys like us, Iceman – we're magnets, aren't we? Magne*tized*. Voyeurs, hangers-on – helpless before our pull. They want to be one with us. They want us to save them. People born without it, they like to be close to those who possess it. "It," you know? Whatever "It" *is*. But in the end, if we let them, they'll suck the life out of us. Because they're psychic vampires. Like that toady of yours, hanging around like shit on your shoes. I need to piss.'

Gecko lifted himself off his wheelchair, unfolding a pair of long, perfectly workable legs and strolling out of the tent. The shrivelly rubber legs still dangled from the empty wheelchair. When he returned, I said, 'You're just a dress-up freak. You're not even a bona fide gimp!'

'Right about now,' added Gus, 'I have to admit I'm feeling kind of screwed and betrayed. After pouring out my guts and troubles.'

'I'm a card-carrying misfit,' said Gecko. 'Just because I was born with limbs doesn't mean I'm any less an outsider. Don't judge me by a genetic accident. Gecko's my doppelgänger. He's everything I am on the inside. A perpetually humiliated, debased character. Condemned to watch helplessly as the woman he loves betrays him, over and over . . .'

The girl threw a quick sideways glance at the handsome cocoa dude, then stared fixedly at the ground. She sat with her arms crossed, as if protecting herself from a chill wind no one else could feel. I thought I heard her tell Gecko, 'Please,' under her breath. 'I love you. Please . . .' Begging.

I noticed the tent had emptied, save for the Gecko, his girl, the cocoa dude, Gus and myself.

'In moments of clarity,' said Gecko, pulling the tent's canvas flap shut, 'I realize that I'm not really in love with her. Being an artist, I'm in love with a blank slate onto which I've projected my fantasies. The beloved becomes a kind of canvas on which one works. The artist is forever using his own soul as a laboratory, combining combustible elements. If you've ever studied the artistic temperament, you'll recognize the phenomenon. The appetite for self-delusion is endless.'

After a while the girl closed her eyes and let the cocoa dude climb on top of her. All through it she barely moved. Under her breath I could hear her singing the Beatles song about the octopus who makes his garden under the sea. Tears streamed down Gecko's face as he watched and typed furiously on his PowerBook.

CHAPTER 24

Night cloaked the desert now and the wind outside was picking up and screeching like a wounded animal over the sands and pounding the sides of the tent, ruffling the canvas thwap-thwap-thwap, thwap-thwap-thwap. Through a little air-vent in the tent needle-bursts of sand blew in. I could hear row after row of freaks trooping by outside, beginning to gather at the Head for the coming Burn . . .

Inside, the tent was thick with smoke from a big tiki-torch Gecko had lit, and his face flickered yellow and anguished in the flame. He was back in his wheelchair, in his gimp-outfit, bent over his PowerBook, oblivious to Gus and me, typing maniacally and occasionally swigging from his water bottle while those rubber limbs dangled in front of him. Now and then his brow knotted violently and he muttered a string of curses; other times he whimpered, shuddered, and shook his head over the screen . . .

'I told Marvin I'd meet him for the Burn,' said the girl, wrapping herself in a blanket against the chill. 'It's in five. Are you coming?'

'Pathetic,' said Gecko without looking up.

'You're protesting the Burn too?'

'Go join the lemmings, you lemming! Go ahead! You were always one of them, anyway! Just a common backstabbing slut lemming!'

The girl ducked through the flap and disappeared, leaving us alone with Gecko, the chill deepening in my bones minute by minute and the smoke dribbling up black from the tiki-torch, stinging my lungs, making everything around me hazy, Gecko's face writhing slowly in the shadows, and back there in the corner of the tent, big, unmoving, breathing hard, Mad Dog Miller in his mask waiting for his bone . . .

In the desert legions of voices were rising and falling, begging for fire, the Burn imminent, Gus probing for his piece beneath the great swell of his belly, Gecko looking up finally and in a voice fearful but resigned said, 'They sent you, didn't they?'

'Burn the Head! Burn the Head! Burn the Head!' cried the freaks outside.

Suddenly I felt the weight of the Smith & Wesson in my hand. Gus's mask was off and his big face was wretched with failed nerve. His eyes pleaded with me, ashamed. They said: *Now you know why I brought you. Because I was afraid I couldn't.*

I stared stupidly at the gun sticking out of my fist for what might have been a second or an hour. From behind his PowerBook, Gecko's puffed, watery face glared at me with sudden respect, with terror, and the new dynamic was not completely unsatisfying. Then he flung himself at me head-first. Light exploded behind my eyes, and I was on my back, and the gun was out of my hand, and I felt his fingers scrabbling for my eyeballs as we thrashed. We tumbled into Gus's shins and the big man's whole brick-avalanche mass crashed down on top of us, pinning us both. Then there was a chaos of limbs, teeth and nails and elbows, all of us thrashing – Gus face-down trying to right himself, Gecko screaming, Benny screaming, freaks outside screaming, the wind leaving me, a terrific pain blasting up from below, someone's knee in my groin, all of us tangled and trying to extricate ourselves. Then, somehow, Gus's leg was splayed over Gecko's chest, the convict presenting the poet with the bowie knife in his boot. Gecko was not about to ignore such a gift; he unsheathed it and started hacking the air wildly; and as Gus rose to one knee, the blade slashed across his eyes.

'BURN BURN BURN! BURN BURN BURN!'

Gus struggled howling to his feet, staggered into the tent wall and brought down a section of the roof. He careened about the tent, hands clapped over his face, fat fingers glistening with blood like black ink, his mouth open in a roar dwarfed by the din.

'BURN BURN BURN! BURNBURNBURNBURNBURN—'

Gus caught fire then; the torch-flame must have touched his shirt – it started with one small tongue jumping from his back, and then a moment later it had multiplied and his whole body was crawling with flame, his hair, his hands, his beard, the old sauce-head could have been sweating kerosene for as fast as he went up, and he crashed blindly through the tent flap into the desert.

Through the smoke Gecko lunged at me knife-first and I scrambled for the gun, which I had forgotten was supposed to be useless. Then it was in my hand and I squeezed it and felt the kick shudder through my arm. Gecko dropped to his hands and knees. I could see liquid dripping from his mid-section. He craned his head to look at me, his lip petulant. He crawled across the floor, groping with absurd tenacity not for the dropped knife but for his water bottle, as if a good draught would save him, dissolve the burning lead in his abdomen, erase the world's hypocrisies and diddling priests and vanilla-soul posers, fix everything.

'BURN BURN BURN! BURN BURN BURN! BURN BURN BURN!'

From the desert there came a tremendous roar of joy.

I ran through the ghost town of empty tents and abandoned slagheaps smoldering in the sand, while behind me the Head crackled and splintered and all the freaks bellowed ecstatically, and I thought I heard a strain of horror – hysterical horror – rising and falling among the other screams.

Then I was bumping over the desert in the Dodge, and there

was blood on the driver's side window where I smashed it with a rock in my fist, blood all over my shirt, blood on the seat beside me, except it was not mine, most of this blood was not mine, and all the way out of the desert I watched the tower of flame burning and diminishing in the rearview. The gun was gone; I must have dropped it. *Blank rounds*, Munoz had said. *Safe as a squirtgun. No one gets hurt*. But there had been a mistake somewhere, a definite fuck-up somewhere, because a real round had gone into Gecko's real gut and splattered real blood. Had the gun Gus handed me been the one I'd handed him? Had Gus brought a real one, one he'd had all along? *Blank rounds, Benny, safe as a squirtgun . . .*

On a highway, going somewhere, black desert flying past, and there must have been an ocean nearby, because after a while all I heard was the sound of water rising and crashing in my ears – *thoom thoomthoom thoomthoom thoom*.

I fled the desert, driving all night. As the sun came up I watched the road bulging through mile after mile of terrifyingly serene, sun-dappled grids of apples and grapes and artichokes, and I kept all the windows open to dispel the scent of my friend, which seemed to saturate the van – his boozy, smoky, sweaty-big-man's stink living on in the upholstery and the dash, and the dead dog's fart-foul stench living on too, two ghosts and their murderer trapped on a pirate ship, and the gibbering in my head unceasing:

Why didn't you save yourself? Why didn't you stop, drop and roll, you sonofabitch?

Because you sensed an opportunity, that's why. An unexpected little gift from the universe, a chance to sear yourself like a scar into all those skulls. A little piece of you living on in 12,000 nightmares . . .

No: ridiculous . . . you didn't want to die . . .

I kept looking in the rearview mirror and it was a long time before I became conscious of what was drawing my attention. There: Gus's waist-high freezer, half concealed behind the van's junk.

The freezer he slept beside, there in his room at the bar.

Which he'd been carrying with him the day he arrived.

Which he always kept locked.

I had to pull over to catch my breath.

I dragged the freezer into the desert and fished a mallet from the van and busted open the padlock with three square blows. I smoked three or four cigarettes, standing there, looking at the closed lid. After a while I opened it.

The guy inside was squeezing his knees up against his chest, like an Inca sunk into a mountainside grave. He was bald and missing his eyebrows and sunken-cheeked, but he looked peaceful. The tattoo on his arm said '173rd.'

CHAPTER 25

In the movies a dying man holds up his finger and says, 'Wait, Bonehand – stand down a minute,' and death obeys, allowing the nearly departed to explicate the burning mysteries that surround his life.

A man props himself on his elbow and generously clears it all up, even as the last of his blood soaks into the dirt; he can always find a few minutes for his listeners; death doesn't begrudge him that much.

In real life, the dead decamp with their secrets. People are greedy that way. They don't want to clear anything up, not even their real names.

He called himself Gus, but his name wasn't Gus. It wasn't Evel Sanders, Quentin W. Cash, or Dale Delacroix, either. And it certainly wasn't the Iceman. The ink on his arm gave as accurate a tag as any: Hardluck Bastard. But Gerry Finkel was anyone's best guess at his real name.

How Gerry Finkel, the drifter, came to meet the Vietnam vet, Gus Miller – and how he came to steal his name – are problems I've run through my mind a thousand times.

All I had were a handful of clues, retrieved from the intestines of the van, arrayed before me on the coverlet of a Motel Six mattress somewhere in California's Central Valley.

A medical examiner can determine a lot, studying the digestive tract of the dead: what he ate, when he ate. A poor man in a fairy tale slits a fish-belly to find an Arabian ruby. So what did I find in the Dodge's teeming bowels? What did it gobble, on its travels? What gems did those musty guts yield?

A peace button.

A dogpiss-yellow section of the *Arizona Republic*, dated two summers back, which contained an ad circled by red pen in the classifieds: *Vietnam Vets Support Group 6 p.m. – All Welcome*.

A matchbook from a Phoenix bar called the Stag.

A snapshot of a gaunt, sick-looking man sitting on a couch, his eyes dead, his smile weak, his face exactly that of the man in the freezer.

A driver's license bearing the same man's face, identifying him as Gustavo Emmett Miller of Fischbach Court in Phoenix.

A dog collar that read 'Jimmy Jingles.'

A multiple-choice questionnaire, scribbled on a cafeteria napkin, detailing a life gone amuck.

All these objects trying to link themselves together, trying to magnetize, trying to tell me a story.

If I closed my eyes and concentrated I could see my friend taking shape, a big, shaggy figure in a cammie jacket lumbering down the streets of downtown Phoenix with a rucksack slung over his shoulder. It's a mean, sprawling, furnace-hot town, the latest of 20 or 30 cities he's drifted through in the last decade, working his way steadily from the eastern states to the West Coast.

Only recently has Finkel become aware of his trajectory; his unconscious has been steering him inexorably west for years, one hitched ride and odd job and jail stint after another. He remembers the salt smell of the Pacific, the ocean he grew up alongside, and finds himself aching to smell it again. Sometimes he thinks of the ocean as Hope; other times he's certain it will be the place he snuffs himself. He's in no hurry to get there – knows, in fact, that he's afraid to arrive. Because what if the ocean holds no magic at all? What if he finds himself standing before all that cold beautiful blue, aware that nothing's changed, that he's still trapped in a bloated body with a bum ticker, a poisoned liver, and a tired, sick soul? What if Hope's just a lie he keeps telling himself? No choice left, then. Head into the surf and keep walking.

Finkel stops now in front of a window in a strip mall. A small stucco church. Under his armpit there's a folded newspaper with the Nam Support Group ad. It's the ad he looks for first in every new town. Instant friendship. Understanding souls ready to extend a few bucks, a job, a hot shower, a couch. And of course there's always an audience: love in the form of a listener's rapt attention – sometimes, strangely, the only love that feels pure and uncompromised, even as he wins it with extravagant and multilayered lies. Will this be the city where the universe gives him a sign? Will this be the place where he learns who he's supposed to be?

I see his blocky scum-nailed hand with its riot of faded tats, pushing open the door and leaving an imprint of oily sweat. I follow his boots as he heads inside, the wooden stairs creaking under his Army-surplus shitkickers as 300 pounds of guts and muscle descend to the basement meeting room, his belly preceding him like a heavyweight's medicine ball. Men with yellowed fingers are already beginning to fill the circle of foldout chairs, smoking and cradling Styrofoam coffee cups. The same crowd he's seen in a hundred such basements. Weathered smoke-leached skin, rutted faces, rheumy eyes, bandanas, the stench of underpasses and pay-by-the-hour motels. There's a tattoo on a stringy arm that says 'From Crank to Christ.' The kind of men he's known all his life: chasers of Jesus H., blow and ludes and demon weed, E and Big H and Special K, and anything else named in the Periodic Table of Human Hungers.

Scanning their faces, Finkel realizes with a surge of outrage that at least half of them are fakes. Never saw The Shit. Probably never spent a day in the armed forces. His jaw tightens with contempt; bile rises in his throat. The gall! He's looking at a bunch of broke-dicks who've botched their lives by one of the

10,000 available methods, who come for the comfort of a shared fiction, for absolution. Yeah, if the government's dirty war had fucked their lives, put all those demons in their heads, maybe they weren't entirely to blame. Maybe it wasn't their fault that they slept on a slab of concrete and spent their days picking lice from each other's scalps. *You are beneath contempt*, he thinks. Then he remembers that he's a fake too. Been at it so long he sometimes forgets. His cheeks are suddenly hot with shame. He swallows, trying to put it out of his mind.

It isn't that Gerry Finkel lacked the stones; it isn't as if he didn't try to get to Southeast Asia. In this, at least, he feels superior to the other impostors. In his teens, watching broadcasts of American soldiers carried out of the jungle in body bags, he thought, 'That's a fine death.' While he envied their sacrifice, he also possessed the secret conviction that the soldiers might have survived had they been more ruthless, had they refused to allow the hippies back home to sap their mojo. In those days he could close his eyes and imagine the hot weight of heavy artillery vibrating in his hands: a gorgeous snap-snap-snap-snap-snap of rounds slashing through gook foliage. Gunning down hundreds of gooks, strafing them from the air, smoking them out of their rat-tunnels, striding between their bayoneted corpses, finishing off the ones that twitched. Sometimes it was the hippies streaming over the border to Canada that he imagined himself strafing: Didn't they give a shit about Duty? Didn't they understand World Freedom was at stake? He understood. Once he got to the jungle, to The Shit, he'd be a model of dedication and ruthlessness. The best killer the US government ever saw. They'd put medals on his chest, maybe put his picture in a book; he'd have friends and admirers. He was 18. He dreamed of having the thousand-yard stare before his twentieth birthday.

And then his life vaporized before him. What had been the recruiter's name? Scandini? Monterastelli? Something Italian. He remembers standing on a busy Redondo Beach street in the hazy daylight, bodies passing in a blur while he stared in his humiliated stupor at a business card imprinted with the recruiter's name and tried to make sense of the words the man had just told him. *A man with a bum ticker is a liability out there.* Standing outside the recruiting station in the bad-ass knee-length black leather jacket he wore in those days, feeling suddenly it was a ridiculous jacket, a badge of idiotic pretension, he studied that card as if it were a death warrant for a crime he didn't know he'd committed: exiled, excommunicated, cast into outer darkness, stripped of his country's love and of his ability to serve it with the best of his love. Murdered – yes! – murdered before he even became a man. Had a bitter life of bungled criminality been avoidable after that?

Yes, if Finkel's life is a botch in every particular, and he knows it is, he suspects his failures might have unfolded from that moment in the recruiter's office. Of course, he considers further, if a man goes looking for candidates to explain his crippled soul, who lacks the luxury of multiple-choice? In moments of self-scrutiny, he sometimes reaches for the nearest napkin and lays out the possibilities:

A. Genetic predispositions to depression/mood-altering chemicals
B. Anger management/impulse control issues
C. Bum ticker
D. Fear of the Pussy
E. Missing The Shit
F. All of the above

He circles F, then crumples the napkin and stuffs it in his jeans.

Now Finkel sits in a church basement among other ragged men, sipping black coffee and listening as they ramble, some of them barely coherent, of napalm, sonofabitch sergeants, fragged friends, loneliness, drug habits, divorce, adjusting to The World, wretched mistreatment by the VA.

Finkel introduces himself, says he's passing through. He speaks slowly at first, in a voice he knows is barely audible. Tells how he always wanted to be a soldier. Got to the jungle full of piss and vinegar, drunk on John Wayne. (Murmurs of assent around the circle.) Tells how he was ambushed on long-range recon. His best friend blown up beside him . . . crazy-brave Arkansas kid named Theodore Piper. As his story mounts toward its climax, he is orating with the full range of his lungs, tears are streaming down his cheeks, and he's staring at the big hands cupped in front of him, bellowing, 'Teddy's brains! His fucking brains, man! Teddy's fucking brains!' Several of the other men are weeping too. It's a command performance. Quietly he sits back in his chair, shaking off the memories, feeling their love, their reverence, their pity for him and for themselves. Someone gives him a handkerchief and he says, 'Thank you, brother. Thank you, man.'

Finkel has barely registered the presence of the emaciated man who sits quietly across from him, his face shadowed by a baseball cap. Wan and pallid, he has a long, hard-looking, stubbled face, hooded eyes, broken Roman nose. On the lapel of his flannel shirt is a tiny peace sign.

The man has an air of great gentleness about him, but his eyes are dead.

'I'm Gus, but most of you already know me,' he says in a soft voice when his turn comes to speak. 'I just wanted to tell you all how much this group has meant to me. My time's almost up. I dunno if I'll be back next week. If I'm not, I just want to say to you all: Be good to one another. Love each other, alright?'

The man is different from the others. The real McCoy. Finkel notices it now. Such men draw him magnetically.

'Big C, huh?' Finkel asks him after the meeting as the men file toward the street.

Miller lifts his cap to disclose the bare lumps of his scalp.

'Being bald's part of the bitch of it,' he says, smiling dimly. 'Especially for an old cocksman who was proud of his mane. Here's what it used to be.'

He lets his wallet fall open on his skeletal palm. His driver's license photo shows the same man – same hard-looking face, hooded eyes, long jaw, broken nose – only considerably younger and heavier, with thick luxuriant hair. Finkel catches the writing on the license:

MILLER, GUSTAVO EMMETT
139 E. Fischbach Court
Phoenix, AZ
Date of Birth July 1, 1946

Finkel blinks at it. They have the same birthday. They both came into the world on the day the bomb fell on Bikini Atoll. He takes this as a sign. He doesn't know what kind of sign, not yet, but he doesn't believe such things are just coincidences. Hadn't he been praying for a message, a clue, an oracle – something? Something to tell him whether to put a bullet in his head, at long last, or wait a while longer? So he asks the vet where he was born, and it turns out they came into the world in the same Venice, California hospital. They might have shared the same nursery, laid side-by-side in it. Now they're both intrigued. They discover further linkages. It turns out their families had lived just a couple of miles apart in Venice; turns out that Finkel's mom, a janitor, had serviced the bowling alley that Miller's dad had run. Both men have vivid memories of roaming the bowling alley as boys; it's possible they even played together.

It's clear they must talk further. Finkel asks where in this hot, shitty city a man can get a drink. Miller says he knows a place. They climb into Miller's Dodge. An old gray German shepherd, head resting on its forepaws, looks up savagely from its place on the floor of the van, growling belatedly at the drifter. 'Jimmy Jingles is the world's sorriest guard-dog,' Miller says.

By the time they reach the Stag, the dog is lazily licking Finkel's hand in friendship. As the dog's tongue passes slowly and repeatedly over Finkel's palm, insistently tasting his sweat, his poisoned glands, his accretions of bad years, Finkel is surprised to realize he feels like weeping. He is aware of his immense loneliness. He would like a dog like this.

Miller leaves the windows of the van cracked and they head inside to drink. He explains that he's been a pacifist since he returned from the war. It was traceable to a specific incident. Some very bad shit. Wounded and alone in the Delta for three days and three nights, pieces of his buddies floating in the malarial puddles around him, he'd become convinced God had selected such a ghastly death for him as punishment for the killing he'd done in Nam. So he promised God that if He brought him home to The World, he wouldn't hurt another living thing, ever.

So he returned from that bloody shitstorm with the absolute determination never to inflict an ounce of injury. Got heavily into Zen. Became a vegetarian. Wandered a lot. Lived mostly on his VA checks and odd jobs. A couple of wives, a couple of divorces, no kids, no hard feelings. Then cancer got him. That was pretty much his life story.

He asks Finkel where he's keeping himself.

'Loose on the streets of the world, brother,' Finkel says. 'I'm on borrowed time, too. Headed back to California for a last look at the sea, I guess.' Finkel taps his chest three times with the tip of his beer and adds, 'They've been telling me for twenty years the pump could crap out any minute.'

Miller nods, and his weak hands lift his beer to his thin lips with difficulty. They talk most of the night, two doomed men on borrowed time, sharing their scarred souls – Finkel careful about what he says, careful not to expose himself as an impostor. Finkel wonders at the long odds against them meeting like this, having been born at the same place and time, only to ramble about the world on their respective ways, thousands of miles apart, suffering mightily, clawing for rare moments of grace, getting older, surviving, finally nudged together in that basement by forces that couldn't just be chance . . .

Miller puzzles over that and says, 'Well, maybe it's not so strange. We're born in the Vietnam Era, so we're gonna go to the jungle. And when we're back, we're gonna go to the vet centers. And if we're West Coast boys, well, probably we'll settle near home eventually, and there's only so many of those centers in the western states. So if you think of it like that, the odds of us meeting there go way up.'

Finkel sags a little inside, but he refuses to let go of his idea, his good and strange feeling that he is somehow situated on one of fate's axial lines. Miller tells how his wives left him because he wouldn't give them babies. 'Genes,' Miller says. 'I don't trust the ones they gave me. I watched my dad kill himself and my brother kill himself and my sister die of acute alcohol poisoning, and I don't feel so terrific myself, and I decided, "I'm not passing on my warped genes to an innocent kid." So both times I said, "I can't, baby, I'm sorry but I can't." So they skipped. Who could blame them? But I've been flying kind of solo since, and that sucks.'

It might be then, during that pause in the conversation, that Miller says it. Or it might be later, after a few more drinks. But sometime that night he comes out with it: 'I got friends in California. How about we head that way together?'

(Scratch that. It's Finkel's idea. Yes. He's an angler for advantages, after all. He needs a ride; he connives to get one. Maybe makes Miller think the idea is his own.)

They'll take the scenic route, hit some bars on the way there. That's the plan. There are a few great dives in LA and Orange County, Miller says, that he has a yen to revisit one last time. 'Funny to see if they're still telling stories about me,' Miller says.

'What kind of stories?'

'I was supposed to be some major bad-ass,' Miller says, and the recollection seems to amuse him. 'They called me Mad Dog Miller. I chewed eyes out of people's skulls and picked my teeth with their bones. Can you believe that?'

The thing of it was, he explains, he came back from Nam a changed man, a man who had thrown down his sword. He had the thousand-yard stare, sure; he was big and ripped and hard-looking; he swaggered, a walking provocation to the toughs. But he was a man who had lost the physical and mental ability to inflict harm on other human beings. It was more than the promise to God. The thought of doing violence made him physically ill. Even if he'd wanted to, he could not throw a punch. A man might swing on him, and he'd just take it. It was a dangerous character trait to bring into the dives he frequented. One of his favorite places, a bar in Costa Mesa run by a Nam buddy of his, Dorsey, was particularly rough. Numbers guys, shylocks, professional arm-breakers. Dudes pulling knives over nothing at all. You might get stabbed for taking the last peanut from the bowl or for blowing your smoke in the wrong direction. So to protect him, his pal Dorsey – good old Dorsey – started calling him Mad Dog Miller and let people guess where the name came from. Soon he was being spoken of as a berserker killer, a time bomb, practically a cannibal. The stories spread and multiplied and sprouted spontaneous appendages, the regulars vying to outdo each other with tales of violent madness they had personally witnessed Mad Dog perpetrate. Which allowed the man who wouldn't, *couldn't* throw a punch to drink without threat, while the legends around him grew.

(Finkel files this away. His brain does it automatically, with no immediate notion of how it might benefit him. A seeker after angles, advantages. Years of practice. A snitch can tell you: you never know how a dollop of random information might come in handy.)

That night, Miller opens the foldout sofa in his one-bedroom apartment and puts some sheets on it for Finkel. At the kitchen table they share a Stouffer's microwave pizza, a Coors 12-pack, and a fat Oregonian blunt. The place is filthy. Miller refuses to kill the bugs. Finkel watches as he corners a lizard and, rather than kill it, carefully carries it outside in his quivering cupped palms.

'You don't molest God's creatures,' responds Miller. 'Not when you're this close to meeting Him. Whatever you want from the fridge, take it. We'll hit the road tomorrow.' He disappears down the hall to his bedroom, the dog lurching alongside his master's slow, shuffling slippers.

Alone in the living room, the mattress sagging under his bulk, Finkel listens to Miller's tortured breathing from the next room and wonders what his being here signifies, what he's being called on to do. Then he's convinced meeting Miller is a pointless accident, signifying nothing except the universe's cold sense of humor, its way of disguising randomness in significant-seeming get-up, mockingly sending you what looked like a scrap of meaning, a Virgin Mary on a tortilla, and watching you scrabble hungrily for it, only to reinforce your utter adriftness, your worthless aloneness. Finkel decides: Fuck it, I'll just steal his van and get out. After chewing it over, he decides finally against it: mystic link or no, the man had taken him in, done him a kindness. And he could use the guy's company.

In his dreams that night, Finkel has a vision of them being swapped at birth, of doctors stealing his strong good heart and giving it to Miller, blessing him with it; of doctors snatching Miller's bum baby ticker and planting it in Finkel's own chest, cursing him with it. Yes, somehow Miller had stolen his life, took the body that was rightfully his and the war experiences that were rightfully his, consigning him to a shadow-life, a gelded, squishy half-life.

Sometime during the night, Finkel wakes to sense Miller near him in the dark.

As his eyes adjust, he perceives Miller sitting several feet away on a foldout chair, facing him, his head in his hands. From time to time he can hear Miller sobbing softly. Finkel doesn't know what to say. He sits up slowly and listens to the choked sobs, realizing that Miller has left his breathing apparatus in his room. Finally Miller says, 'Look, I'm pretty much a lone wolf, and . . . And I'm real close and . . . I got to thinking you were right about being sent here . . . And, look, I know it's unorthodox, but . . . maybe if . . . some human contact . . .'

Finkel hears himself roar, 'I dunno what you take me for, but my faggotry's strictly situational. Strictly in the joint, where it don't count.'

Miller lowers his head dejectedly, shaking it slowly from side to side, aware that he misjudged his guest. 'That ain't what I had in mind. I'm just askin' not to die alone, brother. I'm sorry.'

Miller starts to get up, to return to his room, when Finkel walks over and puts his hands on the man's sharp-boned shoulders. He carries him, all bones, no more than a hundred pounds, and sets him down on the mattress. He holds him all night, Miller sobbing and shuddering against Finkel's chest, babbling ancient nightmares of jungle and monsoons and pieces of friends bobbing on malarial puddles, before going quiet and still . . .

As he sleeps, Finkel dreams of Miller, an even skinnier and older Miller than the one in his arms, dreams of him wearing the long white hair and shimmering robes of Gandalf in *Lord of the Rings*, handing him an amulet of some kind, he can't tell what – a sword or necklace or power-wand or Army dog-tags or handgun or grenade . . .

Finkel wakes the next afternoon in a shaft of dismal sunlight, paralyzed by a vicious clawhammer hangover. He realizes dimly that the dog, Jimmy Jingles, has been frantically licking his cheek for some time; that he has been listening to the dog's whimpering in his sleep; that he perceived hours ago, half-consciously, that the man slouching against his chest wasn't breathing.

CHAPTER 26

In a Motel Six, somewhere in the Central Valley, I lay staring at the ceiling with my hands clapped over my ears, the world's oceans massing and hammering against the insides of my skull . . .

In the motel lobby I poured myself cold black coffee and tried to figure out what day it was, blinking against the awful sun daggering through the blinds. Mid-afternoon and my bones felt ancient, heavy with a thousand years of accumulated crypt dust. The boil-faced man behind the counter was saying, 'They're showing it again. Watch how this hippie buys it.'

He pointed to the television, where an earnest anchorman was saying, '. . . DEATH in pagan bohemia! . . . Warn viewers about the graphic and very disturbing nature of the footage you're about to see . . . ' Then a flaming figure ran through the desert amid a chorus of screams. '. . . What was supposed to be a desert celebration became a NIGHTMARE as one of their own was INCINERATED before their horror-struck eyes . . .' the anchor said. '. . . man not yet identified BURNED to death in what appears a FREAK accident . . .'

Back in the studio, a brunette co-anchor with a fashionable white skunk-streak in her hair was shaking her head slowly, as if stunned by the horrors the world contained: 'Dick, that is highly disturbing footage.'

'It *is*, Michelle,' said the anchorman. 'It *is* disturbing. And fire experts say it's a grim reminder of the danger of incendiary devices.'

'Well,' said skunk-streak, 'let's take one more look . . .'

'Seen this yet?' the boil-faced proprietor asked me. 'They been showin' it for three days. "Freak accident." Ask me, freak's the right word. I'd see 'em all torched.'

'In a possibly related incident,' the anchorman said, 'police are looking for whoever is responsible for the MURDER of a well-known festival performer . . .'

The coffee rushed up my throat and I choked it down, stumbling down the hall to my room. Behind me boil-face said, 'Hey, your forgot your jo—'

For hours I paced the tiny room, trying to figure, trying to plot my next move. I decided to call Munoz and picked up the phone. Then I decided he was the last one to call. I was in the center of some monstrous fuck-up. At least until I understood what was happening I should disappear – get on the road, go north, head to Canada. I got to the parking lot to find the van listing to the left, the front tire dead-flat. I rummaged through the van and found no spares. I went to the counterman and said, 'I need a tire. I'll pay you.'

He chewed jerky. 'Alright, sure,' he said. 'I got a buddy. Let me call him.' He dialed and said into the phone, 'I got a man here needs a new tire. How fast you figure you can get out here? He's in the lobby right now. Yeah – *right now*.' Then I saw the way he was looking at me and I saw sweat glistening on his boils, and I knew the police would be swarming the lobby in minutes.

They caught me about two miles down the road, on foot.

Which is everything that happened until now, Goins.

PART IV THE FIX

CHAPTER 27

On the day before my preliminary hearing, Goins walks into the interview room with bags under his eyes, yesterday's soiled clothes, and a complexion like the scum-bottom of an ashtray.

'All-nighter,' he mutters, sounding a little froggy as he opens his briefcase. 'Now. Good news is, they're not charging you with the *real* Gus Miller's death. Once they thawed him out and cut him open, it was cancer.' He shakes his head wearily. 'Sick shit, to carry a war hero's corpse in your van all that time. Why do you think he did it? Finkel, I mean.'

'He was filching the dude's VA checks.'

'Sure, but why keep the body around? You think he had some kind of perversely sentimental attachment to the man he was impersonating, the man he wanted to be?'

'Shit, Goins, this isn't an Edgar Allan Poe story. You've seen pictures of that van. He was a packrat. He couldn't get rid of anything.'

Goins shrugs, removing his yellow notepad from the manila folder labeled *California v. Bunt*. He's already filled dozens of pages with notes of our conversations; reading upside-down I can see, as he rifles through the pages to find a fresh one, endless underlinings, double- and triple-circled words, marginal exclamation points, question marks. He writes a few more words and then turns the notebook toward me. It reads:

THEORY: frame-up
MOTIVE: fuck-up

'Boiled down,' Goins says, 'this is where we are. Their theory, as far as I can make it out, is going to be that you were an active participant in this murder-for-hire scheme from day one. *Our* theory is they're railroading you because their harebrained plan blew up in their face. They're covering their asses, because what they did – giving you a gun and trying to follow you to a hit – was highly unorthodox and dangerous. It invited exactly the kind of mess we got.'

'"Safe as a squirtgun," he called that fucking piece.'

'Well, far as I can figure, there are several explanations for what happened. One: even though ballistics says the fatal bullet came from the Smith & Wesson recovered from the tent, the gun you fired wasn't the one they gave you. Say there was another gun in the tent – maybe Nastahowsky's or a piece that Gus wasn't telling you about – that you grabbed in the melee. Of course, if that's the case, where's the first gun?

'Explanation two: the cops gave you a gun they knew was real, knowing you'd pass it to Gus, as a little insurance. If the investigation petered out, if they never found out who Gus wanted to kill, at least they'd be able to bust him as a felon in possession of a firearm and send him away forever. They knew they could count on you to deny giving it to him, if they wanted you to.

'But what's most likely, I think, is that this is simply another episode in the teeming annals of police incompetence. Maybe not *the* most spectacular example I've ever seen, in a long career spent observing police botches, but it's pretty close. Hubris and ineptitude are a very scary mix: a law-enforcement specialty. And they didn't have to do any of it. They could just have grabbed Gus at the start. This Munoz was after headlines, obviously. A glory move, and you were his pawn.'

'How are they gonna explain my having a police-issued gun?'

'They'll deny they ever gave it to you, which makes it your word versus theirs.' Goins looks at me silently for a long time before adding, 'You may have to testify tomorrow.'

'Okay. I want to tell my story.'

'Ordinarily I hate to put clients on. It gives the prosecutor a chance to skip rope with your intestines, and the guy they've got – Cal Buckhorn – he's rabid as they come. But I don't see any other way to get your story into evidence. And you're a lot brighter than most of my clients. Crazy as your account sounded at first, I think you'll be able to hold your own up there. You sold me.'

I want to weep into my hands, I'm so grateful to hear this.

'Anything else I should know, before we go to battle?' he says. 'I don't want to be caught flat-footed.'

I study Goins for a long time, his pallid, puffy face, his tired eyes shining with purpose, and say, 'I've told you everything.'

He starts packing up his briefcase. 'I need a few hours' sleep. You're first on the docket, eight a.m.'

When he reaches the door I say, 'What they're saying doesn't make any sense. If I'm a for-real hit-man, how did they even get turned on to this thing?'

'Funny you should ask,' Goins says. 'They say they had a snitch, and it wasn't you.'

CHAPTER 28

Down through the aisle of the Inyo County District Courthouse, felony division three, comes the gray old vampire, gaunt and slinking in ancient snakeskin cowboy boots, an off-the-rack Salvation Army sportscoat, and Chuck Norris crotch-flex jeans agleam at the waist with a bronco-buckle. Looking straight ahead with fanatical concentration, as if an errant glance in such rarefied air might doom him, Telly Grimes marches nervously past the empty visitor gallery, past the lawyers' oak tables, and pauses before the heavyset clerk, who makes him hold aloft a crabbed, trembling right hand and swear to tell the truth. When he settles himself behind the witness stand, right under the great golden seal of the State of California, his neck emerging like a shrunken ginseng root from the collar of his ill-fitting shirt, I see his eyes flicker over the courtroom, for an instant touching me, his old drinking chum, fellow mole man, pal of a thousand nights in another universe, now planted behind the defense table in a ridiculous robin's-egg-blue suit Goins has supplied for me from the Public Defender wardrobe closet (crammed hanger after hanger, I imagine, with all the pastels of lamblike innocence). For the second that he looks at me, I think I see the twitch of an involuntary smile in Telly's otherwise petrified expression: the two of us here in cheap impostors' clothes playing roles in someone else's absurd game. He gets to be Judas.

Goins, for his part, is looking earnest, wearing shiny black shoes, a fine blue suit with a patterned tie – no bullshit on game day – and as he sits beside me I can smell his fresh-soaped skin, shampooed hair, and cologne. A public defender, sure, and his voice a little scratchy from a sleepless week preparing my case, but for the first time presenting himself thoroughly as a pro, a gladiator: mine. I like that he detests the prosecutor, since this will make Goins fight hard and nasty.

'State your name,' says Assistant District Attorney Cal Buckhorn, a tall, broad-shouldered Aryan with a lipless, unforgiving mouth and an air of corn-fed righteousness.

'Telly Grimes,' the witness rasps so quietly and hesitantly you can barely hear him.

'Lean into the microphone, Mr. Grimes. Speak up,' says the judge, whose placard reads 'The Honorable Barbara D. O'Brien.' She's in her mid-forties and voluptuous, with an abundance of raven hair flowing over her robed shoulders. To be adjudged innocent by her, I think, would redeem a lifetime.

The prosecutor jabs the air as he asks questions. On one finger he wears a fat college football ring. 'Isn't it a fact,' he asks Telly, 'that your vocation is that of a fence – someone who buys and sells goods on the black market?'

'Not anymore, sir,' Telly says, every syllable squeezed up from his agonized bronchial tubes like marbles through a straw. 'Because I fell on my face and asked Jesus to help me stop sinning. And since then, sir, I haven't besmirched the statute book of the great State of California in even the most minuscule way, sir. I see loose change, I put my hand in my pocket. Girls pass, I turn away. Not even a parking beef.'

'How long ago were you Saved?'

'Off and on for years, sir, but the big one was a number of weeks ago.'

'I remind you that you enjoy immunity for the statements you make in this court today. Up until several months ago, you were still engaged in black market activity, were you not?'

'I did so engage, sir.'

'And did a man you knew as Gus Miller ask you to procure a gun for him?'

'Sir, yes.'

'Did he tell you why he wanted one?'

'Only that someone needed wasting, sir, and he was getting fifty grand for it.'

'And what did you do?'

'I didn't want anything to do with whatever he had in mind. I got enough on my conscience, sir, without helping to get someone shot up. Killing's a mortal sin. You go to hell for it. Plus, I didn't feel like helping such an assh— such a man.'

'He tried to yank you through the window of your car once, correct?'

Telly's lip twitches at the humiliating memory. 'That was *after* I told him I wouldn't get him a gun. I think he did it as a warning, because he was afraid I'd go to the authorities.'

'And did you?'

'Not at first, because I thought maybe he was joking, and I thought snitching was wrong, sir. Then after he tried to hurt me, I figured all bets were off. That's when I realized the greater sin would be to let a murder occur.'

'What did you do then?'

'I called El Guapo, Detective Al Munoz of the Costa Mesa Police Department. I told him Miller was trying to get a gun, and the authorities would be behooved to keep an eye out.'

'Why Munoz?'

'I consider him a personal friend. I gave him information once in a while, and he helped me on some beefs. Some legal violations I'd been accused of, sir.'

The prosecutor suddenly looms over me, his fat ring shining as he points down at me. 'Are you familiar with the defendant, Benjamin Bunt?'

'I know Benny, sure. I know Benny.' He lowers his eyes and

coughs violently into his fist. It takes him forever to clear his throat. 'This isn't easy for me, because I always considered him a buddy.'

The prosecutor plows on, showing no concern for old Telly's stricken conscience, no interest in the burdens of friendship or the pang of perpetrating betrayal. 'Did he do anything unusual around the time Gus Miller was speaking of this contract murder?'

'Benny, sir, he – he wanted me to get him a new ID. I got him a California license. A really good-looking one. You'd have to look real close to tell it wasn't bona fide. I remember the name he wanted on it, too: John Romita.'

That hangs in the air forever, and I can hear Goins's breathing stop.

'No further questions,' the prosecutor finally says, folding his big arms across his chest as he sits.

'Any cross, defense?' says the judge.

Goins sits there blinking into dead space, his brow clenched, and the judge has to ask the question again. Goins catches himself and bolts to his feet, sputtering, 'Yes, your honor.' He looks disoriented as he walks up to the podium. 'Mr. Grimes,' he says. 'Mr. Grimes.' Goins glares as hard as he can at Telly, breathing like a big starving cat. 'Isn't it true . . .' he begins. 'Mr. Grimes, you admit to a history of depravity, criminality, and gutter-dwelling treachery, do you not?'

'Objection, your honor!' cries the prosecutor. 'Compound question.'

'Restate your question, counselor.'

Goins pounds his fist on the podium. 'You swim in life's gutter, do you not?'

'Sir, I would ask that you not judge my past.'

'Isn't it true, as the single example of your coldblooded huckster nature that I find it necessary to invoke here, that you once tried to counterfeit the likeness of a beloved Mexican saint on a flour tortilla?'

'If I did something like that to any beloved likeness, sir, I have no recollection of it.'

'Are you being paid for your testimony here today?'

'No, sir.'

'Are you being given a break on one of your criminal cases?'

'No, sir. I'm here because of my conscience.'

Goins snorts dramatically, pounds the podium with a sneer, and sits down beside me. Under his breath he snarls, 'I should have known about the fucking ID, Benny.'

With a look of infinite relief, Telly shuffles his bones down the aisle, breathing with difficulty, and disappears into the hallway.

Next through the door is Detective Al Munoz. As he strides toward the witness box, steely-eyed and beautiful in his crisp short-sleeved black uniform, with its knife-creased slacks and shining badge, there's no swagger or self-promotion in his step, only noble purpose. His walk conveys his absolute conviction that he's in a holy place, the Temple of the Law to which he's given his life. His ramrod-straight posture connotes incorruptibility, the fine and unimpeachably American habits of a West Point instructor. As he raises his hand to be sworn in, with those delicate tapering fingers and heroic arms, he looks like a glossy cop-recruitment poster. And when the clerk asks him if he swears to tell the truth, the whole truth, and nothing but the truth, he says, 'I do,' in a tone of voice that makes you want to cry with gratitude that God ever made a man so fine. He settles into the witness box. A vein bulges lengthwise down one of his absurd biceps like an IV tube, like a junkie's dream.

'After Mr. Grimes contacted you about this murder plot,' the prosecutor asks, 'what action did you take?'

'Because we did not know who the intended target was, we decided to conduct surveillance,' Munoz says.

'Your honor,' says the prosecutor, 'I'd like to play Exhibit Number One for the court.'

He pops a cassette tape into a player. Out pour the sounds of a dull mechanical hum and crackling static, like a far-away radio station. Voices rise and fall. Through the interference two men who sound vaguely familiar are talking about a gun.

'Do . . . ladies' weapon . . .'

'Auh?'

'. . . forty-five . . . essentially . . . chick's gun.'

'. . . blue-collar, meat-and-potatoes . . . you wanted . . . bazooka.'

One of the voices booms, loud enough to hear clearly: 'You and me are gonna kill us one motherfucker today. How you feelin'?'

'I'm feeling really positive about it.'

After a few moments I realize this last voice is my own.

The prosecutor removes the tape and holds it before Munoz. 'How did you obtain this recording, Detective?'

'We planted a bug in the dashboard of Gus Miller's van.'

'And your plan was to follow Mr. Miller and Mr. Bunt to the target and intercept them?'

'Yes. Tragically, we lost sight of the van in a thunderstorm. And we were staking out the wrong place. It cost a man his life. Two men, if you count Mad Dog Finkel.' With tremendous dignity he adds, 'I – I take responsibility for it. As an American, as a Californian, as a police officer, and as a human being, it weighs heavily on my conscience.'

'Scumbag!' mutters Goins. It's his turn. His knuckles are white as he clenches the podium.

'Isn't it true,' he cries, 'that you obtained this recording because it was my client, Benjamin Bunt, who was wearing the wire on your behalf?'

Munoz looks genuinely perplexed. 'I'm sorry?'

'Isn't it true that my client was your snitch on this? That he's merely playing a role on this tape that you assigned to him?'

'Is that what he told you?' Munoz looks at Goins pityingly. 'I'd like to see some evidence of *that*. We're dealing with a very cunning little conman here. A career hustler. In prior cases, it's true, he has supplied information, though its reliability was always iffy. What makes him dangerous is he knows how to lie. He'll weave his fabrications in among facts that can be verified. He knows the best way to hide a lie is between two truths.'

'Isn't it true,' Goins trudges on, 'that if you'd simply arrested Mr. Finkel immediately on learning of this alleged hit, none of this bloodshed would have happened? Isn't it true that, but for your bungling, two people would still be alive?'

Munoz clenches his jaw. 'We made a judgment call,' he says.

'In the interests of your own personal glory, isn't that right, Detective?'

'We needed to know—'

'All to resurrect your fading career, correct? You were on your way out, thanks to a stack of use-of-force complaints, and this was your last gasp, wasn't it?'

'No, sir,' Munoz says evenly. 'Unless we knew the intended target, we would never be able to piece together who issued the contract.'

'It turned into a complete and utter debacle, didn't it?'

'It bounced out of our control, sir. In hindsight—'

Goins is sputtering angrily, 'And isn't that why you are now blaming my client? As a smokescreen for your complete incompetence?'

'We erred, sir.'

'Isn't it true that you actually supplied Mr. Bunt with a gun, with the promise that it was inoperative? Isn't it true that you botched that, too?'

Munoz doesn't reply, but his look says the question is too preposterous, too desperate, too stupid to answer. He glances at the judge, as if to say, 'Am I supposed to take that one seriously?' She looks at him sympathetically and darts her eyes away so suddenly I become convinced she is in love with him. And who wouldn't be?

'Well?' demands Goins.

'There's another one,' he says, 'I'd like to see some evidence of. We would not give a dangerous weapon, under any circumstances, to a criminal.'

When Munoz steps down, the prosecutor stands beside me and jabs his finger in my direction some more.

'Your honor, we believe the evidence plentifully demonstrates that this man conspired to commit the murder of Matt Nastahowsky, and was in the commission of this felony when his confederate, Mr. Gerry Finkel, a.k.a. Gus Miller, suffered fatal burns, which makes Mr. Bunt responsible for felony murder in that death. We believe the evidence is ample – more than ample – to bind Mr. Bunt over for trial in Superior Court.'

'What says the defense?'

Goins stands at the podium, shifting from leg to leg as he gazes down at his notepad. 'This is a conspiracy, your honor, perpetrated by rogue cops intent on whitewashing their role in a ghastly foul-up—'

'Counselor,' the judge cuts him off. 'You are making an argument for which you have furnished no testimony, no evidence. Do you have any to give? Are you putting your client on the stand?'

Goins looks at me grimly. He shakes his head. 'No, your honor.'

'Okay,' the judge says. 'I'm binding it over. You will stand trial for murder in Superior Court, Mr. Bunt. You will get a fair one. Next case.'

When my attorney sits down beside me I say, 'What the fuck, Goins? What the fuck?'

'Buckhorn would have disemboweled you,' he says hoarsely. 'What you say here is admissible at trial, and I couldn't risk it. If we want to have any shot before a jury, we have to get your story straight.'

'My story's straight as a ruler, man. You said so yourself.'

'I thought so until today,' he says. 'Best way to tell a lie is to squeeze it between two truths, isn't it, Benny?'

CHAPTER 29

The next day Goins comes into the jailhouse interview room and opens his briefcase without a hello.

'Just got back from a tête-à-tête with the prosecutor,' he says coldly. He writes on his notepad as he talks, his eyes never meeting mine. 'Good news. They're willing to take the death penalty off the table, if you cooperate.'

'Cooperate?'

'Plead guilty to all charges and offer your testimony against Helen Langley, explaining how she set this up.'

'Cloe's mom?'

'She's a fat cat, and happens to be a big contributor to the guy running against the Orange County DA in this year's election, and they want her a lot more than they want you.'

'But I never talked with the lady about . . .'

'Lucky for us, gas stations use surveillance cameras, and some use digital, which means they keep them for months. Based on the dates you gave me, my investigator tracked down the tape of your encounter with Helen Langley at the PCH mini-mart. You're shown in the parking lot having an animated conversation with her – an argument – which culminates in her slapping you. Now, there's no audio, but it's proof you've met. All you have to do is testify that she was talking about the murder.'

'The thing is—'

'I'm not suborning perjury here. I say *if* this happened, you testify to it. Otherwise, they put a needle in you. You want a needle in you?'

'I thought you believed in me, Goins. I thought we were gonna fight this.'

Finally he looks at me, and in such a quietly ferocious way that I can't look at him.

'Finkel told Telly Grimes it was a fifty-grand contract,' he says. 'What do you make of that?'

'Gus blew everything up.'

'How long does it take for symptoms of chocolate toxicosis to set in, Benny? Reach into your mansion-house memory and pluck that out for me.'

'I don't know. Who cares?'

'I looked it up on the Net this morning. Three, four hours before a victim of chocolate poisoning will start showing symptoms. And yet in your version, Jesse James dies almost on the spot.'

'He had a bad heart. It was cardiac arrhythmia, something like that.'

'I'm asking myself, "Why is Benny lying to me about how that dog died?" I'm asking myself, "Who would falsely cop to a thing like murdering a dog? What bigger thing does it hide?"'

He lets his questions hang between us, until I start stammering helplessly.

'Shut up,' Goins says. 'My investigator has been talking to people. One guy at the bar said the dog kicked off a couple days *before* you and Finkel left for the hit. Heard Finkel blubbering into his booze about burying him at the beach.'

'I swear to you, Goins – that's dead wrong. Because we took him into the mountains. I put him in the ground. Check my shoes, analyze the mud: I was there!'

'I think you went up into the mountains, and I think you dug a hole. But I don't think it was a canine carcass you put down there. You needed an explanation for why you went up there, because you believed someone might have seen your van. So you made yourself a despicable dog murderer.'

'You're not even a real lawyer, Goins.'

He smiles humorlessly. 'Well, maybe you can draw a map, send someone to fetch that fifty grand out of the dirt and hire yourself a bona fide private attorney you can try to bullshit.' He crosses his arms and strokes his jaw, his face all sour victory. 'The worms can't spend it. I'm thinking you convinced Finkel to bury the money before heading out, for safety's sake – just in case you got caught on the way. And when he took the fall for the hit, you would circle back and use the cash to start all over as John Romita. A whole new life. A snake shedding his skin.'

I start crying. 'You think I meant for anyone to die?'

'I don't know. I believe you thought you could outsmart everyone. Maybe you were their snitch, and you just didn't count on a real gun. Or maybe you were the guy with the murder contract all along, and things just bounced bad. I'll tell you this – you read me pretty well. You had me going with the poor-schmuck-in-over-his-head thing. It's the kind of story sentimental suckers like myself have a weakness for. A law-enforcement conspiracy that's virtually vertical? In the light of day, well, it's all just so wildly implausible that to risk it on a jury would be pretty stupid. And I was ready to do it, which is a measure of your imagination and my stupidity.'

'I want another lawyer! A real lawyer! I'm firing you!'

'I'm not here to blow sunshine up your ass. They're going to kill you if you don't tap-dance for them. Your record doesn't help your credibility, Benny. If I can save your life, I can look in the mirror and say I've done my job.'

'I'm not pleading to anything.'

'It doesn't really matter, legally speaking, whether it was you or Finkel who whacked Nastahowsky. Under the law you're both principals. "When you run with the wolves, you share in the kill." Jack London.'

I clasp my hands between my legs to stop their sudden violent shaking.

'Occam's razor,' Goins says. 'The old philosopher, Occam, who said, "Let's cut the horse puckey. The true route between A and B is the straightest line between A and B, all else being equal." Which is what Cal Buckhorn is going to tell the jury. "Ladies and gentlemen, which is the more believable scenario? That these veteran law-enforcement officers, these decorated officers who risk their lives every day, have concocted this elaborate plot, have knowingly destroyed evidence, have railroaded an innocent man? Or, scenario two, that this low-life Benny Bunt got caught in a murder scheme and is trying to save himself by inventing, out of whole cloth, a ridiculous story meant to beshit the names of these sterling officers? Occam's razor. Which story is so much cleaner?"'

'Those pricks staged Munoz's shooting so they could waste a drug dealer, and got me to lie to back it up. That's sterling?'

'I'm sure you're going to tell me you have some independent proof of that, right? Physical evidence? Videotape?'

When in response I offer nothing but silence, Goins shakes his head at me with an expression of weariness and disgust.

'I can live with whatever you wanna do here. Fight this puppy? I'll do it. You're the client. You get the needle. Thanks to the ACLU and civil-liberties saps like me, it doesn't even hurt much these days.'

I listen to the humming of the air vents in the interview room for a long time. After a while I start crying again and I listen to the snot sucking in and out of my nose. Finally, numb, depleted, I nod. Goins gives a small, tight smile.

'Like I said, they want Helen Langley. In a sworn deposition, you're going to describe how she propositioned you to whack Nastahowsky.'

'Even if it's not true?'

Goins frowns. 'Sorry? I missed that. Come again?'

'Even if it's—'

'I'm sorry, I keep missing that. Too many Grateful Dead concerts. I didn't hear you.'

I take the message. 'That's the price for my life?'

'You have a problem with that?'

'Tell me something, Goins. You're a smart dude. You know how the world works. What happened to you?'

'Sorry?'

'You're just a PD. You make pennies next to what other defense guys make. You drive a Honda or a Yugo. You look like shit. Your clients insult you. I'm betting you left law school wanting to be Clarence Darrow or Johnnie Cochran, and you're not either. I mean, where'd you go wrong?'

He shrugs; he is not even offended; he will be rid of me soon. 'That's a funny thing to hear, from a man sitting where you are. You're a bright one. Why didn't *you* ever do anything with yourself?'

'Society. Bad breaks. Nobody throwing a line. I don't know.'

'Sure. Everybody's got a list.' He packs his briefcase with a blank face. 'I'll be back with your plea papers.' He rises and buzzes for the guard. 'Who's John Romita, anyway? Why that name?'

'A guy I wanted to be, a long time ago,' I say. 'He drew Spider-Man.'

In his face: a flicker of pity. Yet as he stands waiting near the door, ungainly and stoop-shouldered, ridiculously I feel sorry for him, sorry for his raped hopes.

'What was life gonna be like, as John Romita?' he says. 'You must have pictured it.'

'Every day for months,' I say. 'Find a girl who was nice to me and treat her like gold. Never go into another bar or talk to another cop. Come home from some job, whatever it was, with clean hands and a clean conscience. Maybe Mexico or Canada or Florida – one of those places people disappear to.'

I'm about to tell him more when the guard opens the door. Goins jerks his head quickly in my direction, says, 'Back tomorrow with your plea papers,' and disappears.

CHAPTER 30

From the deposition of Dean W. Langley, taken at the office of the Inyo County District Attorney:

Q. So it was her idea?

A. From the beginning. It had been floating out there, kind of unsaid, before she came out with it.

Q. And what specifically did she say?

A. The word was 'exterminate.' Like a bug.

Q. What was your reaction?

A. I was appalled, naturally. This is a human life we're talking about.

Q. Yes, it is.

A. So naturally I was appalled. I stood up to her. I said, 'You're a crazy woman, you're insane.'

Q. She wanted you to find someone to kill Mr. Nastahowsky?

A. She kept pestering me. Day in, day out. All day, every day. Are you married?

Q. This isn't about me.

A. That fat little harridan calls my office seven, eight times an afternoon. She pages me on the golf course, on the yacht. She stands over me while I'm trying to work my bowels. Even there!

Q. Relentlessness itself.

A. I was appalled all the way through it. I'm appalled now.

Q. A Fury, you might even say.

A. What's appalling is how I let her treat me all those years. She liked to tell people she kept my balls in a little mason jar on her nightstand. Do you understand?

Q. Let's, uh, please continue with the chronology . . .

A. I mean, where does a man like me start looking for a killer? There's no one like that in our social circle. Here we are, blessed with money. Envied. Active in the community. The Daily Pilot puts our New Year's party in its society page. The American Dream. And yet—

Q. No friends of that sort.

A. Who would want one? Well, Helen maybe.

Q. At some point you meet a man who called himself Gus Miller.

A. I found him on the road. When I hit him.

Q. The universe is so funny that way.

A. I'm coming home on PCH, and I guess I'm not looking, and I slam into this – I'm thinking it's a bum. He's reeking of booze, he's covered with blood, his dog's hurt, he's threatening to tear out my pancreas and eat it.

Q. Describe him.

A. Big and grubby, big outlaw-looking type. Beard. Tattoos that said, like, hardluck bastard and a bunch of war stuff. He doesn't want to go to the hospital, he just wants me to pay him, and I say, 'Sure, let's go to my ATM.' Because I don't want any trouble. And on the way he starts bawling.

Q. Crying?

A. But in a kind of weird, hostile way. Raving about the government, and how he had to do unspeakable things in Vietnam, and how fat cats like me were the American dream, but he was the American nightmare. How yogurt-eaters like me in our safe little worlds, in our Benzes, we didn't want to acknowledge there were guys like him. So I give him five hundred dollars so he doesn't sue me, and he calms down, and we go for donuts.

Q. Then what?

A. I threw some work his way. He was good with his hands. We needed our deck redone.

Q. Which is how he meets Helen.

A. I never should've – I mean, I felt sorry for the big old guy, okay? I had a friend whose uncle was in Vietnam, and my heart goes out. How am I supposed to know he's a psychopath?

Q. They strike up a rapport.

A. You could call it that. She jumps right in with the questions. 'You're versed in the dark arts? How interesting! How do you use a garrote? When do you use piano wire? What cutting implements do you find preferable? In what circumstances is strychnine or oleander tea the best tack?' It seems like he likes the attention.

Q. Were you a participant in these conversations?

A. No! I was appalled. I just listened. From the other room, listened. I didn't know what I should do, I – I didn't know—

Q. So then?

A. So then she says, 'I have this problem, and I've exhausted the usual remedies.' She says, 'I'm in the market for non-traditional solutions. I'll pay whatever. I'll pay in advance.' He says, 'I'm on borrowed time, I wouldn't know what to do with the money.' I mean, he's acting like this is going to be a lot of trouble for him.

Q. He expressed reluctance?

A. Almost like he's throwing out excuses. So Helen starts bawling. She says, 'I'm desperate. My daughter's been kidnapped by a sociopath who calls himself a poet.' Shows him Cloe's picture and says, 'This is what he took away from us.' The big guy gets really emotional. She takes him up to Cloe's room – what used to be Cloe's room – which we haven't changed – and shows him all her things. Yearbooks, music, stuffed animals. And explains how Cloe skipped college, to live with this, this *creature* . . .

Q. Nastahowsky?
A. Yeah. When Helen turns it on, she can turn it on. (Pause.) I just couldn't believe any of it was serious . . .
Q. Or else, being appalled, you would have contacted the authorities.
A. Absolutely! I wrote her off as hysterical. (Pause.) Look. If anyone deserves the gas chamber for this . . . Is that how they do it these days?
Q. Let's not—
A. Or is it, what? Lethal injection?
Q. Try to keep this—
A. If anyone deserves it, I mean – you told me if I testified I wouldn't . . . Because this thing was never my idea anyway.

(Break in interview.)

A. Helen had the idea that Cloe was supposed to go to Harvard or Juilliard, some place Helen could brag about to her friends. She'd have them over for hors d'oeuvres, Tiffany Bren or Emma Colby or Sasha Rubelstein – this whole museum charity-ball set. And all they'd talk about was their kids. Sasha Rubelstein saying, 'I flew up to see Sarah at Harvard this weekend, she's rooming with a senator's daughter, can you believe it?' And Tiffany Bren saying, 'Julie's on the swim team at Brown, she made the papers!' And Helen with that smile plastered on her face, gulping down Bloody Marys, waiting for them to ask, 'So what about Cloe?'
Q. What did she say?
A. Some lie or other. That Cloe got into Harvard, but was taking some time off to decide. Traveling in France. These amazing, elaborate lies. Anything but the truth, you know. Which is that she picked Greensward Community College—
Q. Which is where?
A. This rinkydink place up near Castaic. Which didn't even have

a website. We go up there for a tour, and it's this sad little place where Mexicans and Arabs are trying to learn English. Stucco dorms and wilting flowerbeds – they don't even have the budget to water them. Helen's face getting tighter and tighter, and Cloe finding it all delicious. It was payback.

Q. For . . .?

A. Private tutors, violin instructors, fencing lessons, riding lessons, ballet, SAT prep courses, summers in Europe, French lessons, Spanish, German. The childhood Helen insisted she have, so that Cloe could compete. (Pause.) Helen's raving about those flowerbeds for days. How Sasha Rubelstein and Tiffany Bren get to walk under Corinthian columns when they visit their girls, and she gets these sickly flowers and this shitty school with no reputation, and how she'd rather die than admit her daughter goes there.

Q. What was your feeling?

A. I told her, 'Look, she's baiting you. She picked this place to make you insane, and you're letting her.' And it turns out, Cloe dropped out in the first semester. She never planned to stay. Just wanted to make a point. That was the first really ugly thing she did. She calls and says, 'I was hoping the Hydra would stroke out.' After that, things got really ugly . . .

Q. Is this when Nastahowsky enters the picture?

A. We found out from our private eye she was up in Berkeley doing experimental theater, but we didn't meet Nastahowsky until we went up there. She invited us to a show at the Andy Gibberstein Theater. An Evening of Performance Art. And that's when it got extremely ugly.

Q. How so?

A. It became clear the only reason she invited us was to humiliate us. Helen likes to pretend she's hip to the whole bohemian thing, that she's not stuffy and conventional, but God forbid it's her daughter . . . The first girl to go on stage builds the Statue of Liberty with Tampax and chicken-wire and sets it on fire.

The second girl does a monologue about being molested by her uncle and the postman and a drama coach, and God knows who else. Nastahowsky comes on and does this horrible sex thing. I'm not gonna get into it, but the finale is he shoots hot Lubriderm at the audience from a squirt gun.

Q. Does Cloe perform?

A. She comes on with her violin. There's a projector screen, with a family photo. Of us! Me, Helen, Cloe, with these disgusting labels. Helen's 'The Hydra,' as usual, and I'm 'The Gelding,' and Cloe's 'The Chattel.' She's ripping her violin apart with a pair of pliers and screaming from the stage about how much she hates us. 'I'm not your property! I hate, hate, hate you!' It was a big hit.

Q. And you meet Nastahowsky?

A. He has this weird energy about him, and this grin. 'Look,' he says. 'You shouldn't take it personally. That wasn't really you guys she was talking about. It was "mom" and "dad." Understand? With quotes. It was characters. It was important for her to do it. It was catharsis. You'll get along on more honest terms, now.' And then we knew he'd put her up to it, that she'd never conceive of such a cruel stunt on her own. 'You're the kind of people who don't care at all about art,' he says. 'It's just some status badge to you. A Picasso or a Lexus: which will impress my idiot friends more?' Helen refused to look at him. She wouldn't acknowledge him. She's shaking. She can barely stand. Her hair's full of Lubriderm. She tells Cloe she's coming home with us, and that was the worst thing to do, the worst possible thing, that just starts a shouting match . . . He starts going off on Helen's jewelry. She's wearing these pearls, and this little crucifix necklace, and he starts quoting the Bible about the eye of the needle and calling her a hypocrite, and how Africans were dying over those pearls . . . Finally Helen says, 'How much do we have to pay you to leave our daughter alone?' But she still won't look at him. 'Name your amount! Name your amount!' she keeps saying. And he says, 'If you want to bribe me, you can at least look at me.' But she won't. She says, 'Dean, pay him. Have him name his amount.' What does the kid do? He takes out his checkbook. 'How much do I have to pay you to get out of her life?' Winning points with Cloe up and down. I could tell, she absolutely loved it . . .

Q. So ill feelings are in the air.

A. My thinking was, 'It's just a phase, let's lie low, let's ride it out.' Because Cloe had been through phases before. In high school she was a Marxist, and you know, behaved like, I'm sorry, but, promiscuously. With our pool men and gardeners. To make some point about God knows what. Colonialism. Helen got them deported, which only made Cloe angrier. (Pause.) I remember, she learned about homelessness when she was ten or eleven, and for a week she slept on the floor. To empathize. That was Cloe. She took meals to bums. She brought all kinds of misfits home. Paraded them before Helen and made her insane.

Q. Misfits?

A. In junior high, high school. Skinny guys who were into Dungeons and Dragons and, you know, robot books. Guys who had harelips, guys with terrible zits. The guy she took to the prom – Helen didn't approve of this at all – he was missing a few fingers. Nice enough kid. But they always broke her heart, you know. And then Nastahowsky came along.

Q. Being in her twenties, legally she could live with whomever she chose.

A. Helen was convinced he had her under some kind of evil spell. So we got deprogrammers. Three guys in Encino. Supposedly experts. That cost us twenty grand.

Q. They abducted her?

A. Yes. They locked her in a cabin outside Merced, and we could hear them screaming at her – we're in the next room, and we're listening to them scream at her, trying to break this spell. Shock treatment. 'Your name is Cloe June Langley. You've been brainwashed. Nastahowsky isn't your family. Your parents are your family. You come from a wonderful, loving home. You're a citizen of freedom-loving democracy. Your name is Cloe June Langley.'

Q. Did she respond?

A. She went into herself.

Q. I'm sorry?

A. She just – disappeared into herself. Like she always did when . . . when what was around her . . . was . . . you know . . .

Q. Was too much?

A. Helen, she . . . with all the pills, you know, and the drinking . . . and everything she wanted Cloe to be that she hadn't been because she married me . . . Cloe liked that Beatles song, 'Octopus's Garden,' and she'd pretend to be the octopus, you know. When it got rough. Safe down there in her little stone garden she'd made at the bottom of the sea, where no one could get in to hurt her. She told me that's where she went . . .

Q. And in this cabin—

A. I had to stop it. I couldn't stand to hear her voice. They'd been screaming at her for five, six hours, and I came through the door and I said, 'Stop it! Christ, enough!' And I hugged Cloe, and she didn't seem to recognize me at first, and then she said, 'Hi, Daddy.' And she said, 'I have to get back to Matthew. He's going to be missing me.' And then she saw Helen through the door, and she started shaking. She's in my arms, and she's shaking like she's in a nightmare . . .

Q. And after that?

A. She went back to him.

Q. Where's your daughter now?

A. In a facility. I see her every day. She's getting better, thank God. She'll be coming home soon. We're going to rebuild our relationship. It's my top priority – my only priority.

Q. Did your wife ever tell you she had actually put out a contract on Nastahowsky's life?

A. Not directly. She knew I'd call the authorities. (Pause.) And yet I can't help feeling guilty, because I was the link. Because I'm like my daughter. I feel sorry for people. And I wanted to give this vet a hand. Is that a crime?

Q. I'm not aware of any crime you've committed.

A. A man loses his wife and gets his daughter back. That's some trade. (Pause.) You know Helen had the family dog's throat cut open? The barking made her jittery.

CHAPTER 31

A letter comes from my wife.

She writes that she cried every night the first few days I was gone. Eventually she went looking for me. Nobody at the bars around town would tell her anything; neither would the cops. One day a lady at the drugstore saw her weeping and said, 'Girl, you need to get on with your life. He no good.'

Finally someone told her my name had been in the paper and she found out I was locked up and probably wouldn't be getting out. She was sorry she missed my court appearances, she said, but she didn't have a car, and it wasn't as if I'd left her any fucking bus fare. She burned all my comics and moved to Ocono Falls, Wisconsin, to live on her aunt's farm. There were no barking dogs there, thank God, and she guessed it was alright, though the goddamn pollen was making her sneeze.

'At first I thought you'd gone gay, but I bet whatever you did, you did for pussy, if I know my Benny,' she writes. 'I guess you decided you didn't love me anymore. Maybe I was not the world's best wife, but maybe you weren't the world's best husband, either. I don't know what to say except it definitely sucks and I think I hate you. Please don't try to contact me. I don't want my heart broken any more or any worse. I mean it. Please.'

Six weeks later another letter arrives.

'I can't believe you haven't written, after me pouring out my heart to you! FUCK YOURSELF AND GO TO HELL, YOU CRIMINAL! YOU JEFFREY DAHMER CHARLES MANSON FREDDY KRUEGER PREPARATION H FAGGOT MOTHERFUCKER!!! WE'RE DONE, DONE!!! KILLER!!!!!'

CHAPTER 32

Another letter arrives, this one from a 'crime journalist' named Chuck Boyle Rivett. He wants to visit me. I'm wary, but excited. This might be my chance to tell my story.

'Despite the horrible and horrific crimes of which you have been convicted, I believe there is a core of humanity in you, Mr. Bunt,' his letter goes. 'I want to give you the opportunity to show the world that you are not the monster you have been painted and portrayed as. Give me that opportunity, Mr. Pfister!'

The Pfister name puzzles me until I realize it's probably a form letter. The box of his books Boyle sends along confirms it. The most recent is *Call Me Og: Og Pfister, the Nation's Most Prolific Claw-Hammer Killer Discusses His Shocking Crimes*. Others are *Shanked! The True Story of a Prison Murder*; *Sisters on Ice: The Grisly Meatlocker Murders at the Sacred Heart Convent*; *Bucket of Guts: The Shocking True Story of a Ritual Disemboweling*. They're full of gory photos. The bio says Boyle used to be a private eye. The author photos show a stocky, balding man with a tough-guy scowl and a big bad-ass eye-patch.

'Billy, hello,' Boyle says on the day he visits. His face is fleshy. No eye-patch. I study him through the windowpane of the visiting pod, looking for signs that one of his eyes is fucked up. It doesn't seem so.

'I'm Benny,' I say.

He looks harried and sweaty. He explains that he doesn't have much time, he's got just three weeks to finish this book – he has most of it written already – plus two other books due next month.

'I'd like the chance to put on the record that I'm a decent guy,' I say. 'I feel terrible Nastahowsky died. I never should've been there. But he came at me.'

'I've interviewed dozens of killers – hundreds. I'm not afraid of looking into the eyes of evil. I can look right into the lamps of a guy like you and not flinch at all.'

He gazes at me hard through the glass, unblinking, barely breathing, his nostrils flared. He holds it for a good 10 seconds, then exhales slowly and sticks a piece of gum in his mouth.

'You see?' he says. 'I don't even blink. So don't try to con me. I can't be taken in. Now, talk to me. Your ex-wife says she was always afraid of you.'

'Donna?'

He fishes out a notebook and pen. 'She told me about the bed-wetting, the arson, and how you killed slugs as a kid. Care to confirm or deny that you set your apartment on fire?'

'I was trying to light a joint! Maybe I did it in a stupid way, touching a newspaper to the stove, but it was still an accident.'

'And the bed-wetting?'

'It doesn't count when you're drunk.'

'The slugs?'

'I was a kid, dude.'

'Sure, I understand. But stack it up, we have a classic pattern. Looking back on your life, it seems pretty obvious you were headed toward this. How long did you feel this hunger, this irresistible compulsion, to kill?'

His pen hovers above his notebook, and it becomes clear to me that any details I give him are going to wind up in print as ammunition against me, twisted beyond recognition as further confirmation of my loathsomeness.

'So how does it feel,' he continues, 'to take another human being's life?'

'I'm not telling you anything. You've made up your mind.'

'Look, I don't have time to listen to some I-got-railroaded sob story. You pled guilty. That closes that. I'm lawsuit-proof on you. I don't even have to worry about calling you "alleged" killer, alright? The facts are in. I'm here mainly because I wanted to get a read on you. A feel. A vibe. I always go on gut. My readers trust that.'

'Your readers? The ones who think you took a knife in the eye?'

He crosses his arms over his chest, moving his jaw truculently around his gum. 'That photo was taken two days after retinal surgery. That's what the patch was for. I never pretended otherwise,' he says. He licks his lips. 'Look, your wife gave me the skinny on you. At least tell me this: who was the pitcher, and who was the catcher?'

'What?'

'You and Finkel. Who wore the choke-collar, and who gave the reach-around?'

CHAPTER 33

From *Murder on the Edge! The Shocking True Story of Sex and Death in the Mojave Desert* by Chuck Boyle Rivett (Knife-Kill Publishers, 232 pgs):

When the human eye soaked in fabled Orange County, California, when not dining in its ritzy 5-star dining establishments or enjoying world-famous attractions such as Disneyland, the Richard Nixon Presidential Library and Birthplace, or the gigantic brass likeness of John Wayne at the airport bearing his immortal name, it bounced eagerly along the sparkling beaches – a Shangri-La of perfect 10s soaking up golden daydream sunsets with dental-floss bikinis and world-class breast jobs from the finest surgeons money could buy (not to mention a plethora of eye-catching 9s, 8s, and 7s). Ironically, the orange orchards that gave the county its name were nowhere in sight, though the delectable bosoms gleaming with quality tanning creams on its miles of scenic coastline put one in mind of oversize versions of that delicious citrus commodity, as well as other produce, including casaba melons, honeydews, cantaloupes, and many exotic varieties.

Hidden beneath the heaving, heaven-sent bodies, there was another Orange County – a back-alley world of crime, depravity, prostitution, drugs, seedy nicknames, lethal back-stabbing danger, degenerate perversions, and egg-sucking moral scumbags waiting to prey on law-abiding citizens, though equally without oranges.

Benny Bunt and Gerry Finkel were losers who had never 'fit in.' They always seemed to be together, literally glued to each other like Siamese twins, from soon after they met. Most nights, they were seen getting three sheets to the wind while tying one on and burning the midnight oil at both ends at a Costa Mesa bar on Harbor Boulevard.

They made a kinky and dangerous pair. Finkel was the big one. He had a disgusting beer gut, with hands the size of Major League Baseball catchers' mitts made of pre-oiled premium steer hide and treated with Glovolium Glove Treatment™, or honey-glazed Christmas hams, or perhaps long-shank hickory-smoked Smithfield hams suitable for any occasion, plus forearms the size of Harley Davidson mufflers that shattered the silence of serene law-abiding suburbia for miles. With his big beard, he looked much like Santa Claus, though Saint Nick never was a substance abuser with a terrifying array of tattoos. Nor had the real Father Christmas spent a third of his life behind prison bars for violent felony acts. Finally, no storybook ever alleged that the actual beloved holiday icon possessed a 'sex dungeon.' Finkel lived in the room behind the bar, and some regulars suspected they heard sounds of sadistic pleasure and sick masochistic 'kicks' coming from behind the door – flesh being slapped, oiled, lathered, leather-whipped, lashed, spanked, scarred, and burned.

Bunt, in all likelihood his secret sex-slave, was short and sleazy-looking. He was a drug addict and a dishwasher and tried to impress people with a memory for pointless facts. He was known to memorize Trivial Pursuit cards to give himself an unfair advantage in the game. 'He'd put a knife in his mother's back for a nickel,' said Costa Mesa Police Detective Al Munoz, who boasted a puma physique women found irresistible, eyes that shot daggers at criminals and love-darts at the willing ladies, who were always willing.

Recently, during an exclusive investigative prison interview with Bunt, this writer looked into the killer's eyes and forced him to tearfully confess that he had long suffered from what FBI profilers term the 'Homicidal Triad' – a history of arson, bed-wetting, and animal abuse. He was clearly a bomb waiting to go off. These findings are presented in this book, exclusively, and for the first time.

Bunt and Finkel dreamed of the 'big score' that promised the easy money. The grapevine had it their dream was to buy a place together and live as man and wife. So when a wealthy Newport Beach woman, Helen Langley, approached them with a murder contract, their twisted ambition suddenly seemed within reach . . .

CHAPTER 34

scritch-scritch-scritch—

scratchscritchscratchscritchscratchscritchscritch—

At night the cellblock is full of the sounds of inmate industry. Prisoners very patiently working: making lethal wonders with Plexiglas shards and soup ladles, forks and bench struts, nail files and hairbrushes. It starts every night about 10:15, after the guards have made the final headcount and retired to the control room on the other side of the range. I stick wads of cotton in my ears so I can sleep.

scritch-scritch-*scritch*

A letter came from Dickie Pincus, an old friend from the Greasy Tuesday, informing me that the bar burned down last month and Telly Grimes went to Peru to die in a botched surgery. Telly needed a new set of lungs and the American doctors refused to give him one, since he'd already destroyed the set they gave him from the Mormon kid, Billy Cannon, and there were more responsible people who needed them. Every day at the bar, Telly would sit crying with his cigarette and wheezing monologues to Billy's ghost, saying he'd let him down, he'd been such a good kid, why couldn't he have been worthy of his gift? Finally he got a line on a 'doctor' outside Lima who might be able to hook him up for five grand. Too weak to hustle up any money, he pleaded with his pal Sal Chamusco for help. Sal came through for his friend. He financed Telly's trip to South America and accompanied him while he got butchered. He even paid to fly Telly's body back and sunk in a plot at Forest Lawn. Apparently El Chupacabra knew his chances. One of the last things he said was, 'Say so long to Benny for me and thank him for all the drinks.'

And the Greasy Tuesday burned down. Circumstances were suspicious. Accelerants were detected. Junior made sure a couple of dozen people saw him in a bar across town on the night it happened. Junior? I imagine he just wanted to be free of his gloomy sawdust cage, and the ghost he was trapped in there with. A couple of weeks before the fire, he'd removed his father's pictures from the walls and left them in the trash bin, along with his box of mementos. Maybe all those stories of his gook-killing dad soured him on the place. Maybe the bullshit king who called himself Mad Dog Miller broke Junior's credulous heart. All that was left was the insurance payout.

Another historic dive vanishes. At least my ghost won't be trapped there. Maybe even poor Tony the Money – I met him once – gets to go free.

scritchscritchscratchscritch—

On the tier I keep mostly to myself, trusting no one. At breakfast one morning a sinewy old hillbilly sits across from me and starts talking, casually inserting a rolled-up slice of baloney through his cracked, cigarette-stained lips into the gash between his missing lower teeth. He calls himself Snail; he's been in for 30 years for some stick-ups. He's got a chessboard, he explains, and some nice wooden pieces that he carved at the woodshop. He needs a new partner, since the guy he'd been playing with got paroled. We start playing in the rec room, five, six games a day. He gives me cigarettes and coffee and paperbacks and becomes my only friend. He likes to recount mysteries he's read, snickering at the futile strivings of the characters, the riotous doomwardness of their ambitions. One day as we're setting up the board he smiles and says, 'I heard this hilarious story. I forgot the names, but they don't matter. There's this Rich As

Croesus dude and his Insane Bitch Wife, and they'd like to get rid of some Motherfucker, right? The Wife is on a warpath, poking under every rock for someone to do it. Now Croesus would like to get rid of two people: his Wife *and* the Motherfucker.' He cackles. 'So what does he do? He knows this Scum Cop who needs some of Croesus's cash, and so they put their heads together, and they say, "Let's pin it on some loser no one will miss and no one will believe if things go wrong." Croesus knows a Crazy Handyman Killer, and all he's gotta do is put him in the path of the Wife, knowing the Wife will sic him on the Motherfucker. Follow? It gets even funnier when Crazy Handyman Killer tries to get some help from his Little Buddy, who rats him out to the Scum Cop, who says, "Little Buddy should go down too." Lets him think he's the Law's Little Helper. The trouble is, after it's all done, the Scum Cop takes off with his big fat cut *and* the cut that belongs to the Other Cop, who helped him arrange it and is now left holding his dick.' Snail grins at the richness of that. 'But the Other Cop knows Little Buddy buried some of Croesus's money before he got busted, so he gets Little Buddy a message. It goes, "That cash ain't doing anyone any good. But if you draw a map, half will get to anyone you want."'

My larynx tastes of dust. I stare at our pieces ranged across the chessboard, at the pawn he jabs forward. When I can taste a drop of saliva in my mouth again I say, 'What if the guy who buried the money doesn't have anyone left to give it to?'

Snail doesn't smile. 'Everyone's got someone.'

I'm on my feet, hurrying from the rec room to the lidless steel toilet of my cell. Wave after wave of nausea keeps me planted there, on my knees, my brain making linkages while onrushes of bile scald my throat. At last I realize it was Dean Langley wearing that bottomlessly sad expression I saw once, while a cop disguised as a surf punk – one fond of striking up special relationships with those he arrested – led him in cuffs from the Pomona Park bathroom.

scritchscritchscratch-scrapescrapescrape—

Prisoners are resourceful and patient men. Combs, forks, spoons, shards, mop handles: objects scraped and honed methodically through endless solitary hours, hunched men on bunks running fingers up the jerrybuilt blades to desperately sharp tips and smiling in the darkness. Sounds rising through the steel and concrete guts of the cellblock; sounds loud enough to reach me in my dreams, even through the wadded cotton.

Goins informs me that the FBI will be visiting me soon, pursuant to a probe of suspected corruption at the Costa Mesa Police Department. A circle of cops, including several high-ranking members of the department, is under investigation for fixing cases, shaking down suspects, and planting drugs and 'drop guns' on them. Dozens of cases are being reopened. Of particular interest to the authorities is what I may know about the circumstances surrounding the death of a crack dealer named Ivory 'Daddy Glock' Williams. The Feds are also keenly interested in speaking to Detective Al Munoz, whose recent disappearance, weeks after his retirement, has aroused suspicion; they are eager to learn whether his vanishing has any connection to a $500,000 deposit that had been wired to an offshore account he secretly maintained, and why a Swedish lawyer linked to the Langley Mustard Co. was the source of those funds.

'This could be just the break you need,' Goins says, sounding shocked and abashed to learn that I might have been telling the truth all along.

scritchSCRITCHscritchSCRITCHSCRITCHSCRITCH—

A rat flew through the slats of my cell last night and landed on my chest. Disemboweled, throat cut. No note attached. The rat being the note.

Word of the incident reached the warden. He offered protective custody. I'd trade in my bright orange General Population scrubs for light blue ones; I'd live safely in a wing with smiling monsters who rape kids.

In the end they'll try to take all your pride, snuff out even the sick little flame you've managed to keep alive, cupped somewhere inside you. I told the warden to fuck himself, I'd take my chances in orange.

The man who called himself Mad Dog Miller taught me a few useful things. Such as: First light is when they come for you. He also taught me how to improvise a weapon in a cage.

From the commissary I buy a cheap watch and break it against the floor of my cell, removing the stainless-steel bottom: a quarter-sized disk hard enough to cut most metal. Standing on my mattress, I can reach the light fixture in the ceiling. After an hour's careful work I manage to shave off a four-inch sliver of the lip. I sharpen it against the concrete floor, hour after hour, until I can run my thumb along it and draw blood. I sink it into the molten tip of my toothbrush, and as it anneals I hold it against my chest, listening to my tier-mates' labor through tight wads of cotton, waiting for the 6 a.m. electric charge that sends my cell door sliding open to expose me.

All night they work methodically in their cells, honing their weapons with slow, implacable hatred, saying prayers to their personal gods, their Christs, their Virgins of Guadalupe, their Allahs, their Santeria pantheons, their Hitlers, their Mansons, kneeling before their foot-locker shrines and little plaster saints and handmade clay totems lined on concrete windowsills and praying, all of them praying for a little bit of luck, a little bit of grace, asking: Let me be the one to do the snitch.

Scritck, scritch, scratch, snickt.

A thousand shanks, sharpening.